A Lady in Shadows

A Lady in Shadows

A Madeleine Karno Mystery

LENE KAABERBØL

TRANSLATED BY ELISABETH DYSSEGAARD

ATRIA PAPERBACK

NEW YORK   LONDON   TORONTO   SYDNEY   NEW DELHI

ATRIA
PAPERBACK

An Imprint of Simon & Schuster, Inc.
1230 Avenue of the Americas
New York, NY 10020

Copyright © 2013 by Lene Kaaberbøl

Originally published in Danish in 2013 as *Det levende kød* by Modtryk

English translation copyright © 2017 by Elisabeth Dyssegaard

First Atria Paperback edition December 2017

ATRIA PAPERBACK and colophon are trademarks of Simon & Schuster, Inc.

For information about special discounts for bulk purchases, please contact Simon & Schuster Special Sales at 1-866-506-1949 or business@simonandschuster.com.

The Simon & Schuster Speakers Bureau can bring authors to your live event. For more information or to book an event, contact the Simon & Schuster Speakers Bureau at 1-866-248-3049 or visit our website at www.simonspeakers.com.

Manufactured in the United States of America

10 9 8 7 6 5 4 3 2 1

Library of Congress Cataloging-in-Publication Data
Names: Kaaberbøl, Lene, author. | Dyssegaard, Elisabeth Kallick, translator.
Title: A lady in shadows : a Madeleine Karno mystery / Lene Kaaberbøl ; translated by Elisabeth Dyssegaard.
Other titles: Det levende kød. English.
Description: New York : Atria Books, 2017. | Series: A Madeleine Karno mystery | Translated from the Danish.
Identifiers: LCCN 2017027810 (print) | LCCN 2017031070 (ebook) | ISBN 9781476731445 (eBook) | ISBN 9781476731421 (paperback)
Subjects: LCSH: Women forensic pathologists—Fiction. | Homicide investigation—Fiction. | France—Fiction. | BISAC: FICTION / Historical.
| FICTION / Suspense. | FICTION / Mystery & Detective / Historical. | LCGFT: Detective and mystery fiction
Classification: LCC PT8177.21.A24 (ebook) | LCC PT8177.21.A24 L49 2017 (print) | DDC 839.813/8—dc23
LC record available at https://lccn.loc.gov/2017027810

ISBN 978-1-4767-3142-1
ISBN 978-1-4767-3144-5 (ebook)

The idea is now hovering before me that man himself can act as creator even in living nature, forming it eventually according to his will.

—JACQUES LOEB, BIOLOGIST, FEBRUARY 26, 1890

A Lady in Shadows

She stood awkwardly, stooping to dip the sponge into the hot water. The steam from the copper tub rose up around her stocky figure, clinging moistly to her hair and skin, imprinted still with the marks left by the stays of her under bodice. She had retained her pantaloons, and he permitted it. For the moment, it was of no significance, just as it did not matter that she was neither handsome, nor slender, nor young.

"Sit down," he said.

"Monsieur?"

"Sit in the tub."

She did as she was told, albeit slowly and uncertainly. She looked as if she had never bathed before, and indeed it was possible that she had not, at least not like this. He imagined that for most of her life, her ablutions had been scant and hurried, performed at a washstand with a few splashes of cold water.

"I just want you to be clean," he said. "Everywhere."

"Monsieur. Might I do this . . . alone?"

"No," he said simply.

She had been standing under the streetlight outside Les Étoiles, with her shawl tied under her heavy breasts in order to present them to their best advantage. She was probably in her late twenties—not young, as noted, and there was a weariness even in the smile with which she tried to lure him closer. A narrow smile, with her mouth closed—later he discovered that she was missing several teeth—followed by a batting of the kohl-smeared eyelashes that did not have the seductive effect on him that she probably imagined it had. Her hair was so darkly auburn that it was nearly black, except for a russet sheen where the light fell; her dress was stained and threadbare, the hem fraying at the bottom.

They had agreed on four francs. He had therefore not expected her to be bashful about bathing in his presence.

"Wash yourself," he said. "What are you waiting for?"

On a chair next to the tub lay the worn dress and bodice, the black stockings, the blue shawl. She glanced in that direction as if she would have preferred to get dressed again.

"Listen," he said, with some annoyance, "you were willing to give yourself to me for four francs. If bathing first is such an inconvenience to you, I am prepared to raise the sum to five." That had been her original price.

"And then you wish that I . . . give myself afterward?"

He could tell she was making an effort to speak more properly than she was used to. He had noted the yellowish-brown stains that seemed ingrained in the skin of her hands, especially around the nails and in the folds of skin by her knuckles—a tobacco worker, he concluded. She might have been fired after the strike, or perhaps her meager factory wages simply did not stretch far enough to cover the rent. That was equally insignificant; he had no particular need for affected speech or parlor manners.

"Yes," he said, though that was not, in fact, what he had in mind. He had learned that the women became calmer when they knew the exact nature of the transaction. Or thought they knew.

It seemed to have the desired effect on the tobacco worker too. She sat down in the copper tub and ran the sponge over her upper body and neck, even managing a clumsy attempt at coquetry. The water was high enough to provide her pale, blue-veined breasts with a certain buoyancy, and the air trapped under the fabric of her undergarments caused them to balloon around her hips and thighs.

He made no attempt to hide his arousal—merely sat there in his armchair, legs apart, feeling his erection push against the fabric of his trousers. Foam clung to the nape of her neck where her hairline made it downy and dark. He did not touch himself, not yet. It was enough to see the sponge slide over breasts borne up by water, and when, in a moment of inspiration, she began to nip playfully at the sponge with her lips, he had to look away.

Waste not your seed on the ground, he admonished himself. *You have better uses for it.* He glanced at the tall glass that stood within convenient reach on the mahogany humidor next to the chair.

She raised one arm up out of the water, soaping it with long, near-graceful strokes. The sight of the dark hair in her armpit aroused him further, and one of his legs began to tremble. He breathed heavily through his mouth and placed a hand on his thigh in an attempt to keep the offending limb still.

Now she clearly felt that she was in control of the game. She arched her back and thrust her breasts forward, and let her right hand disappear into the water for a moment. In the thinly misted mirror at the foot of the bath, he could see that she was touching herself through the white cotton of the pantaloons.

"No," he said sharply. "Not you. All you have to do is . . . bathe."

The correction brought back her nervousness. She snatched her hand out of the water and reached for the soap instead, but it slipped from her wet fingers and skated across the floor, ending up at his feet.

"I'm sorry, m'sieur." She looked at him with widened eyes. Kohl bled into the half-dissolved face powder that still clung to her cheeks, and any attempt at grace had evaporated. But it did not matter. The scent of lavender soap, the wet trail across the floorboards, the smell of a woman's body and wet undergarments . . . he only just managed to get hold of the glass in time.

Later, he sat hunched over the microscope for almost an hour, observing them with an excited fascination infinitely more intense than anything the half-naked body of a woman could ignite in him. They looked like tiny, wriggly water creatures, darting tadpoles that raced in every direction in their drive toward life. One half of the moment of creation. A miracle so precious that five francs was a scant and almost insultingly low price to pay.

June 24, 1894

I t was an unusually hot and torpid night in June. Every window in the house had been left open, not just the ones overlooking our small rooftop garden, but those facing Carmelite Street as well, and yet not a breeze stirred. I lay dozing with only a sheet across me, but the heat made it difficult to fall deeply asleep.

Something was happening in the city. I could hear a faint murmuring unease, distant shouts, dogs barking, hoofbeats. A certain curiosity nudged my drowsiness. What had happened? Great disasters, great defeats, great victories . . . it had to be something like that, something that could move many people at once.

Oh, Lord. Had war broken out again?

Now wide awake, I listened carefully. The commotion was drawing nearer. There were footfalls and voices in our street now, so hushed that I could not distinguish any words, and yet somehow a sense of anxiety and anger seemed to communicate itself through the rising accents. Doors slammed. In the house across the way, the lights came on.

I sat up. Even as I did so, I heard steps immediately below my window, and then someone knocked rapidly at our door.

My father was away, he had been called to Saint Bernardine to do emergency surgery on a little boy who had been kicked in the head by a horse. Instead, Elise Vogler was staying over, sleeping on a cot in the living room as she so often did when he was not here. For some reason, no one seemed to believe that I was capable of sleeping alone in the house.

There was another knock—a long, insistent series of small, hard raps.

I leaned out the window and thought I recognized our neighbor, Madame Vogler.

"Elise," I called. "It's your mother."

I threw a shawl around my shoulders, out of consideration for propriety rather than any need to cover myself from the chill, and went downstairs to see what Madame Vogler wanted.

She was no more properly dressed than I. A skirt, to be sure, but under her shawl the blouse was no blouse at all, merely a sleeveless nightgown, and her blond hair, usually neatly pinned, hung limply down her back in a long braid. Her face was entirely dissolved into tears.

"Madeleine," she said, even though she rarely called me by my first name anymore. "Dear Lord, it is a terrible thing."

"What has happened?" I asked.

When the answer came, it hit me like a blow to the chest.

"Someone has murdered the president."

Madame Vogler was right. The president of the Third Republic, Marie François Sadi Carnot, had been stabbed by an Italian anarchist. The details reached us gradually. That Sunday, President Carnot had begun what was intended to be a three-day sojourn in Lyon to attend the great national exhibition being held there. After a banquet in his honor, he had just set off in the landau that was to take him to a gala performance at Lyon's theater. The vehicle was surrounded by cheering crowds who broke into "The Marseillaise" when they caught sight of the popular president. A young man made his way toward the carriage, waving a piece of paper that most people presumed was a petition of some kind. The cheering and tumult may have been a source of distraction for the president's escorts because the young man, Sante Geronimo Caserio, succeeded in reaching the landau without being stopped. He leaped onto the carriage step, clinging to the door with his left hand, and plunged the knife with his right, hitherto hidden by the paper, into the president's stomach.

The prefect from the Rhone district, Monsieur Riveaud, felled the young Italian with a single blow, but by then it was too late. The knife had penetrated the president's liver, and the internal bleeding could not be stopped. Some hours later, at twelve forty-five in the morning, the president of the Republic was declared dead.

The authorities sought to prevent the news from spreading too rapidly by stopping all telegrams dealing with the president's tragic plight, but there were enough phones in France now for this to be a forlorn effort. *Varbourg Gazette* had the first broadsheet on the street shortly after midnight—while the president still lived—and could cite the préfecture's latest bulletin: "The president's condition is critical, but far from hopeless. The wound is in the liver region. The bleeding, which at first was profuse, has now been stopped." *Varonne Soir* was slightly less timely, but more precise: "THE PRESIDENT MURDERED" shouted the succinct headline, above the scant details about his assassin that sufficed to ignite the spark of xenophobic rage even in peaceful Varbourg: He was an anarchist, and he was Italian.

That night, in the major cities of France, few people slept. Varbourg was no exception. Around the Italian consulate in Rue Picaterre, an agitated crowd had gathered, and the gendarmes had to be called in to protect the blameless office workers who lived and worked there. Several of them were not even Italian, but merely locals earning a living, stamping travel documents and expediting export permissions.

Madame Vogler made us coffee.

"I do hope the Doctor does not try to come home," she said. She almost always called my father "the Doctor," as if there was only the one in all the world. "It is not safe to walk the streets tonight!"

Going to bed was unthinkable. I was reminded of childhood summer visits with my aunt and uncle in the country. When there was a thunderstorm, everyone—from the smallest child to the oldest farmhand—would sit in the kitchen until the storm had passed, and my aunt and the kitchen maid would make coffee and put out bread and cheese. I remembered feeling indulged and anxious at the same time. It was exciting and unusual to be allowed to stay up so late and eat with the grown-ups, but also frightening with the thunder rolling and crashing overhead. The sudden pale flashes made the faces around the table appear stark and unfamiliar.

Madame Vogler, Elise, and I gathered in the salon, drinking our own "thunder coffee" while we waited for the human storm outside to subside.

Around four in the morning, there was a boom very close by, with a tinkling echo of glass falling to the ground.

"What was that?" Elise asked anxiously.

"I don't know." I got up, opened one of the windows, and leaned out to look. On Carmelite Street, there was nothing to be seen, but . . . did I smell smoke?

"Mademoiselle, be careful . . ." Madame Vogler was on her feet as well.

"Yes, yes." Definitely smoke, but not the comforting kind from fireplaces and hearths. This was a hostile reek—black, bitter, and acrid—and in the windows at the end of the street, I saw the reflected glow of flames.

"Someone has set fire to something," I said. "In Rue Perrault."

"Sweet Mary and Jesus," whispered Madame Vogler with quiet sincerity. "It's not a house, is it?"

"Perhaps it is just a bonfire . . . ," I suggested. I was too young to remember the Paris Commune and the unrest of 1871, yet I had some vague memory-like flashes of barricades and fires in the streets, which my imagination must have created from the stories I had heard. Such things seemed to me to accompany riots and outrage and public unrest.

"Oh no. I hope they light no fires here . . . ," said Elise.

There was yet another boom from Rue Perrault, and all at once the crowds came surging around the corner and down Carmelite Street. Our narrow, peaceful alley was suddenly filled by a tangled darkness. It was not possible to distinguish one darkly clad figure from the next, and I saw only a black wave, broken in glimpses by a flaming torch here, a hatless head there, and a lone upturned face, mouth open, like a drowning man gasping for air.

"Find them!" roared a mouth somewhere in the maelstrom. "Those bastards are not getting away from us!"

There was pounding on doors—ours as well. I had instinctively pulled back from the window already, and now Madame Vogler slammed it shut so hastily that there was a squeak of protest from hinges and hasps. But someone had seen me, apparently.

"Open up!" a second voice roared. "We'll get those murdering bastards, you just see if we don't!"

My heartbeat accelerated abruptly, and I felt a bitter dryness in my mouth. What murderers? It was absurd. They could hardly imagine that we were sheltering someone who had anything to do with the assassination. Or could they? There was a madness, an irrational violence in the shouts, the torches, the heavy fists that pounded on not just our door but also on random doors and windows down the entire street.

"Death to the anarchists!" someone shouted. "Death to the traitors!"

Anarchists?

"We aren't anarchists," whispered Elise. "What do they want?"

"I don't think they mean us in particular," I said. "I just think we happen to live in the wrong place . . ." I had realized that it might be the neighborhood itself that they wanted to wreak their vengeance on. It wasn't a purely working-class community; tradesmen and accountants and other families of the lower bourgeoisie lived here too, but in the old, narrow medieval streets, rents were considerably lower than along the boulevards in the city's modern center just a stone's throw away, which was also the reason my father and I lived here. And it was true that in Rue des Maisoniers a few streets away, there was a dilapidated half-timbered building that housed a Socialist society with its own printing press, but that had never caused us any trouble before now.

A flat crack echoed between the houses, and then another. The sound sent a galvanic spasm of fear through my entire body.

"Was that a shot?" gasped Madame Vogler.

"I'm afraid so." I hoped with all my heart that no one told Papa about the trouble here, or he would undoubtedly try to come home. I could barely stand the thought. Although the fractures he had suffered in the spring were more or less healed, he still could not walk without limping, and it seemed to me that in the press and surge of the crowds, his fragile body must inevitably be trampled and broken like a dry twig run over by a wagon wheel.

Shots. Though I was attempting to maintain my composure for the sake of Madame Vogler and Elise, the fearful jerk that had shuddered through my body at both the first and the second had no doubt been visible.

"It's probably just some hothead shooting into the air," I said, a little too late to maintain the relaxed and carefree demeanor I had meant to present. Not so long ago, someone had shot at me, deliberately and with the intention to kill, and certain natural reflexes were still hard to restrain. I turned away from the window to get my impulses under control and instead caught a pale flash in the French doors that led out to the little courtyard garden my mother had established on the flat roof of the kitchen many years ago.

For a second—no, a fraction of a second—I simply tried to make sense of what I had seen. Was it the lights in the salon that had created a peculiar reflection, or perhaps a bird, or a wayward scrap of paper caught in the wind?

Then I could not hold back a scream.

A face. A bloody face right outside the window, cupped by two bloody hands. A gaping, gasping mouth and two staring eyes wilder than those of a crazed horse.

Madame Vogler turned and screamed as well, but more quietly. One might think she had seen a mouse, not that she was about to be attacked by a madman. I think she recognized him almost at once in spite of the blood and the wild look. I realized who it was only some moments later when he knocked lightly on the pane with one hand, surprisingly politely, considering the circumstances.

It was Geraldo, dishwasher and errand boy at Chez Louis, the little bistro where my father and I usually went for dinner. Less than eight hours ago, we had been comfortably seated in the wicker chairs under the awning, enjoying an excellent coq au vin.

"Oh, the poor soul," exclaimed Madame Vogler, and I hurriedly opened the garden door.

Geraldo all but fell into my arms.

"Thank you," he sobbed, his speech wheezing and blurred. "Merciful Madonna, thank you."

I was not his "merciful Madonna," but his gaze clung to me almost as if I had somehow interceded on his behalf and saved him from a fate worse than death.

"What happened?" I asked. "Elise, get me some bandages and a basin. Is that kettle still hot?"

"Devils," gasped the wounded young man. "They were like devils. Shouting, screaming at us, calling us murderers, but they were the ones who wanted to kill. What is it they think we have done? We did not kill the poor president."

"Sit down," I said, and arranged for him to be seated as closely as possible to the lamp. There was so much blood that at first it was difficult to determine the extent of the damage, but it looked as if most of it was coming from a lesion on the forehead, right above his left eyebrow.

"We had to flee across the roof," he said. "Monsieur Marco went back when he had helped me down the wall. He took a washing line from one of the lofts . . . I was so afraid it would break."

"Where is Monsieur now?" Marco had become the owner of Chez Louis some years ago and had chosen to let the restaurant keep its more French-sounding name. Still, someone had apparently known that he had Italian roots.

"He stayed. He said . . . he said he had to keep an eye on the restaurant."

That sounded worrisome, but there was nothing we could do for our plump little café host now, other than hope and pray.

When I had washed the blood away, a cut was revealed that was almost nine centimeters long but luckily not all that deep.

"It needs stitching," I said. "Would you allow me to do it, or would you prefer to wait for my father?"

His eyes widened again into the wild stare that had made his arrival so frightening.

"Will it hurt?" he asked.

I thought quickly. We had a little ether, but it was probably better and safer to use nitrous oxide.

"Have you heard of laughing gas?" I asked.

He nodded. "I was at a variety show once, in Napoli." It was as if the recollection of his home sapped his last strength, and his lips, plump and full like a child's, began to quiver. "People could pay to come up on stage and try it, but I did not have the money . . ."

"Under the influence of the gas, you will not feel pain," I assured him. "You will probably just find my stitching entertaining. Afterward, the pain will be significantly reduced."

"Then . . . I would be grateful if it could happen quickly."

I brought him down to the laboratory. The sight of glass beakers, Bunsen burners, and our ancient microscope unfortunately did nothing to calm his fears, but it was much easier to create sterile conditions here where the tiles, tables, and floor could be wiped down with alcohol or sprayed with carbolic acid.

I prepared the gasbag, filled a test tube with ammonium nitrate, and placed it over the Bunsen burner. The gas bubbled up through a water-filled rubber hose and gradually filled the bag.

"Please have a seat," I said to my tense patient and indicated the long zinc-topped workbench. It was not the first time it had served as an operating table. Geraldo hauled himself up to sit obediently, if somewhat nervously.

"Breathe in through your mouth and out through your nose," I said, and held the mouthpiece of the gasbag toward him. "Can you manage that?"

He nodded. Silence descended while we watched Geraldo's breathing. His concentration on the mouthpiece was so intense it made him squint almost comically, but he settled visibly right away. I did not think this was solely the effect of the gas—it was as if the effort to control his respiration in itself had a calming effect.

"You may lie down now," I said. "But continue to breathe through the mouthpiece."

He was slow now and beginning to show the effects of the nitrous oxide. Elise and I had to help him get his legs up on the table, and Madame Vogler folded a clean cloth and placed it under his head.

"Elise," I said, "you have to hold the bag."

Elise nodded. She had grown used to assisting with various emergency procedures, though it was the first time she had stood in as an anesthetist. That was usually my responsibility when my father performed surgery at home.

I stitched the cut with care, but also as swiftly as I was able. The shorter the anesthesia, the milder the aftereffects. Geraldo was humming as I stitched. Occasional words emerged from the humming, luckily in Italian, because based on Geraldo's own giggles, I sensed that the content might not have been entirely appropriate.

"Thank you," I said to Elise and her mother, once I was satisfied with my work. "Would you open the window and give us some fresh air?" I took the now deflated gasbag from Elise. She let go only reluctantly.

"May I try?" she asked. "They say it is hilarious."

I shook my head. "It is for medicinal use only. Regardless of what Geraldo may have witnessed at the variety show, no one should inhale this for fun."

I bandaged the wound with surgical gauze treated with carbolic and felt quite uplifted and satisfied with the results of my effort. There was, I felt, a good chance that the cut would heal without infection and leave only a faint scar.

I had been so intent on my task that the disturbance outside and my worry about my father had receded from my awareness. Now both reasserted themselves. Through the open window we could still hear shouting and noise and the tinkling of broken glass, though it sounded more distant here than upstairs in the salon.

Geraldo had stopped singing. He raised his hand to his forehead, but I caught it before he could touch the bandage.

"Please remain still. Do not attempt to sit up before you are ready," I admonished him.

The effect of the gas was fading, but he was not yet quite himself.

"Mamma," he moaned in his own soft native tongue. "I want to go home . . ."

Two days later, he did just that, with an admonishment to see a doctor in ten days and have the stitches removed. Marco did not dare keep him in town, or even in the country, given the current atmosphere. But let us not get ahead of ourselves. The long, tumultuous night might have been coming to an end, but the day had barely begun.

June 25, 1894

I n the morning, when the night's unrest was tapering off, a message came from the hospital. My father was fine, but he had gone out to Petite Napoli, as the neighborhood between Pont d'Elise and Rue d'Artois was referred to colloquially. This was where a large part of Varonne's Italian immigrant population lived, which had led to street fighting, attacks, and fires. I should not count on seeing him before evening.

"Terrible," said Madame Vogler. "What a horrific night."

Elise dared to go down to see if there was any bread to be had. She returned with four-day-old croissants, but reported that Monsieur Margoli, our local baker, was planning to have fresh brioche within the hour.

"Anyone would think there had been a war," she said, her eyes shining with distress. "There is rubble and broken glass everywhere, and it stinks of soot and ashes."

"Did you see Monsieur Marco?"

"No," she said. "But all the windows in the restaurant have been broken, and the mob dragged the chairs and tables into the street and set fire to them."

"Dreadful," said Madame Vogler. "What is the world coming to?"

Geraldo was still lying in my father's bed sleeping, exhausted after his ordeal. Elise, Madame Vogler, and I made tea and ate stale, sticky croissants smeared with strawberry jam.

I had just poured myself a second cup of tea when there was a knock at the door—not an aggressive drumming like the one we had experienced the night before, but nonetheless quite authoritative. The caller was a tired, middle-aged corporal of the gendarmerie, who had clearly had a trying night—two buttons were missing from his tunic, and one sleeve was blackened with soot. A little farther down the street, an entirely civilian hansom cab was waiting.

"Mademoiselle Karno? The Commissioner requests that you and your father accompany me."

The Commissioner was not an officer of the police or the gendarmerie, but Varbourg's Commissaire des Morts, the man ultimately responsible for all of the city's dead. There was thus no reason to ask why our services were needed, so I simply informed the corporal that my father was busy with the living right now and was not expected home until later in the day.

The man glared at me with visible irritation. He just wanted to carry out his orders and be done with it, I sensed.

"Then we shall have to make do with you, mademoiselle," he said. "If you would be so kind . . ."

A job half done, it would seem, was better than nothing.

Daylight was a dubious blessing. Had it still been night, the sight that met us might have led even a rational soul like mine to fanciful fears of the shadows. Now nothing was hidden. Every gruesome detail was revealed by the morning light, with the sort of prurient clarity certain painters lavish on pseudoclassical half-naked damsels in distress.

She had been found in a narrow yard used by a coal merchant for storage. A length of corrugated roofing ran along one wall, and beneath it fifty or sixty coal sacks had been piled in a row. The coal dust had blackened the wall indelibly, and the cobblestones were greasy with soot and so uniformly black that only the contours of the coins revealed that there were in fact cobbles. Against this sinister backdrop, the sprawled limbs of the young woman appeared alabaster white, and the deep copper glow of her hair was a brutal shock of color, a lone sea anemone in a primal, lightless sea.

Her skirts had been rucked up around her waist, leaving her legs, belly, and crotch exposed, and she was wearing neither stockings nor shoes. Someone had slashed open her lower abdomen with a number of forceful incisions, several so deep that they had penetrated the abdominal cavity. The glistening coils of the colon were plainly visible.

"I'm sorry," the Commissioner said quietly. "It is not a pleasant sight."

I appreciated the fact that he did not add "for a young lady." I fought hard to be perceived as my father's assistant, a professional who merely happened to be female and twenty-one. I knew that the Commissioner did respect my knowledge and my skills, but he had known me since I was a little girl in pigtails, and he still called me "sweet Madeleine" most of the time. His protective instincts were kept in check only by an act of will.

"I would be grateful if you would perform the necessary in situ examination, Mademoiselle Karno," he said with a formality that was directed at the various representatives of the gendarmerie. "We would like to bring her to the morgue as fast as is appropriate before the so-called gentlemen of the press show up."

"I would have thought they had enough to keep them occupied elsewhere today," I said. "But I'll work as quickly as I may." There was already a smaller gathering at the gate, and most of the windows above us had been flung open. Men in shirtsleeves and suspenders leaned out to get a better view, jostled for the privilege by women with their hair still in untidy nighttime braids and even several gaping children sporting only runny noses and nightshirts. If it had been a normal Monday morning, most of the adults would have been at work, but since the factories and workshops and mills were closed for the day because of the presidential murder, we had a large and interested audience. Although the corrugated roof fortunately blocked a part of the view, the fact that a violent crime had been committed in the coal merchant's yard would not long be a secret to the general population of Varbourg.

I opened my father's spare bag, now mine, unwrapped the thermometer from its travel case, and performed an initial measurement of the air temperature. The night had not brought any coolness, and here in the still air between the tall sooty walls the mercury crept up to indicate 33.1°C.

"Is the photographer coming?" I asked.

"He has been sent for."

In spite of this, I took out my drawing pad and began to sketch the body's position—the arch of the upper body across the toppled coal sacks, the loose-limbed opened legs, the rucked-up skirts. Photographs are a wonderfully objective source of evidence that may be useful in any court case, but my own sketches give me something more. They sharpen my powers of observation and push emotion into the background, and later they may help me to recall colors, depth, and detail that the camera's flattened black-and-white representation does not have the power to re-create.

The Commissioner waited, patient and silent, while my charcoal stick flew across the paper. First two general overviews, then details: the lesions, naturally, but also the feet—bare, and pointed like a dancer's—the hands, not clenched, just with faintly curled fingers. And the face.

In view of the brutality of the attack, one might have expected a contorted grimace, wide staring eyes, a gaping mouth. There was nothing of the kind.

Her eyes were closed. I could not make out even a glimmer under the thick, dark lashes. Her features were relaxed, almost smiling, her lips only slightly parted. She had the classic oval face of a Botticelli Madonna, the forehead smooth and high, the chin soft and feminine. Her lips were full, her cheeks round. Despite the lividity, one could still imagine the warm glow her skin must have had when she was alive, now faded and yellowed, like paper left too long in the sun. There were no marks or lesions on her face. No broken nails or traces of blood on her hands. From the waist up she was flawless, serene, without disfigurement. In contrast, her lacerated abdomen was brutal.

The photographer arrived, and I stepped back so he could do his work. Varbourg's police had only the one, a young man named Aristide Gilbert. He could not survive on police work alone, and had a portrait studio on a side street off Rue Germain, where the common citizen could have himself and his family immortalized for a relatively modest sum. Gilbert was no artist, no aesthete. He could not arrange and light his subjects so that the ladies could catch a glimpse of their own faded beauty, had no power to portray the glue manufacturer and the brick master with a dignity that suggested noble ancestors. He photographed what was in front of the camera. No more, no less. He would never be the preferred portraitist of the bourgeoisie, but his police photographs were technically without fault.

"Mademoiselle Karno," he said, and raised his derby politely. "Your father is not here?"

"No, unfortunately not," I said. "He is busy. But the Commissioner wanted the body brought in before . . ." I nodded at the gathering crowd on the other side of the wrought-iron gate.

"I understand," he said. "Is there anything special you wish me to photograph?"

"The lesions, of course, but also the hands and the face."

He nodded and began to mount his apparatus on the tripod.

While he worked, I crouched down and scratched at the sticky mixture of coal dust and ordinary dirt that covered the cobblestones.

"Are there any footprints?" I asked the Commissioner.

"Too many." He sighed. "During the day, a lot of people have reason to be here, and it's not possible for us to distinguish those of the killer from the others."

"The soles of her feet are completely clean," I said. "I think I might extract some textile fibers from between her toes, that is all. And they will most likely be from her stockings."

"Do it anyway," said the Commissioner. "If we succeed in finding the stockings, we might at least be able to prove that they are hers. Was she killed here?"

"I should think not," I said. "Because of the coal dust, it is difficult to determine precisely how much blood is here, but . . . it is not enough. I am sure lividity will tell the same story when we get her undressed."

A minor tumult had broken out by the gate. A clear young voice cut through the general susurration.

"Monsieur le Commissaire! Let me see her!"

The Commissioner turned his head sharply, and I saw that he recognized the person who had called out.

"Will you excuse me for a moment," he said, and headed toward the gate. He returned a little later followed by a sparrow of a young girl, small, light, with lively dark eyes and black hair and a body that, except for the breasts and a certain fullness around the hips, could have belonged to an eleven-year-old. She barely reached his chest.

"Let me see her," she repeated. "I have to see if it's Rosalba!"

When she came closer, I noticed that she was not quite as young as I had at first assumed—but rather my own age or perhaps even a few years older. She was wearing a flowered cotton dress that emphasized her little-girl proportions, and the heels of her button boots were of an extremely modest height. Her dark hair was put up in a simple chignon, and her face was almost free of makeup—a light touch of powder across the cheeks, that was all. It was mostly her hips and the faint crow's-feet by her eyes that revealed that I was not, in fact, facing a schoolgirl.

"You must wait a moment," I said. "Mademoiselle . . ."

"Fleur," she said. "My name is Fleur."

It was only then that I realized she was probably a prostitute. Most young women would have presented themselves with their last name, but among the ladies of the night it was common to use only their first name or an alias.

"Mademoiselle Fleur. You will have to wait a few more minutes before we can allow you near the body."

"Oh, oh. I must know, can't you see that?"

She was gray with emotion, and there were tear tracks on her powdered cheeks.

"In a moment, mademoiselle. As soon as we are ready, I promise you."

The Commissioner cleared his throat and handed her his handkerchief. She took it but then simply held it in her hand, as if she had no idea why he thought she should need such a thing.

The photographer moved the camera into position and ducked under the hood. I could hear the click from the shutter mechanism. After a few moments his upper body and head appeared again.

"I think that is that," he said. "I can have the pictures ready tomorrow."

"Thank you," said the Commissioner slightly absently. "Madeleine, could you . . ." He gestured vaguely in the direction of the body, and I nodded. I understood. No one who had known the young woman with the Botticelli face should see her as she was now.

I ducked under the corrugated roof. Now that we had photographed the body as it had been found, I could do two things. First I measured the body temperature—35.0 degrees—and then I pulled down her skirts quickly so that they covered both the exposed abdomen and the terrible lesions. There were dried bloodstains on her petticoat, but not as many as one might have expected. I smoothed the blue dress as best I could, but otherwise there was not much I could do to soften the impact of her death.

"Please, mademoiselle."

Now that we had agreed to her demand, she hesitated for a few seconds. Then she nodded with pale determination and approached me and the body. Recognition was instant. I could see it in her shoulders, in her entire body. She hid the lower part of her face in her hands while the dark eyes still peeked out above her fingers.

"Oh, God," she said. "Oh no. Oh, God."

"What was her name?" I asked gently.

She swallowed and had to clear her throat. "Rosalba. Rosalba Lombardi."

"Italian?"

"Yes. From Parma. Oh no. Do you think . . . ? Is that why? Has someone . . . because of the president . . . ?"

"It is too soon to tell," I said. I could not rule it out. Not when I thought about Monsieur Marco's broken windows and Geraldo, who had had to flee for his life.

A deep shudder went through her slight shoulders, followed by a violent broken sob that came all the way from her diaphragm. Instinctively, I placed a hand on her shoulder.

"I'm so sorry, mademoiselle. My deepest condolences." I did not ask if she was a close friend or perhaps a relative. Her grief was obvious, and the police would soon be pelting her with such questions. There was no call for me to lead the attack.

"Would you come to the morgue later?" I asked instead.

"Why?"

"To sign a formal declaration of identification. And to help me go through her personal belongings to see if anything is missing."

She nodded. In one sudden movement, she knelt next to

the body and reached out for the dead woman's hand. When I stopped her, she looked up at me in confusion.

"Not yet," I said. "But you will be able to say good-bye later."

The Commissioner gallantly assisted me onto the box of the hearse as if he was offering me a ride in an elegant carriage.

"What are your first impressions, Madeleine?" he asked. Still somewhat formally because the driver was listening.

I thought about it for a moment.

"Contradictions," I said. "There is something inconsistent about it all. The brutality of the incisions, and yet no fear, no signs of struggle, no resistance. The violence is solely directed at her abdomen; there is not so much as a bruise anywhere else. Of course it is possible that we will find something when we undress her, but, as I said, I don't think she was killed here, so this is not a case of a sudden rage and an attack on the spot. At least not this spot. Rage and planning. Peculiar mixture, don't you think?"

He bowed his head lightly. "It has been known to happen. But not often, I admit."

The driver clicked his tongue and slapped the reins against the hindquarters of the two powerful Ardennes horses that were pulling the wagon. With a jerk, we began to move. The gate was opened, the mass of people moved to the side so we could pass.

"Who is she, Commissioner?" someone in the crowd shouted, possibly one of those "gentlemen of the press" whom the Commissioner had been so anxious to avoid. The Commissioner ignored the question with his usual granite impassiveness.

"The time of death?" he asked me quietly, without taking his eyes off the horses.

The journalist, however, did not give up that easily. "Mr. Commissioner. Do we now have our own Jack the Ripper in Varbourg?"

I could not help reacting. How did he know that? How could

he have such knowledge of the lesions on the corpse? He had to know, why otherwise the comparison with London's notorious serial killer? I scanned the crowd to find the man who had yelled. It was the notebook that gave him away. The straw hat, silk vest, and the casual shirtsleeves were, in my eyes, more suitable for a flâneur on his way to a rowing excursion on the Var River.

The Commissioner placed a hand on my arm.

"Say nothing," he admonished me quietly. "Even an unvarnished no can become a confirmation of some spurious theory before they have finished reworking the truth. Madeleine—the time of death? What can you say about that?"

I knew he was insisting not just because he needed to know—a piece of information of vital importance both for his own report and for the consequent police investigation—but also to get me to ignore the crowd and especially the man with the notebook. It worked. I had to turn my attention inward, recall the details.

"Her body temperature had dropped to thirty-five degrees," I said. "And rigor mortis was pronounced." I hesitated and thought of the heat, the heavy, oppressive heat that had made sleep difficult even before the riots had started. Had it remained that hot all night? That might be the case. The temperature could have been even higher than the 33.1 degrees I had registered for the morning air. In that case, the body's temperature did not tell us much. Once it reached the same level as the surroundings, it would not drop any further. Ordinarily, it took about twelve hours for the temperature difference between the body and the surroundings to halve. But I also knew that the smaller this difference was to begin with, the slower the body temperature would drop. Other factors played a role as well. I did not know how long she had lain here, only that she had been placed where she was found before rigor mortis set in, that is, within a few hours of her death. *If* you assumed that the temperature in that airless space between the blackened walls had held constant throughout the night, which in itself was a considerable if . . .

I calculated as best I could in my head. The Commissioner did not disturb me.

A difference of two degrees. Was that a halving?

Rigor mortis was full-blown—the bare pointed feet had been as stiff as the rest of her. Thus it was at least eight hours since she had been killed and possibly as much as twelve. But again, the heat must have affected this process, just in reverse—where the body temperature fell more slowly because of the heat, rigor mortis progressed more quickly.

"She probably died between eight in the evening and two in the morning," I said.

The Commissioner growled. "Could you narrow that down in any way?"

"Not right now," I answered. I did not dare to give up the margin of error I had added. "The contents of her stomach might be able to help us if we can discover when she had her last meal."

The horses clip-clopped down Rue Colbert, with a few curious observers still bringing up the rear, primarily street urchins who ran alongside and shouted in high, singsong voices: "It's a dead 'un, it's a dead 'un, come and look, it's a dead 'un . . ."

Annoyed, the driver lashed out with his whip at a few of the more daring ones.

"Let them be, Jacques," said the Commissioner. "They will get tired of it soon."

He was right. When we turned the next corner and continued down toward the Arsenal Bridge, most of them dropped away. Only one stubborn—and silent—boy followed us for the length of another street before he also gave up.

"It would be nice to know if the killing happened before or after one o'clock," said the Commissioner. "Or rather, before or after it was generally known that an Italian had assassinated our president."

"I know," I said. "Perhaps my father can be more precise."

For some reason that simple remark silenced the Commissioner. He glanced at the driver and rubbed the sweat from his neck with a broad and damp hand.

"Yes," he said at last, as if he had continued the conversation somewhere inside himself. "How is he?"

"Papa?" I said, a bit surprised. "Perfectly well. Or I assume so; he has no doubt had a hard and busy night without sleep. Why?"

"Does one need a reason to ask after the health of a good friend?"

"Of course not. I merely thought that . . . Well, I assumed you knew about as much about the subject as I do." Hardly a day passed without the two men seeing each other, professionally or privately. The Commissioner had a habit of dropping by the house in Carmelite Street most days of the week, quite frequently at mealtimes.

Or . . . That is . . . I realized that it had in fact been a while since he had taken his usual place in the plush armchair. At least a week, perhaps even more than that.

"Have you two had a disagreement?" The imprudent remark shot out of my mouth, though I knew that so direct a question was unlikely to receive an honest answer.

"Not at all," declared the Commissioner.

No more was said about the matter before we reached the morgue and he helped me down from the hearse. While Jacques unhitched the horses, the corpse was carried from the wagon by two gendarmes into the cool cellar where most official autopsies took place. I turned automatically to follow, but the Commissioner stopped me.

"Madeleine . . ."

"Yes?"

"There is something I want to ask you."

I smiled encouragingly. "Please do."

He stood there and seemed almost . . . well, if it had been anyone else, I would have said embarrassed. He was a large, solid man, broad in all directions, with round legs and big hands, a ruddy, roughly carved face, and thick graying hair. I did not know exactly how old he was but assumed he had to be over fifty. To see him standing there, blushing like a schoolboy, was an odd experience.

"I . . . have become engaged to be married," he said.

"Utter shock" probably expressed my feelings best, but I tried not to let it show.

"Congratulations," I said. "What a surprise! Is it someone I know?"

As long as I had known him, the Commissioner had lived in the same guesthouse, a nice and clean but not especially exciting establishment in the Arsenal district. I had thought that Papa and I were the closest he would ever come to a family.

"In a way," he growled. "In a way. It is Marie Mercier. Louis's mother."

He looked at me with a mixture of pride and uneasiness, and I completely understood why. In the spring, my father and the Commissioner had been sought out by Marie Mercier, who was in a state because her nine-year-old son had disappeared. That part of the story ended fairly happily. We found Louis alive, and Madame Mercier had literally kissed the Commissioner's hands out of sheer gratitude. I had noted even then that this made an impression, but Marie was also an uncommonly beautiful woman, though it required more and more effort to maintain her wasp waist, the carefully dyed hair, and the youthful glow. "Prostitute" was really too coarse a word to use about her refined person, and she was hardly a simple streetwalker. But that her warmth and her beauty were for sale, and had been for some years, there was no doubt.

"Congratulations," I repeated because I did not know what

else to say. Perhaps it was a form of salvation for both of them, a chance to experience security and companionship and love in a way that neither had dared to dream of. Perhaps. But that was probably not the way the world would see it. "When is the wedding?"

"The seventh," he said. "We saw no reason to delay any longer. Just a simple ceremony at the *mairie*, but it would make us both extremely happy if you and your father would attend."

"Does Papa know?"

"No." He blushed once more, this rock of a man who never revealed his emotions. "I hoped . . . Would you tell him, sweet Madeleine?"

"Would it not be better if you yourself . . . ," I began.

"Marie has written an invitation," he said before I could finish my hesitant sentence, and pulled an envelope from his inner pocket. It had been there for a while, I judged, based on the slightly concave shape, the dog-eared corners, and certain other signs of wear and tear. The handwriting was neat and feminine, and care seemed to radiate from every pen stroke. *To Dr. Albert Karno and Mademoiselle Madeleine Karno.*

"Please make him come," the Commissioner asked. "It would mean so much to Marie and me."

"I will do my best," I said. But I had absolutely no idea how Papa would react to this news.

They had placed Rosalba Lombardi on the autopsy table. Due to rigor mortis, her legs were still parted, and her back still arched in the awkward curve formed by its contact with the coal sack, but the stretcher bearers had felt obliged to smooth her skirts so that they covered the horrors below.

Two kinds of corpses ended up in the public morgue: those whose identity could not immediately be determined and those who had clearly lost their lives under unnatural circumstances.

Here death was not softened by the comfort of rituals—here were no candles, flowers, or priests, just a brightly lit basement, which even now in the sweltering summer heat was cool bordering on the chilly. The floor was covered in glazed white tiles, and under the paint of the bare white walls one could just make out the contours of the raw bricks. But there was running water and several well-functioning drains and, high on my list of priorities, electric light.

In the course of the past few months, the staff had grown accustomed to my presence, so Jean-Baptiste, the place's porter and handyman, merely nodded at me and asked if I would like coffee or tea. His wife, Marianne, a curt but not unkind woman in her fifties, helped with the cleaning and was also the one who brought the hot drinks that kept the chill of the basement at bay.

"Oh, that would be nice. Tea, thank you, Jean-Baptiste."

"Of course, mademoiselle."

He disappeared up the stairs—he and Marianne lived in a room behind the porter's lodge. In the meantime, in spite of the cold, I removed not just hat and gloves but also the chiffon blouse and the gray serge skirt I was wearing and hung both in the changing room. The smell had a tendency to cling rather tenaciously to my clothing and my hair. I had thus made a smock for myself, not unlike the Bernardine Sisters' habit, from coarse cotton twill and supplemented it with a white scarf and apron that, like the smock, could be boiled. The outfit made me look like a cross between a convent novitiate and a charwoman, but I consoled myself with the thought that the dead cared little for such niceties.

When I emerged from the changing room, Jean-Baptiste had returned with the tea.

"When can we expect the doctor?" he asked.

"I don't know, Jean-Baptiste. Probably not until sometime this afternoon."

He smiled.

"It is almost one, mademoiselle."

Was it? The time had passed more quickly than I had realized. Had three hours really gone by since I walked into the coal merchant's courtyard in Rue Colbert?

That reminded me of something.

"A young lady will be coming by in a little while, a Mademoiselle Fleur. Would you and Marianne take good care of her until I am ready down here? She was very close to the deceased."

"Of course, mademoiselle." He hesitated a moment. "Terrible about the president," he then added, as if two people could not meet on this day without at least mentioning what had happened.

"Yes. A tragedy."

He looked as if he might have said something more, but he just placed the tea tray on the little desk by the door before he disappeared upstairs to Marianne and warmer climes.

I sipped the tea, but it was still too hot to drink. Then I turned to Rosalba Lombardi.

Even when a definite identification is believed to have been made, Lacassagne's excellent procedure, presented in *Vade-mecum du médecin-expert*, prescribes an initial physical description of the body. Take nothing for granted, he admonishes. You must learn to doubt.

Thus I measured the length of the thigh (46.3 centimeters) and established by way of Lacassagne's tables that she must have been just about 163 centimeters tall—the height of a prone and dead person will always diverge significantly from the standing height the person had while alive, and it is therefore better to base one's calculation on the length of the femur, tibia, fibula, radius, humerus, or ulna. I opened both her eyes to see the color—brown. Noted her nutritional health—good—and the outer signs of her age. I then proceeded to list the details of her garments—a crêpe de chine dress in a fashionable midnight blue that complemented her titian hair admirably. An expensive dress, I thought, though possibly bought secondhand—there were signs that it had been let out at the waist. If she, like Fleur, made a living satisfying men's desires, then she had lived quite well.

The most noteworthy thing was that she was not wearing a corset. Under the dress there was just a thin white camisole and a petticoat, but since the dress had been made to fit her corset measurements, it had not been possible to hook it up completely at the back.

I had difficulty imagining that a woman with Mademoiselle Lombardi's sense of style would appear in public in a dress that was open at the back. Likewise, it was hard to believe that she would go anywhere without a corset. Add to that the missing stockings and shoes, and—upon looking more closely—the cuff on one of the tight-fitting sleeves of her dress that was buttoned crookedly.

It was an obvious assumption that she had not put on the dress herself, that someone—possibly her killer—had dressed her after she died. This would also explain why there was blood on the underskirt but not on the dress. I imagined her dressed only in her petticoat and camisole, in a bed—it had to be a bed, didn't it? And most likely not her own. A lover, a client? Would there be any trace of semen?

I made a note to look but did not depart from the procedure. I must not get ahead of myself. It was far too early to form a hypothesis.

I began to undress the body. It is often possible to ease rigor mortis by manipulating the limbs, and I did so, partly to make the undressing possible, partly thinking of the promise I had made to Fleur. Taking leave of the dead was always painful, but might be made at least a little easier if the corpse had been allowed some dignity, some appearance of repose.

Unclothed, the corpse's brutal molestation was apparent.

Less than twenty-four hours ago, this had been the body of a beautiful woman, alive and breathing, with gentle curves and blushing skin. Now the lacerations in her abdomen, garishly black and brown and purple against the pallid skin, were so numerous that only close examination allowed one to distinguish the individual lesions. The intestines had been perforated in several places, and I could smell the partially digested contents which, from what I could see, appeared dark and sparse. I did not want to start on the actual autopsy until my father arrived—not unless the Commissioner asked me directly to do so and thus authorized me. At the moment he was off again, to register a different and more peaceful death in the home of a master builder on Place Tertiaire. I was not a qualified physician in the eyes of the authorities, and I was not going to let my lack of official status cast even a shadow of a doubt on the evidence of the prosecution if it ever came to a trial. But we had an unspoken agreement that, for the sake of propriety, it was up to me to undress female corpses, and thus I could at least perform the initial examination. If Papa wished, he could check every fact I noted in the autopsy report. But he rarely felt that that was necessary anymore.

I undertook a minute examination of Rosalba's undressed body, from the crown of her head to the soles of her feet. Postmortem lividity indicated that she had been lying on her side for some time after death had occurred, but her back was more vividly marked. In her mouth, besides a substantial amount of slime, I found a yellow substance that looked like wax—not a lot, just several thin flakes. I took a few samples, mostly because I was curious. How did a corpse end up with wax in its mouth? People did not usually go around gnawing on candles. A cheese crust, perhaps? I noted my findings but did not draw any conclusion.

Under her nails, I found nothing except a whitish mixture of soap residue and cast-off skin cells. Her feet too were just as clean as they had looked at first glance. Under the magnifying glass, the textile fibers that I had noticed during my first examination looked as if they had come from a towel rather than ordinary stocking lint, which would disappoint the Commissioner. And when I carefully brushed her hair, I found nothing except more soap residue. She did not have lice, which in itself was noteworthy. All in all, it seemed as if her sense of personal hygiene was well above the norm. And in spite of my initial assumption about how she had spent her last hours on earth, I found no traces of sperm, on her body or in her undergarments.

Jean-Baptiste knocked quietly on the door. "Mademoiselle Fleur has arrived," he said.

"Thank you." I looked around quickly. "Would you offer her a cup of tea and ask her to wait for a little while? I'll come get her when I am ready."

Rosalba's face was already so peaceful that I could not add or subtract anything. So I merely fetched a clean white sheet and covered the rest of her. I sprayed a bit of carbolic around the room, in a sadly inadequate attempt to alleviate the ever-present smell of death. On a last impulse, I found two candles from our emergency stash—the electricity failed during our work quite often—and placed them in candlesticks on the instrument cabinet next to the examination table. I hoped that the soft candlelight would throw a meager glow of spirituality on the morgue's patently concrete and practical approach to the decay of the flesh.

I washed my hands and face and took off the head scarf, telling myself that it was so Fleur would be able to recognize me more easily, but I knew deep down the real impulse—I did not wish to look like a washerwoman.

She was sitting on the small porch that led into the laundry yard, with the freshly washed white sheets as a billowing backdrop in the shimmering heat of the sun. She too had changed her apparel: She was now dressed in a dark gray walking suit with black trim, a flat-crowned black hat trimmed with a light veil, gray lace gloves, and high-heeled black ankle boots with spats of gray suede. No one would take her for a schoolgirl now. She balanced the saucer on her right hand, a few centimeters under the teacup she was sipping from. One got the impression that she was afraid of spilling.

"Thank you for coming," I said. "This way, please."

She looked up with a glittering dark and observant gaze. Then she carefully put down the teacup and rose.

"I think I am still trying to convince myself that it did not happen," she said quietly.

"Yes," I answered. "I am so sorry."

She followed me down the stairs. After the blinding white light of the laundry yard, the stairwell seemed like the entrance to a cave, dark and narrow, although the steps were actually quite wide and had been designed to allow coffins to be carried up and down. The temperature fell noticeably with every step. I had to overcome a desire to apologize for both the cold and the general bleakness of the surroundings.

Fleur walked directly to the dead woman, without hesitation this time, and stood looking at her for a long time.

"You cannot tell," she said.

"What?"

"What happened. The way she died. She looks as if she died in her sleep."

"Yes."

"May I touch her now?"

"As long as you do not remove the sheet."

"Thank you."

She placed a hand against the dead woman's cheek and neck and caressed both gently. There was an intimacy to the gesture that made me feel like a voyeur, spying on something treasured and intimate, and I instinctively turned away.

"I can give you a moment alone with her if you would like," I said quietly.

"Thank you," she answered.

I retreated to the long, narrow office located a few steps higher up the stairs. Two windows facing the autopsy room allowed an assistant to take dictation from the autopsy without having to be in the room. It was not an option I normally made use of, but right now it was practical because I would still be able to claim that I had not permitted anyone to approach the body without supervision.

I sat down and began to prepare the certificate of identification, the autopsy report, and our official book of records. In the records, I noted only the date and time the body was brought in, wrote "preliminary identification: Rosalba Lombardi," and gave the case a number. In the report, I detailed the initial measurements and discoveries I had made, though not without having first outlined everything in my own notebook—partly to keep the report free from errors and corrections, partly because this automatically provided me with a copy for myself. The pile of notebooks at home in my drawer went back years; I had been my father's secretary long before he officially agreed to let me assist him with the actual autopsies. I was fourteen when I began the first one.

Every few minutes, I cast a quick glance down into the autopsy room. Due to the difference in floor levels, Fleur probably had not realized she was under observation. From her point of view, the windows were so high up that they were not very noticeable, and she would not be able to see me unless I leaned really close to the glass. This should probably have made the voyeuristic sensation stronger but, paradoxically, I felt less of a spy than I had while standing next to her in the room.

She bent over the dead woman and kissed her. Then she held one of the candles close to the dead woman's face, forced open an eyelid, and tried to peer into the dead eye underneath.

This was not what I had imagined would happen when I allowed her solitary devotions . . .

"Stop that!" I shouted through my hurriedly opened window. "What on earth do you think you are doing?"

Fleur glanced up at me without letting go of the dead woman. Her eyes were very dark and very shiny, her face at once expressionless and intense. I think she was calculating how long it would take me to get down there to stop her. Quickly, she bent over the corpse again and resumed her examination.

I raced down the stairs, pushed open the door, and marched up to her.

"I said 'stop'!"

I had to take hold of her thin shoulders and force her away. I was more than a head taller than she was, and for a brief moment it felt as if I was struggling with a child. But no child could have brought to bear such desperate strength of resistance. We were both breathing rather wildly before I succeeded in dragging her away from the body.

Abruptly, her resistance broke. She did not sob, but the tears were streaming down her face nonetheless.

"I couldn't see anything," she said. "Please, will you do it? You have instruments, microscopes . . . a camera."

"What is it you imagine I would be able to see?"

"Him. The monster who did this. He ought to be there, but I can't see him. Please, please get your photographer to—"

"Mademoiselle . . . ," I said as gently as possible. "It is not possible. No matter what you may have heard or read, the eye does not have the ability to retain an image after death."

The English journal *The Lancet* had attempted to bury this

belief more than thirty years ago, but it kept reappearing, even in the normally well-informed part of the public debate. It was not the first time a distressed relative had demanded that we attempt to photograph the last sight that had passed before the eyes of a loved one, but I had never known someone to try to get that last glimpse with the naked eye.

"It is because her eyes were closed, is it not?" said Fleur slowly. "She died with her eyes closed and did not see him. That is why he is not there . . ."

I shook my head faintly. "There is no scientific evidence that—"

But she did not hear me. She turned to the dead woman on the table.

"You should have fought," she told her. "You should have clawed him with your nails, bit him with your teeth, seen him . . . why didn't you *fight?*"

One eye was still open, the other closed. It looked as if the body was trying to wink at us. I closed the forcefully opened eye and immediately felt better. I tried in every way to handle the dead with respect but without emotional weakness, and normally it took more than this to throw me off balance. But Fleur's behavior had punctured my professionalism and turned Rosalba into something other than another body I needed to examine, I had to acknowledge that now.

"Mademoiselle . . . if you would come with me up to the office. I have prepared the certificate of identification."

She made no move to leave. I had to place a hand on her arm before she turned to follow me.

She signed the certificate with a largely illegible signature. "Fleur" could be deciphered but not her last name.

"I have to ask for your full name," I said. "Otherwise the certificate is not valid."

"Fleur Petit," she said.

I looked at her. Petit was, of course, a fairly common last name. There were no doubt a number of small women and short men who had to live with a last name that sounded more like a jocular sobriquet, but I did not think Fleur was one of them.

"Do you have any identification that I could see?" I asked.

For the first time she looked actively hostile.

"Why don't you just write what I say?" she asked.

I considered my options. I was fairly convinced that whatever name she had been given at birth, it was not Fleur Petit. But on the other hand, it was not really my place to pry and question.

I wrote what she said.

"Address?"

"Rue Vernier. Rue Vernier 13."

"And your relation to the deceased?"

"What do you mean?"

"I have to write whether you are a relative, a friend, or some such. So that it is clear by what right and with what degree of certainty you have made the identification."

"She was my friend," said Fleur with a voice that was full of cracks and breaks. "My loving friend. We shared everything. We took care of each other. Until now."

I wrote "friend," since there was no box for something more inclusive.

"When did you last see the deceased alive?"

"Two days ago. She did not come home as we had agreed, not that night nor the next . . ." She made a small involuntary gesture with her hand, as if she was reaching for something to hold on to. "I was frantic. I had told her she shouldn't do . . . that I would . . ." She looked at me with eyes so dark they appeared completely black. "She was so afraid she would no longer be able to work, but I had promised her that it would be fine."

"Where did she work?" I asked in a neutral tone.

"I think you know that," she said.

"No," I said. "I do not record assumptions or theories. I record only what I find or what I have learned from reliable sources."

Her mouth curled in something that was more of a cynical grimace than a smile.

"*Filles isolées*," she said. "That is what they call us, in their files. Because we want to live in an ordinary neighborhood and walk the streets and breathe the air like other people, instead of being caged in a brothel in the whore district. We have to report for medical examination twice as often as the brothel girls, and if the gendarmes see us in the 'good' neighborhoods, they have the right to arrest us, whether we are soliciting or just buying a pint of milk. Do you know how long we get locked up nowadays if those pigs decide we have broken one of their rules? Three months. In one of their fleapit jails, without judge, without lawyers, without visitors. Before, it was a month, which was bad enough; now it is three. For buying a pint of milk in the wrong place. *Liberté*, *egalité*, and *fraternité*, my Aunt Fanny."

She looked to see if she had shocked me. She had, not so much because she openly acknowledged her profession, but because her daily life suddenly had become vivid and real for me. Theoretically, I knew that the authorities were trying to halt the spread of syphilis by registering and examining Varbourg's prostitutes. The system was not quite as rigid and tightly meshed as its counterpart in Paris, but the thought of the frequent forced examinations was, for some reason, more deeply disturbing to me than the fact that she performed sexual favors for money. Perhaps because it violated something that was more important to me than public decency: the relationship between doctor and patient.

Then a realization followed that I should perhaps have had sooner. There might, of course, be any number of reasons for a prostitute to be afraid of no longer being able to work, but . . . the dress had been let out. Perhaps it was not because she had bought it secondhand.

"Was she pregnant?"

Fleur nodded, a series of minimal head movements barely more than a vibration in her muscles.

"How far along was she?"

"I don't know. You could see it. She said she had felt the child, and that is why she did not want . . ."

"To abort it?"

"You can't, not once it is alive, can you? Then it is a sin. And Rosalba believed with all her heart in God and Maria and a long line of saints." It sounded as if Fleur herself had a more agnostic perspective on the God question.

If Rosalba had felt life, she was presumably at least four months along. If her abdomen had been less brutally treated, I might have noticed the signs of pregnancy at the initial examination of the body.

"Can you give me any information about her family?" I asked, though my thoughts were still circling around the pregnancy, the nature of the lesions, and oddly pristine state of the rest of the body. One might almost think the unborn child was the actual target of the attack.

"I am her family. She has no other." She lifted her chin with a defiant jerk. "When can I bury her?"

"It will take at least a few days."

She looked out through the open window, down at the body.

"It was kind of you to light the candles," she said.

"It is the least we can do."

"Perhaps. But many people would not have thought of it." She glanced at me from under her veil. "You were also the one who helped find Marie Mercier's little son, is that right?"

"Yes. Do you know her?"

"A bit. They say she is getting married. Do you know if it is true?"

I hesitated a bit, at the thought of how difficult it apparently had been for the Commissioner to share the news with us. Or rather, me. Papa was still happily ignorant of the upcoming event.

On the other hand, in two weeks everyone and their mother would be able to read it in the city records.

"Yes, that is correct."

She nodded. And she was apparently also well informed as far as the rest of the betrothal was concerned, because she went on. "The Commissioner is a good man. Proper. To him, it makes no difference whether it is some society lady or one of us; the dead are all the same to him. Not like the gendarmes or those snotty quacks they hire to examine us. They look down on us, but they still help themselves to the goods when they can, you know."

How well did she know Marie? She sounded as if she was somewhat better informed than I was, and I had known the Commissioner all my life.

"Mademoiselle. You can see yourself that your friend was not fully dressed. Can you tell me anything about the garments that are missing? Which stockings and shoes do you think she was wearing when she left home?"

The light in her eyes died again. There was no doubt that the sorrow she felt at Rosalba's death was deep and searing, but though the tears began to run down her cheeks again, she answered my questions quietly and precisely.

Rosalba, she said, would probably have been wearing a corset of the make Evangeline, black silk stockings made in Belgium, a pair of ankle boots in brown calf leather from a local shoemaker, and unmentionables of linen, handmade and without laundry tags. In addition, there was a pair of pearl earrings missing, a hat matching the midnight blue dress and decorated with a single egret plume, a blue lace shawl, and a small chatelaine bag in black silk with pearl trimmings, also in black. I recorded the details carefully. Fleur Petit observed my work.

"Will they find him?" she asked at last. "Or don't they care?"

"They will look," I said. "They will seek the killer, but I cannot promise that they will catch him."

Her little-girl face was distorted in a crooked, mocking grimace.

"If it had been one of them," she said. "Those posh ladies. Then they would look. And keep on looking until they found him."

When Fleur Petit had left, I resumed my interrupted examination and turned my full attention to the lesions. Now that I could clean away the blood, it became clearer what I was dealing with. There were, I determined after close observation, eleven cuts in all. The majority were between twenty and twenty-five centimeters long and looked like they had been made with a knife, albeit an unusually sharp knife. There was no tearing of the skin, no ragged edge to the wounds, no sign that the knife had been turned in the process. One of the wounds caught my attention in particular—a thirteen-centimeter-long vertical cut beginning about six centimeters below the navel and continuing down toward the genitalia. There was something precise and symmetrical about it, in contrast to the other more frenzied-looking slashes, and this was what made me train my retractors and magnifier on this particular wound. It was deep, and there seemed to be an unusual amount of congealed blood, and though I could not be entirely sure before Papa arrived and we could open the corpse together, I was almost entirely certain that my hypothesis would be confirmed.

In Rosalba's abdomen there was no longer a uterus—and consequently, no unborn child.

A sigh went through the Commissioner's entire heavy body when he sank into the faithful embrace of our plush-covered mahogany armchair. Even with a not especially active imagination like mine, it was easy to conjure an image of two lovers meeting after a long separation.

"A horrible night and a horrible day," he said. "So much violence, so much hatred. It is not often that I feel the desire to inconvenience the Almighty with my entreaties, but right now I am praying earnestly that we will be spared more of these meaningless, random attacks."

The doors leading out to the garden were open, and the evening sun fell in golden bands across the worn Bokhara carpet on the floor of the salon.

"Amen," said my father quietly from his own chair, though he was not a very religious man himself.

Geraldo had left the house a few hours earlier, reported Madame Vogler, headed in the general direction of the border. Monsieur Marco had miraculously escaped the riots with no more than a few bruises, but Chez Louis was an empty shell, stripped of its inventory, and hardly a single glass or plate had survived the night. Our recently consumed evening meal had therefore been fetched from the charcuterie in Rue Perrault and consisted primarily of bread, pâté, and cornichons.

I felt exhausted, although a quick bath had provided some restoration. For once I had no desire to discuss lividity or cause of death. My thoughts instead turned to August and his upcoming visit—he usually spent every other Sunday with us and the rest with his grandmother in Heeringen. He had promised—or perhaps, more correctly, threatened—that he would teach me to ride a bicycle. Could that be accomplished in one day?

August. Fiancés. Marie Mercier.

I had not yet spoken to Papa as I had promised. I had put it off, and Rosalba Lombardi's autopsy and the rest of the hectic day had made it easy to forget. I considered postponing the problem yet another day, but the seventh of July would be upon us before we knew it, and since Papa and I had carried out the autopsy together, the Commissioner might think Papa was already informed.

"We have received an invitation," I began, but for now kept the envelope with the careful script to myself.

The Commissioner jerked in his seat. He threw a pleading look at me, but I had already decided to be implacable.

"It is probably best for you to tell him yourself," I said.

"What?" said my father as he straightened from his slumped position.

And so the Commissioner had to tell him. The engagement. Marie Mercier. The wedding on the seventh. He hoped we would come, it would mean a lot, we were, after all, his oldest friends.

Papa listened in silence, his face expressionless. His long, lanky figure remained completely still, a waxen image, a scarecrow, a marionette whose puppeteer had thrown it carelessly in a chair.

The Commissioner ran out of words. Still there was no reaction from my father.

Finally, he cleared his throat. "I will only ask once," he said, "and only because you are my best friend. Is it wise, what you are doing?"

The Commissioner smiled faintly.

"You think I am an old fool bedazzled by a beautiful and much younger woman? My friend, in that case I am a happy fool. But I think . . . I think, dear friends, that this is the wisest decision I have made in my life."

An expression passed across my father's face—sadness, perhaps even jealousy. Upstairs on his bedside table he still kept the picture of my deceased mother, and though I hoped that his loneliness would one day be alleviated by another woman, I did not really believe it.

"Then I thank you for the invitation," said Papa. "We would be delighted."

The Commissioner slapped his thighs so hard that there was a faint echo.

"Good!" he exclaimed. "Excellent! Thank you. Thank you so much."

"It is we who thank you."

We heard the street door open. It was Elise, returning with the evening edition of the newspapers. She came up the stairs with light, eager steps.

"There has been unrest and trouble everywhere," she said when she came in, with reddened cheeks and still with her shawl over her shoulders. "Not just here. Lyon, Paris, Marseille . . . Everyone is so angry. 'Patriotic rage' they call it. But they are calling for 'calm and dignity.'" She handed both papers to Papa instead of placing them in the rack as usual. "And then this was lying in the entryway," she said, and handed me an envelope.

I took it, assuming it might be from August. Even in Heidelberg they would have heard of the murder of our poor president, and possibly also of the disturbances here, so it was not impossible that he might be concerned for my safety.

But it was not a telegram. The envelope was stamped with the motto and emblem of the University of Varbourg—*Per veritatem* and, for reasons best known to the founders, a stylized fish between two stylized waves. It was addressed to "Mlle Karno."

Inside was a brief letter from Professor Anton Künzli, dean of the Department of Natural Sciences. He thanked me for my application and wanted to see me for an interview in his office on Tuesday the 26th of June, at eleven o'clock.

That was tomorrow. The letter had been under way for several days, judging from the date of his signature.

An interview. I did not know if that was good news or bad. If my application had been approved, surely they would have sent a simple letter of acceptance. Much the same if I had been rejected, I supposed, only the other way around.

My father exclaimed, "Those blasted journalists."

"What now?" asked the Commissioner.

My father handed him the paper. At the bottom of the front page, under the dramatic descriptions of the presidential murder and the almost ubiquitous riots, a no less sensationalist headline screamed: "JACK THE RIPPER IN VARBOURG!"

The journalist, bylined simply "Christophe," had squeezed as much out of his few facts as possible. The body of a young woman, a *fille isolée*, had been found in a coal merchant's backyard in Rue Colbert "with her belly slit open like a butchered animal." As many might recall, he continued, no more than six weeks had passed since a young factory worker had been found in the border town of Bruc, abused in the same bestial fashion and with her throat cut. "Has London's infamous Jack the Ripper crossed the Channel? Or has our own peaceful city fostered a monster of the same ilk? Police Inspector Marot refuses to comment on the case, and we have been similarly unable to prevail upon Le Commissaire des Morts to comment on this ominous development." The article was accompanied by two equally dramatic illustrations. One showed a masked assailant in the midst of attacking the factory worker Eugénie Colombe in some bushes behind the silk mill in Bruc. Poor Mademoiselle Colombe turned a desperate face toward the observer, and her hair and dress flapped in a strong wind that did not appear to trouble the assailant's clothes or the bushes behind them. I spontaneously thought of a theater poster that was hanging everywhere in Varbourg right now to advertise a popular melodrama. The other sketch was a bit more realistic—the artist had clearly succeeded in having a look through the gate of the coal merchant's yard, even if the body's position and general appearance diverged somewhat from reality. Under the corrugated roof along the wall you saw a dark shadow and the glinting blade of a knife.

I and the Commissioner both read over Papa's shoulder.

"He has no facts," I said. "He is merely guessing."

"Not quite," said the Commissioner. "The murder in Bruc is real. Do you think there is a connection?"

"Hard to say," my father muttered. "But we need to seek further information about it. I wonder who did the autopsy."

"I will send for a copy of the report," said the Commissioner. "But the method is not identical. Not if it is true that the factory worker had her throat slit first and was maltreated postmortem."

"Most of Mademoiselle Lombardi's wounds were also inflicted posthumously," said my father.

"But she was not decapitated."

"No. It looks as if she bled to death. It probably occurred in connection with the incision that gave him access to the uterus."

"Abhorrent." The Commissioner looked as if he wanted to spit on the floor. "Who would tear a uterus and fetus out of a young girl?"

"I don't know," said my father. "But it is unlikely to be Jack the Ripper."

June 26, 1894

The University of Varbourg had its roots in a seminary from the 1600s, and the Department of Theology was still one of the university's largest and most prominent. Not until Strasbourg had landed on the wrong side of the border after the Franco-Prussian War in 1871—and, with it, the university of that city—was it deemed necessary to expand the natural sciences from an atrophying footnote in the curriculum of priests-to-be to an actual department with its own students. As there was also a need to demonstrate patriotism and national pride following a smarting defeat, the new building achieved a pomposity worthy of a triumphal arch. My hurrying steps resounded between massively aspiring sandstone walls, and the steps by which the main entrance was reached were proportioned in such a way that any normal human was reduced to feeling like a child climbing a too-tall stool.

It was four minutes to eleven, and I was arriving at the very last moment. I had left home in plenty of time, but the city was still marked by the riots, and it turned out that the streetcars on Line 4 were not running between Avenue Deuxième and Réunion Square. A great number of cobblestones had been pried up and used for ammunition, and one of the avenue's trees had been chopped down by rampaging crowds. It was hard to determine a motive for this act beyond simple desire for destruction, and it meant that I was more than twenty minutes later than I had hoped to be. I reached the professor's office a few minutes past eleven, out of breath, with red cheeks and completely damp with sweat under my corset.

"Mademoiselle Karno? Anton Künzli." The professor presented himself politely, with an ordinary handshake, and made no attempt to kiss my hand, which I appreciated. I hoped it meant that he perceived me as something more than merely female.

He was Swiss, I knew, and his French showed his origins— the consonants rolled in a different way, and there was a rising, almost merry melody in even the most ordinary courtesy phrases. Perhaps that was why I immediately perceived him as kind. Though his face and physique still looked robust and relatively youthful, both his hair and muttonchop sideburns were brilliantly white and contrasted with a sunburned, weather-beaten appearance that I would not have associated with an academic. But he was of course a biologist, I remembered, and perhaps he still conducted field studies, in spite of his age and position.

"Please sit, mademoiselle," he said.

"Thank you." I sat down on one of the two chairs by his desk, and for once I sat precisely as the teachers at Madame Aubrey's Academy for Young Ladies prescribed: on the foremost half of the seat, bolt upright, and without touching the backrest at any point. It was not the result of my training in "posture and manners," however, so much as my general tenseness.

The professor considered me for a moment, his gaze in no way hostile or vulgar, yet still assessing, I think, both my physical qualities and my demeanor. He wore spectacles that were probably meant to correct the presbyopia brought on by his advancing years, and he was looking at me over the rim, which somehow underscored the sensation of being weighed and measured.

"Mademoiselle, you wish to be admitted to the medical school here at the university," he said.

"Yes."

"I regret to inform you that the university cannot accommodate your wish."

It was a blow. Perhaps not an entirely unexpected blow, but still . . . The world was changing. Earlier that month the newspapers had been full of news about young Marie Skłodowska from Poland who had not only achieved two degrees at the Sorbonne, but had done so in record time as the best in her year in physics, and the second best in mathematics.

"For what reason?" I asked, and did my best to keep both my expression and my tone neutral and passionless. If he harbored prejudice against the female intellect, an outburst of emotion on my part would only strengthen his conviction.

"You are probably not naïve," he said. "You know quite well that your sex raises certain questions."

"And they are?" I said, because I did not intend to make it easy for him.

"Some think that an academic education poses a danger to the more susceptible female mind," he said. "I am more concerned about my susceptible male students. I do not wish them to be . . . unnecessarily distracted."

I had not thought my back could be any straighter, yet now I felt my tense muscles pull back my upper spine another notch.

"Professor. Is that fair? Should certain male students' putative inability to concentrate exclude women from educating themselves on an equal footing with men?"

"No," he said. "Not if you ask me—and not if the woman in question harbors a genuine and deep-felt ambition to educate herself and is not seeking admission here for . . . other purposes."

"Which other purpose . . . ," I began to ask, having literally no idea what he was talking about. Then, in midsentence, I realized what he was alluding to. "Oh . . ."

"It has been known to happen," he said. "It is a fact, mademoiselle, that inside the walls of this institution we have a broad selection of society's more gifted and well-heeled sons, and I have to emphasize that they are here to be educated, not to find either temporary or more permanent female companions."

What a way with words he had. Friendly and helpful, still, and without batting an eye.

"I am engaged to be married," I managed to utter, among a selection of more explosive exclamations. "To August Dreyfuss, professor of parasitology at Heidelberg University. I can assure you that the sons of the bourgeoisie are entirely free from danger where I am concerned."

Now he was actually smiling, which made my blood pressure rise even further.

"I seem to have insulted you," he said. "That was not my intention."

"How would you feel if—" I bit my lip. "I do apologize, but if the professor were in my place, how would you react to such an accusation? And I apologize once more, but if the Sorbonne does not consider female students a threat to the male population, why should the flower of Varbourg's youth be more vulnerable?"

"Paris is a bigger city, not necessarily a wiser one," he said. "But I accept that you are not, or at least do not wish to be, a distraction. And though your formal education at Madame Aubrey's has certain gaps as regards the natural sciences, I also accept your claim that the work you have been doing under the tutelage of your father has equipped you with a significant practical and theoretical knowledge of human anatomy."

"Why, then?"

He held up his hands in an apologetic gesture.

"The question of female students has been debated passionately for a number of years here at the university. As you no doubt know, this institution dates back to the seventeenth century. There is nothing in the charter that prevents the admission of women . . ."

Probably because no one had been able to imagine that it would ever be an issue, I thought grimly.

". . . and the university administration does not want to prohibit it."

Well, that was something . . .

"It has therefore been decided that it is up to the individual professor or lecturer if he wishes to take on female students. And I regret to say that we have not found a lecturer at our School of Medicine willing to take such a controversial step without an express order from the deanship."

I did not respond. Anything I might have tried to say would have escaped like steam from a pressure cooker, scalding, aggressive, and rash.

"Mademoiselle, if you have such a burning wish to become a doctor—then why not the Sorbonne?"

Because I could not leave my father to the abyss of loneliness he would sink into with me so far away. That the Commissioner was now getting married would not improve matters. And there was the money. If I were to go to Paris, it would be on August's money, and that did not feel right.

"It is not possible at the moment," I said.

"I see. Well, then, there is only one thing to do. Could I convince you to seek admission to the Institute of Physiology instead? There I do have a lecturer who is not only willing but has specifically requested female students."

I had lowered my head to hide the tears that burned in the corners of my eyes. Now I looked up again.

"Physiology?" I asked. "Including anatomical studies?"

"That is usually a part of the curriculum," he said with a faint smile. "You will probably have to dissect more frogs than you care to, but it is still a basic study that may be of use to you. And there is nothing to prevent you from later specializing in human physiology."

If I had tried to embrace him, he would no doubt have misinterpreted it. I limited myself to shaking his hand rather more warmly than at the beginning of the conversation.

"Thank you very much," I said.

"Do not thank me until you are sure you have something to

thank me for. Docent Althauser is not a patient lecturer, but he is a highly capable scientist. Would you like to meet him?"

I do not know if Professor Künzli normally accompanied his new students through the hallways of the university to present them to his staff. Probably not. But I was grateful for his gallant effort, even if it did arise from the unwanted special status my sex gave me here, and even if the introduction itself consisted of a highly informal: "Adrian! She is here. Mademoiselle Karno, this is Docent Althauser. Will you be able to find your way out? Adrian, I will see you after lunch!"

After which he continued down the hall without further ado and left me standing in the door, like a child someone had forgotten to pick up.

The room was high ceilinged and full of light, with windows that had to be close to four meters high. The smells that reached me immediately made me feel more at home than if we had met in an office. Carbolic, methane, alcohol, formaldehyde, and a whiff of ammonia—the laboratory's unique perfume.

Docent Althauser looked up. He was of medium height, with heavy dark eyes under drooping eyelids, lending him an appearance somewhat reminiscent of an English bulldog. His dark hair had been combed across the crown from a side parting that looked as if it had been drawn with a ruler, and he was clean shaven except for a well-trimmed little mustache. He threw a quick glance at me, completely free of the kindness the professor had exuded. Then he turned again to the work I had interrupted.

"Mademoiselle," he said. "Come closer. Tell me what you see here."

What he was inviting me to look at was a set of organs that he had just placed on a white porcelain tray, having removed them from the glass jar in which they had been stored—that was why the smell of formaldehyde was so unusually pronounced. At first glance, it was just a pile of formless pale puce tissue, and it was difficult to determine what animal it came from, let alone which organs were on display.

He held a pair of tweezers in one hand, and a scalpel, probe, and retractors lay ready on the white cloth next to the tray.

"May I?" I asked.

He handed me the tweezers and retreated from the table. I had the clear sensation that he was studying me while I studied the specimen, which was fairly distracting.

If only it had been a human organ. There were by now not many areas in human anatomy that were foreign to me, no matter which angle I considered them from. But this . . . I tried to separate the pale membranes and excrescences in the hope of finding something I recognized. I realized fairly quickly that it had to be something to do with reproduction, but from what had to be the vagina there were two cervixes. Not only one uterine chamber but two . . . A cat? No, wait.

"A rabbit?" I said a bit hesitantly.

"Correct," he said. He stood behind me now and looked over my shoulder, while still attempting to maintain a seemly distance. "But on what do you base your conclusion?"

"The double uterus and the size."

"Good. You clearly have a basic knowledge of anatomy."

I did not know how to respond to that. I had more than "a basic knowledge" at least as far as human anatomy was concerned, but I sensed that it would be a mistake to say so.

"Good," he repeated at last, as if he was also having trouble figuring out what words the situation required. "You may tell the registrar that you have been admitted and be under my tuition in the upcoming semester. You will be informed of time and place."

The conversation was clearly over. I set aside the instruments with careful precision. Did he understand how much this meant to me? He was still barely looking at me, at least not when I was looking at him. Not once during the entire session had he met my eyes. I had no idea whether it was indifference or arrogance, or perhaps even the opposite, though he did not otherwise appear uncertain or shy.

It did not matter, I told myself. He could look at me or not; the main thing was that he had handed me the keys to what I wished for most of all in the whole world: knowledge.

"Good-bye, monsieur."

He just nodded. "From now on, mademoiselle, you should probably address me as Docent Althauser, or Monsieur le Professeur if you prefer."

And that was apparently that, or very nearly. Just before I reached the door, he added, "I understand that your father is a doctor?"

"Yes," I said.

"Good," he said for the third time, with a tone that suggested that this explained a great deal. And perhaps it did.

I was accepted. I was accepted. I was accepted!

This amazing fact kept reverberating inside me, crowding out any attempt at concerted thought. Elise's wild shrieks of triumph, my father's calmer but clearly sincere congratulations, the cream gâteaux that Madame Vogler insisted were indispensable to the celebrations—this was all wonderful and imbued the intoxication with a seltzer-like fizz. But as I was lying in my bed that evening trying to sleep, it was not gâteaux or happy smiles that danced behind my closed eyelids. For some reason, I kept seeing the pale rabbit organs glistening with formaldehyde, followed, as if there was an irrational yet still strangely logical connection between the two, by Rosalba Lombardi's lacerated abdomen.

It finally goaded me back into full consciousness, and I sat up and relit my bedside candle.

Where had I seen . . . Where had I read . . .

I could not wrench myself away from this tenuous thread of a connection. Even though the exhaustion of the day's events made my limbs leaden and unresponsive, I knew I would not be able to sleep now. I threw a shawl around my shoulders and tiptoed downstairs to the salon. I turned up the lamp by the table, fetched a pile of my father's old copies of *Médecine Aujourd'hui* carefully bound by year, and began to turn the pages.

It took me several hours, but at last I found it.

A young Italian woman, Julia Cavallini, had contracted rickets as a child and as a result suffered from a deformation of her legs, back, and hips. In 1876, at the age of twenty-five, she was in a state of advanced pregnancy, with no chance of being able to give birth normally. Until then, the cesarean procedure had had a morbidity of nearly 100 percent for both mother and child, in the case of the mother usually because of hemorrhaging. But Julia's doctor, Eduardo Porro, decided to perform the operation in a new way. He would prepare to take out the entire uterus, performing a full hysterectomy, before he attempted to deliver the child. In this way, he hoped to be able to stop possible bleeding.

He succeeded.

"At 4:51 we began to cut through the abdominal wall, layer by layer, through a twelve-centimeter-long median incision along the linea alba. Having opened the abdominal cavity in this way, we immediately began the incision of the uterus, in the same direction and of the same length as the abdominal incision. Unable to deliver the head with my right hand in the uterus, I instead extracted the right leg and right arm, the left leg and left arm, and the trunk, whereupon the head followed easily. We delivered a large female child, weighing 3300 grams, alive, well formed, and healthy, and she began to cry spontaneously. After we had tied and cut the umbilical cord, we extracted the intact placenta, together with most of the umbilical sac. It was providential that we had prepared for the hysterectomy, because the profuse bleeding from the uterus could not be stopped; otherwise the patient would surely have died."

The article was accompanied by two pictures of Julia Cavallini during her recovery, in profile and en face, standing next to a sofa, which she seemed to need for support. She was naked, and you could see the healing scar from the cesarean clearly, as well as the deformities the rickets had given her. She was only 142 centimeters tall and looked like a child next to the bulky chesterfield, but she was the first woman in the world to survive a cesarean section and receive a living child.

Porro's effort was groundbreaking, and it was far from the first time I had studied the miraculous pictures of Julia Cavallini. Now I did so from a different perspective.

The scar that ran the length of Julia's abdomen looked dramatic, but I reminded myself that she was a very small woman. I knew from the article that the incision had been precisely twelve centimeters long, running with symmetric precision along the midline of her body.

I carefully placed a bookmark in the article before I closed the 1876 volume and carried it with me upstairs. When I passed my father's door, I noticed that there was light from beneath it. I knocked quietly.

"Papa? Are you awake?"

"What is it?" he asked, clearly not fully in Morpheus's embrace. He had always had a tendency toward insomnia, and many years of interrupted nights and disturbed sleep patterns had not improved matters.

I opened the door. He was sitting at the small desk by the window, dressed in a halfhearted combination of breeches and nightshirt, with bare feet in the Turkish slippers that had always seemed to me to be an aberration, far too exotic for a man of my father's less than flamboyant temperament. Furthermore, they were now in such a state of threadbareness that they were barely functional, yet he resisted all efforts to replace them with something more suitable, probably because they had been a present from my mother.

"Julia Cavallini," I said. "Porro's procedure. Papa, might someone have attempted to deliver Rosalba Lombardi by cesarean section—only with less skill than Porro?"

June 27, 1894

"I understand," said Police Inspector Marot, "that Madeleine has a theory about the murder of Rosalba Lombardi."

I could tell that he was listening only to be polite, and that even politeness was wearing thin. There was nothing challenging or questioning in his tone of voice, and the aggressive energy that usually characterized him was noticeably absent. He slumped heavily on the café chair, and his eyes, somewhat sunken at the best of times, were red rimmed with fatigue.

We had found him in a café not far from the coal merchant's yard in Rue Colbert. He and his men had more or less commandeered the back room, and in the course of the short time I was there, at least eight different people came in, made hasty notations on a report sheet, placed the sheet in a tray, took a new one from another tray, and then disappeared again. I had seen at least some of them at work on the way here—they were going door-to-door on Rue Colbert and the surrounding streets, because this was not a neighborhood where the inhabitants went willingly to the police if they had seen something.

The inspector was enthroned behind an improvised desk constructed from a door laid across two beer barrels, and judging by the number of coffee cups and the discarded dottles in the ashtray, he had been sitting there for a long time. His lack of enthusiasm no doubt stemmed from a lack of sleep, I told myself. The walrus mustache hung limp and unkempt, and the pomade shine had gone from the centrally parted hair. There was no reason to take it personally.

"It struck me from the beginning that there was something contradictory about the body's condition," I explained. "There were no defensive cuts on the hands, no bruising, nothing that suggested a struggle."

Inspector Marot nodded heavily. "I am aware of that," he said, in a get-to-the-point tone of voice.

"In addition," I continued, "one of the cuts—the first, we believe—is a very precise incision positioned so as to give access to the uterus. That is, the womb . . ."

"Yes. I have read the autopsy report."

"Inspector, what if what we have here is not a murder at all? What if it is simply an operation that went wrong? A botched hysterectomy? She died of hemorrhaging in connection with the removal of the uterus, the remaining lesions were inflicted posthumously, of that we are fairly certain. Besides, there was more mucus and saliva in the oral cavity than you would normally expect, which could be explained by an anesthetic use of ether."

He sighed.

"It is true that this town has its share of quacks barely worthy of the title of doctor," he said. "And the Commissioner here can no doubt verify that their unfortunate patients do die on the operating table with disturbing frequency. However, I have yet to come across one who then proceeded to carve up the patient even further before discarding the remains in a coal merchant's yard. Why not simply send for my honored colleague"—he performed a small ducking motion, half nod, half bow, in the direction of the Commissioner—"and have the death certificate written up in the normal fashion?"

"Because the operation is illegal," I suggested.

"How so?"

"According to Lombardi's friend, she was pregnant. At least four months along, presumably more."

"And?"

"You could argue that the operation was an unusually drastic abortion. You might be able to consider the mother's death an accident, but not the child's. At that point in the pregnancy, it is an inescapable consequence of the intervention."

"But why?" said Marot. "Why not just perform a perfectly ordinary abortion?"

That question I could not answer.

"I don't know," I admitted. "To abort that late involves significant risks."

"Right now she is dead. How is that less dangerous?"

"Perhaps she thought that it was?"

"Hypotheses, Madeleine. Unsubstantiated hypotheses, to boot. We have no idea what the poor girl thought and believed."

His last comment stung. To accuse me of drawing unscientific conclusions was almost like accusing a religiously raised child of not believing sufficiently in God. I was reminded of my father's constant refrain when I would come to him as a child with a wealth of observations about everything from the number of stars to the reason for weevils in the flour or the peculiar behavior of the boy next door: "Is it something you think, Madeleine? Or is it something you know?" Always said in the same measured tone of voice, not a dismissal but an encouragement to explain and support my claim.

The worst part was that Marot had hit the target even better than he knew. I actually did know a bit about Rosalba Lombardi's beliefs: *Rosalba believed with all her heart in God and Maria and a long line of saints*, Fleur had said. From her perspective, abortion was not merely a crime—it was a sin.

"And what about the murder in Bruc?" Marot continued. "No fetus was removed in that case. The poor girl was not the least bit pregnant."

"Is there any certainty that there is a connection between the two crimes?" I asked. "Apart from the flights of fancy scribbled by the journalists, I mean."

Marot extracted a portfolio from one of the piles on the "desk."

"You can read for yourself what we have received from Bruc," he said. "But read it here—it was hard enough to get one copy, I do not want to have to ask for another."

The door to the kitchen opened, and the café owner came out, or at least I assumed it was the owner—an older, clearly hectic gentleman with a dishcloth tied around his waist, a flaming red face, and a shiny bald pate slick with sweat.

"Is the young lady also going to have something to drink?" he asked. "And the gentleman there?"

It was not a polite inquiry. It was rather presented in the same tone of voice as when a hawker at a market demands the entrance fee from the audience. He was clearly not thrilled that the police had taken over a part of his establishment, but if that was the way of it, he was determined that they should at least support his business.

"Café au lait," I requested. The tea here would probably be undrinkable. The Commissioner sighed and ordered a cognac. The inspector had already immersed himself in the next pile of newly arrived reports and did not look up, so it was left to the Commissioner to pay the man.

I quickly realized that the doctor who had performed the autopsy in Bruc probably did not own a copy of Lacassagne's *Vade-mecum*. The presentation was neither systematic nor clear and was riddled with uncertainties like "approximately," "about," and "circa." Eugénie Colombe was, for example, "between 155 and 165 centimeters tall," which presumably described at least half of Bruc's female population, and if it were not for the accompanying photographs (in a folder marked "MUST be returned to the police department in Bruc!!!"), the report would have permitted me to conclude very little except that the deceased was probably Eugénie Colombe, and that she had probably been killed, and that she was in any case definitely dead.

The police department in Bruc had sent along only five photographs. One showed the place where she had been found, a shrubbery that looked as if it consisted primarily of brambles, thistles, and grass; the second the location of the murder, the adjoining field, the tall grass of which had likely been intended for haymaking. Now an area of seven or eight square meters had been trampled flat and soiled in blood. The remaining three pictures showed Eugénie Colombe herself. She had been dragged into the shrubbery—one could still see the track made by her heels—and was lying on her back among the thistles. Her lower body was completely exposed—her blood-soaked skirt and her unmentionables had been found in the grass near the place where she had been killed. The blouse and camisole—she was not wearing a corset, few factory workers did—had been slashed to ribbons, and her entire torso was smeared in blood. Her throat gaped darkly at me, and her head dangled to the left. I knew from the report that the knife that had inflicted this mortal wound had been used with such violence that the sinews on one side of her throat were sliced clean through. At least she had been dead when the rest of the abuse had occurred.

He had cut off her left nipple. Most of the more than twenty-five subsequent slashes were directed at the abdomen and sexual organs. Even without magnification, I could tell that the knife was not the one that had been used on Rosalba Lombardi—the blade was broader, the weapon much larger and clumsier. The report did not say whether traces of semen had been found.

From the police report, I knew that Eugénie Colombe had left the textile mill where she worked shortly after lunch, with the explanation that she felt unwell and thought a little fresh air might help. The factory overseer, apparently one of the more humane of his kind, had agreed to this and had merely specified that she had to be back within an hour if she wanted to be paid for the day's work. He had told the police that Eugénie was a dependable and skillful weaver who normally did her work quickly and well.

There was "no trouble with Eugénie." When she did not return to work, he noted as much in the pay book but did not give it further thought. It was not until her mother wondered why she had not come home from the factory that a form of alarm was raised. The concern at first was limited to asking around among Eugénie's friends and colleagues. One of them revealed that Eugénie had a "secret sweetheart," a twenty-three-year-old cooper's journeyman from the neighboring town of Saint-Pierre-sur-L'eau. He was not all that secret since most of the factory's girls knew him and had seen him and Eugénie together on several occasions. But he insisted that he and Eugénie had not planned to see each other before Saturday and that he had not heard from her.

On the way to the factory the next day, one of the weavers had noticed a shoe in the grass next to the path. It was Eugénie's. When they followed the trail through the hay field from that starting point, they found first the spot where she had been killed and later poor Eugénie, half hidden in the shrubbery.

The police immediately arrested the sweetheart, just to be on the safe side. But luckily for him he had been at work all day and had then gone out to a tavern with the other journeymen. They had to let him go. For the time being, the authorities had no other suspects and no other leads in the case.

Eugénie was nineteen. She had worked at the mill since she was twelve. She was, according to her mother and the neighbors, a good girl who went to mass every Sunday and every Saturday paid her mother half of her weekly wages for room and board. She had apparently never had any beau except for the cooper's journeyman, and he insisted that his intentions were honorable and that he had not "forced himself" on her. He wanted to get married as soon as they could afford it. One of Eugénie's closest friends said that Eugénie did not feel quite as sure, and that was the reason she had not told her mother about the relationship.

"What do you think, Madeleine?" asked the Commissioner,

who had read the reports behind me and now sat turning one of the photographs in his large hands. "Have we acquired a Jack the Ripper of our own?"

I shook my head and sipped my café au lait. It was lukewarm because I had forgotten it while concentrating on the report.

"I would prefer not to think that in peaceful Varonne there are two men on the loose who would maltreat women and women's bodies in this way," I said. "Two young women, in the same district, within a month and a half . . . one would think there had to be a connection. Yet there are also many differences. No organs are missing in the case of Eugénie. The knife is different. The professions of the two women are entirely different; they are not even of the same nationality."

"Do you think that it is relevant that Rosalba Lombardi is Italian?"

"I don't know. I definitely do not think she was killed in a fit of xenophobic rage; that does not fit the evidence. My point is just that they are so different that there are unlikely to be many people who have met them both."

"You are right," the Commissioner said thoughtfully. "If it is the same murderer, that would be a way to look for him—to find a man who *could* have met them both."

"And if it is not the same murderer after all, that effort would be a complete waste of time," I said.

"That is the way of it with police work," sighed the Commissioner. "But Marot is in charge, not I."

June 28–30, 1894

The following days, the newspapers were full of speculation and comparisons, and the persistent "Christophe" from *Varonne Soir* even related a "conversation by telephone" with Dr. Horrocks Openshaw, an English surgeon and coroner who had examined the kidney Jack the Ripper had reputedly mailed to George Akin Lusk, the head of the Whitechapel Vigilance Committee. Dr. Openshaw had subsequently himself received a letter purporting to be from the killer—that is, if it was the notorious murderer who was the source of the letter, and not, for example, an interfering journalist who wanted to have something to write about . . .

Unfortunately, Dr. Openshaw had not felt like telling "Christophe" very much and almost nothing of medical relevance. Such a pity. As Dr. Openshaw was also the curator of the London Hospital's Pathology Collection, he was someone with whom I would have dearly liked to discuss our own homicides, had I been fortunate enough to converse with him over the telephone.

I did not know if Inspector Marot paid any further notice to what he called my "theory." But as the Commissioner had pointed out, the investigation was now in the hands of Marot and his staff, and there was not much we—he, Papa, and I—could do about it. Life went on—and with it, also death. The following week, I helped my father examine four bodies that are not relevant to this story. One was a weaver, like Eugénie Colombe had been, it is true, but her death was neither violent nor inexplicable. Her lungs were so full of textile dust that she had finally given up the fight to breathe.

Her autopsy was conducted under primitive conditions in a room at Saint Bernardine's Chapel of Rest, since the death occurred in this hospital. My father remained there afterward to look after a living patient while I headed home. It was only a short stroll from Saint Bernardine to Carmelite Street, which was one of the reasons my father and mother had originally moved there. I had walked the route countless times since I was a little girl— knew every house, every sound, every shadow, and every bump in the road. I knew the people who lived there, and they knew me. I nodded to the people I met, called good evening up to an open window, was as usual waylaid by the raucous gaggle of boys playing in the yard behind the old cotton spinning mill.

"I don't have anything for you tonight," I said apologetically. And because they knew me, they believed me and turned back to their game.

I stopped for a moment when I reached Chez Louis. It was still dark and closed, with rough boards nailed across the empty windows. A young man had stopped like I did to take in the sad sight while he smoked a cigarette. It was Paul Tessier, the blacksmith's eldest boy. He and I had played together as children.

"Evening, Maddie."

"Good evening, Paul."

"Idiots," he said after a short pause, presumably referring to the vandals who had ransacked the restaurant. Paul had been a silent boy who did not spare a word if actions would suffice, and as an adult he had not grown much more garrulous.

"Yes," I said. "All this hatred just seems pointless and cruel."

"Geraldo?"

Paul was apparently informed about the rescue action.

"Healing well, but he is going home to Italy."

He blew cigarette smoke out through his nostrils, accompanied by something between a snort and a grunt. I interpreted it to mean that he regretted Geraldo's departure but could understand the reason for it.

"I have to go home," I said. "Keep well, Paul."

A nod.

It was not until I had started walking that he called after me. "Maddie."

"Yes?"

"There's a man."

"Where?"

"At your front door."

"Who is it?"

"Don't know. Some gentleman."

It was probably not August, then, because by now he was known to most of the neighborhood, not least because of the stir he caused when he occasionally showed up in his automobile.

I nodded again and continued. Paul was right. Leaning up against the wall outside the door to our house stood a gentleman wearing a boater and a light tweed jacket, for all the world as if he was on his way to a Sunday lunch in the country. I recognized him from the chaotic morning in Rue Colbert.

"Monsieur Christophe, I presume."

"You are clever, mademoiselle. And brave."

"What do you mean?"

"That you dare to walk the streets alone, and after dark, to boot."

"Why should I fear to do that?"

"And you say that, knowing better than anyone what he is capable of? Tell me, mademoiselle, what was it like to stand there and look at what he had done to that poor young woman?"

I suddenly remembered—perhaps too late—the Commissioner's warning. *Say nothing. Even an unvarnished no can become a confirmation of some spurious theory before they have finished reworking the truth.*

"Monsieur, I have nothing to tell you. Would you be so kind as to move, so I can pass." He was currently barring my access to the door.

"I just want to have a few words with you," he said. "I promise you that if you share some of your experiences with me, then the newspaper will only print what you wish us to print."

"Move aside, please."

"No one needs to know that I have this information from you," he said quietly. I noticed a strong scent of anise on his breath—absinthe, I guessed. He would appear to be a devotee of the green fairy, as they called it. "Don't you think the public has a right to know?"

"Not about everything," I said. "And if you do not move aside immediately, I will scream."

"Mademoiselle, you are hardly the type to scream . . ."

I took a deep breath, perhaps not to scream melodramatically, but a loud yell would serve the same purpose. When he realized I meant it, he was obviously surprised, not to say flustered. He tried to place his one gloved hand over my mouth.

"Mademoiselle, please stop . . ."

"Help," I shouted, rather less positively than I had intended.

But it was enough. I was on my own street, in my own neighborhood. It was a warm evening, and the windows were open. Within seconds seven or eight neighbors were gazing down on us.

"Madeleine?" yelled the typographer who lived across the street. "Is there anything wrong? Who is that gentleman?"

"His name is Christophe," I said loud and clear. "He works for *Varonne Soir*. And I think he is just leaving . . ."

The journalist stopped trying to hush me. He looked up and noted the many eyes and ears. Then he tipped his boater to me with a hint of gallantry.

"Touché, mademoiselle," he said. "You win this round. But if you do not wish to speak with me, then I will have to compose the story myself—and I am not sure you will like what I write."

Upstairs in the salon, Elise had set out some supper—the rest of the pâté with cornichons and toasted slices of the thin dark pumpernickel bread she bought at Dreischer & Son, the small narrow shop next to the market halls.

"I did not want to let him in," she said. "That journalist. I told him that neither you nor the doctor was in. But he just stayed out there, and I did not know what to do."

"You did well, Elise. If he comes back, just shut the door in his face."

I was feeling quite smug about the whole encounter. I had said nothing he would be able to use, and though my actions had mostly consisted of calling for help at the right moment, I had nonetheless vanquished him.

Or so I thought.

Two days later, in the Saturday edition of *Varonne Soir*, it was no longer "Varbourg's Jack the Ripper" who dominated the headlines—at least not directly. On the cover there was a photograph of the coal merchant's yard. You could see the Commissioner standing off to the right, but at the center of the picture knelt a young woman—me, I noted in some shock—next to the only partially shrouded corpse of another young woman. The headline was no less shocking.

MADEMOISELLE DEATH

it screamed, in bold type. The caption was hardly any less alarming:

> *Does it take a woman to catch a killer of women?*
> *Varbourg's own Mademoiselle Death is on the trail.*

My father was predictably furious. At me, at the Commissioner, at the newspaper, and apparently at most of Varbourg's population, or at least at the not insignificant portion of it that bought and read *Varonne Soir*.

"How can they write such offensive twaddle? How can people read it? Why do people continue to support a scandal rag like that? Have they nothing better to do with their money and their time?"

"We buy it too . . . ," I interjected, though I felt little inclination to defend the newspaper or its readers right now.

"Not anymore! I can assure you of that."

He was so angry that his entire body was trembling. I almost wished he would start pacing about the salon, as he sometimes did when he was agitated or annoyed, but the emotional turbulence was apparently too great. He merely stood, on shaking legs, pressing two powerless fists against his thighs, as if he could, by these means, prevent himself from hitting the next person who came close enough.

"Papa, please sit down."

He paid absolutely no attention to my attempt to calm him.

"If your mother had seen this . . ." Even his voice shook. I could literally *hear* his teeth clatter against one another, a faint porcelainlike tinkling.

At least he did not say that he was happy she had not "lived to see this." At least he did not say that.

"How could it happen? How could he do this to you? This time the "he" was the Commissioner. "What would August say if he heard about it?"

"I don't know," I said. "But I suppose we will find out when he comes tomorrow."

I reached for my hat and gloves.

"Where are you going? Madeleine, you are not going anywhere! We have to talk about this!"

I carefully placed my hand on his tense arm. "But, Papa, we *can't* talk about it. Not as long as you are so upset. You are not listening to a single word I am saying."

"*You* are the one not listening to me!"

I kissed him on the cheek. To the great regret of my aunt Desirée, I had grown tall enough to do so without stretching. ("And your mother who was so tiny and lovely," she moaned on a regular basis. "*Une petite. Une vrais petite.*")

"Papa, I love you. And I admire you greatly. But I cannot be precisely as you wish me to be, or do everything exactly the way you wish me to do it."

He looked at me with his mouth half open, caught in the midst of yet another flare of anger. He looked as if I had tricked him with my declaration of love—we did not often talk about emotions in our little family.

"You might at least tell me where you are going," he exclaimed at last.

"I think I know who took that photograph," I said, and pointed at the front page of the newspaper, knowing well that it would probably make his anger erupt again. "I want to ask him why and how it ended up in a newspaper."

"I will go with you."

"No, you will not. You are too upset. I don't want you trying to hit the man."

"Violence is for boors."

"Precisely. Do not expose yourself to that temptation."

"Well, then bring Elise, at least."

I smiled a bit stiffly.

"Isn't it a bit late to equip me with a chaperone?" I said. "Keeping up appearances was never my main ambition in life, which is probably just as well. I am sorry, Papa. I cannot be the sort of well-bred young lady Madame Aubrey would approve of."

"Perhaps you prefer to be known as Mademoiselle Death?"

"No," I said. "But it appears I have no choice . . ."

Abruptly, the anger in him extinguished itself as if someone had flicked the switch of an electric lightbulb.

"It is my fault," he said quietly. "I should never have . . . If your mother had lived, then . . ."

It was the second time he had mentioned my mother. Of whom we never spoke. Never. This time, it was I who found it difficult to keep my voice steady.

"If Mama had lived," I managed to say, "I hope she would have supported and approved of her daughter's ambitions to accomplish something in this life. She taught me to read when I was five years old. If she knew what I was doing now, if she knew that I had been accepted at the university—the *university*, Papa—don't you think she would have been just a little bit proud?"

But I should not have mentioned her, I could see it in his face. It froze. Stiffened. Lost any kind of expression that was not raw pain.

"Well, then go," he said coldly. "I won't wait up for you."

I'm sorry. I'm sorry. Forgive me. Please don't be angry with me!

A year ago, I would probably have said the words out loud. Now I held them in.

"It will not be late," I said, and walked quietly down the stairs.

Aristide Gilbert's studio lay in a narrow passage leading off Rue Germain. The straggly ivy outside his windows lent the otherwise somewhat dismal and unappealing alley a forlorn charm. I had been here only once before, in the company of the Commissioner, who had stopped on his way to the préfecture in order to pick up some overdue photographs.

The windows facing the passage were partially obscured by dusty tulle curtains, and a plaque announced that here resided A. GILBERT, PHOTOGRAPHER. PORTRAITS DONE BY APPOINTMENT. I knew that Gilbert lived in the little apartment above the studio, but it looked as if he was still at work. There was a light on behind the dusty curtains.

I knocked. After a while a boy of about ten or eleven opened the door. He was dressed like a perfect miniature of a bank teller or a law clerk, or perhaps an undertaker's assistant—dark suit, white shirt, silk vest, and bow tie, his hair slicked down to such a degree that it looked as if it had been painted on. All that was missing was the watch chain and the pocket watch.

"Monsieur Gilbert is in the darkroom," he said. "But you are welcome to wait. Is it regarding a portrait?"

"For now I only wish to have a few words with Monsieur Gilbert," I said vaguely.

The boy pulled up a chair for me and offered me "refreshments," as he called it, but since all he had to offer was absinthe or lukewarm white wine, I abstained. The young man remained standing at attention, some meters from me, observing me with an unrelenting interest that was rather unnerving.

"What is your name?" I asked, in an attempt to dispel the awkwardness.

"Bruno," he answered without taking his eyes off me for as much as a fraction of a second. He clearly preferred looking to conversing.

I ended up being the one to break eye contact. My sense of embarrassment was simply better developed than his. I tried instead to get a sense of the surroundings without letting myself be too distracted by the undertaker's gaze.

The room was larger and lighter than the façade had suggested. One half of it was pretty clearly a later addition to the back, somewhat like the laboratory at home. Here, there were skylights and large windows facing a courtyard that might well be full of latrine sheds and garbage cans, but was wider and more open than the alley in front of the house. The floor in that half of the studio was painted black and seemed to be raw cement under the paintwork. The shutters and thick black curtains made it possible to close out the daylight, and a clever set of pulleys operated a shutter system for the skylights. Along one wall stood a number of painted backdrops and assorted furniture—a white garden bench, a plush ensemble of two armchairs and a chaise longue and, somewhat surprisingly, a tandem bicycle, attached to an iron stand so it would not fall over. There was also a miserable-looking palm tree in a pot, a pair of enormous baskets filled with dried flowers, and a not especially lifelike stuffed dog. Who on earth would want to be photographed with that? I wondered. It was a kind of spaniel, with a reddish coat and long shaggy ears hanging too limply, and its brown glass eyes glittered at me lifelessly, like a visual echo of the boy's persistent staring.

I heard a faucet being turned on, and there was a clatter of glass behind the door that I assumed led to the darkroom. Shortly afterward, Aristide Gilbert emerged, in his shirtsleeves and a canvas apron, an embroidered smoking cap perched rather rakishly on his head. He stopped abruptly when he saw me.

"Mademoiselle Karno," he said. "To what do I owe this honor?"

"I would like to speak with you," I said, "regarding a certain newspaper photograph."

I cannot claim that he grew pale with guilt, but a certain resignation settled on his already somewhat morose features.

"Yes," he said. "Bruno, you had better go home now. Your mother will be expecting you."

The boy fetched his jacket and a peaked black cap from a row of hooks by the door.

"At what time should I come tomorrow, monsieur?" he asked.

"Not before five," said Gilbert. "You have school, don't you?"

"Yes, of course, monsieur. Au revoir." There seemed to be a hint of disappointment in the way he trudged to the door and closed it quietly and politely behind him.

"He is an odd sort of boy," the photographer apologized. "But he is polite to the customers, and he is precise and thorough when he helps me mix the chemicals. I think his mother is very happy that he has something sensible to do elsewhere, so that he doesn't disturb his father's sleep. The poor man is a baker and must get up at two in the morning."

Aristide Gilbert might be described as a presentable man. Broad shouldered and well built, with regular smooth, clean-shaven features, dark combed-back hair without a hint of gray, well-kept hands, and precise pleats in his pants. The smoking cap was for me an exotic surprise. When he was working, he invariably wore an entirely ordinary round felt hat.

Despite all these advantages, he was not someone one would notice in the street. Much less prepossessing men strutted along with self-confidence and aggressive virility, convinced of their own powers of attraction. Gilbert seemed to have no such conviction. At any rate, his manner was so quiet and modest that few people noticed him before he spoke. If he had once possessed youthful male panache and boldness, he had shut down both long ago. There was a sadness about him, somehow underscored by the smell of chemicals and the scent of anise that probably originated with the absinthe the boy Bruno had offered me.

"*Varonne Soir*," I said.

"Yes." He made no attempt to deny it. "I am truly sorry. I had no idea that he would use the picture in that way."

His confession deflated my anger a bit. Most of my self-righteous indignation died for lack of resistance.

"Why did you do it?" I asked.

"For the money," he said without demur. "I have debts, you see. Monsieur Christophe offered me a hundred francs for a picture of the incident that showed you as well."

"Me?"

"Yes. He offered me fifty for a picture of the corpse, but if you also were in it, it was a hundred."

One hundred francs. That was a considerable amount—for many people several months' wages. But still . . .

"Monsieur Gilbert, if the Commissioner finds out, you will be fired. The police will never use you again."

He smiled sadly. "The pittance they pay is no sort of living. Unfortunately, there are not enough crimes committed in Varbourg."

Was that irony? An attempt at jocularity, even? I thought so, but his general air of depression made it hard to be certain. My eyes fell randomly on the stuffed spaniel with the stiff blank gaze. It must be difficult to make a living as a portrait photographer when one so blatantly lacked the ability to imagine how other people wished to appear, I thought.

"I assume you will now inform the Commissioner," he said. "I am really sorry that my unfortunate circumstances have also caused you embarrassment, and I can assure you that I had no idea that the newspaper would present you in this . . . bizarre way."

I realized that I was actually wondering if I might be able to convince the préfecture to pay a little more for the poor man's services so that he would not be tempted to resell his pictures to the highest bidder. And I, who had come to . . . in fact, I did not know quite why. To make him admit it, first and foremost, but he had done that within the first minute.

"If I refrain," I said, "will you promise me never again to sell photographic evidence to Monsieur Christophe and his ilk?"

He looked up, evidently surprised. I once again caught the scent of absinthe on his breath.

"Do you mean that?" he asked. "That is . . . far more than I could expect."

"Of course I cannot guarantee that it will not come out anyway," I said. "Even though the picture is taken at a distance, the angle of it makes it clear that the photographer was not at the gate but in the actual courtyard. If I can make that deduction, so can the Commissioner. But if you give me your word, then you have mine that such a revelation will not come from me."

"My word? Of course. And thank you."

The scent of absinthe brought an unwelcome association.

"When did Christophe come here?" I asked.

He considered. "It must have been Thursday afternoon. Yes, it was. A little before five. Bruno had not yet arrived."

"And I imagine you offered him a glass of absinthe?"

"How do you know?"

"Because he still smelled of it when he came to see me later Thursday afternoon."

He looked at me with intensified misery.

"It is a very distinct odor, isn't it?" he said. "Perhaps I should attempt to change my habits."

"That is none of my business," I said firmly. "As long as you keep your word about the other point that we have discussed."

He merely nodded.

I left him with an oddly downcast sensation, as if Gilbert had infected me with his melancholy. I now knew that Christophe had been planning to write his article about Mademoiselle Death even before I refused to supply him with a comment. Beyond that, I was not much the wiser.

It was shortly after nine in the evening when I arrived home. My father was sitting in the salon—he had not yet managed to carry out his threat of going to bed without saying good night—but he was not alone.

"August!"

"Are you surprised?"

"I didn't think you were coming until tomorrow."

"I decided to take the afternoon train."

He stood there entirely untouched by the rigid tension that I still sensed in my father. His tall athletic figure exuded a relaxed vitality. His dark hair fell across his forehead in its usual untamed fashion, and he must have taken a bath at his lodging before coming here, because it was still damp, and he smelled of eau de cologne and soap. A burst of heat shot through me, spreading from my abdomen into my entire body so that I had the sensation of being pink all over, like an infant just plucked from its bath. My entire being unfolded and made itself ready, in a way that Madame Aubrey and her academy would definitely not have approved of.

He saw it. Blind though he was to my father's repressed anger, where I was concerned, his acuity was complete. He took my hand and kissed it, all very proper, and yet . . . I could feel him inhaling, taking in my scent, and his lips parted lightly in midkiss so that his tongue touched the skin between the third and fourth fingers on my right hand.

"I hear that the good Commissioner is getting married. He is overtaking us, Madeleine. Don't you think we should soon follow suit?"

Yes. Now. Tomorrow. No, even better: tonight.

I had to control myself not to say any of this out loud. My legs had begun to shake a little, and I was afraid he would notice the slight movement of my skirts. There had actually been a short course for the senior class where Madame Aubrey herself had explained to me and my blushing schoolmates what marriage involved, in her opinion. Nothing she mentioned seemed to acknowledge the existence of a female sexuality, and her florid and strongly metaphorical account left the impression that my body was a flower meadow, which my future husband would feel a certain need to water at regular intervals, and that I would have to put up with this watering process as a "happy duty." Nothing was said of shaking knees and overheating in a considerable area south of my navel. Yet he had only kissed my hand . . .

I attempted to force my decidedly unfloral impulses back where they came from.

"Perhaps this fall," I said cautiously.

He lit up. "Do you mean that?"

It was the first time I had come close to setting even an approximate date, but his very eagerness immediately made me a bit more reticent. The old litany began to echo somewhere in the back of my head: married, impregnated, conquered by biology. What if I conceived? The thought cooled my blood considerably. I could not risk it. Not now. Not when I had finally been admitted to the university, not when I stood on the threshold to everything I desired even more than . . . the other thing.

"We will have to see," I said. "Perhaps you will not feel like being married *or* engaged to Mademoiselle Death."

I could tell that he had read the story.

"If you ignore the journalist's bizarre choice of words," he said, "then there is nothing in that article that I did not know already. Besides, the engagement is now official—it has been announced in the newspaper."

He was right. I had no idea how the journalist had unearthed the fact, but the article noted that "young Mademoiselle Karno is engaged to Professor August Dreyfuss of the University of Heidelberg."

August smiled at me and kissed my hand again, not quite as lingeringly this time. Perhaps he sensed it would not be to his advantage to push me off this particular ledge. His words were similarly light and jesting: "You are not getting away that easily, Madeleine!"

I inadvertently looked at my father. He had not risen when I came in, as August had. He still sat brooding and grim in his usual armchair, only minimally softened by August's presence and the cognac that made the bottom of his glass glow golden in the lamplight.

"August thinks that we should not take it too seriously," he said reluctantly. "He thinks people will forget it as soon as the next sensation catches their attention."

"Let us hope so," I said firmly.

When he thought of his father, his teeth hurt. It was an inescapable fact, even though he knew perfectly well that a dentist would find neither cavities nor abscesses. This morning, the monthly Sunday visit was upon him, and he could literally feel his gums pull back and expose the sensitive neck of the tooth so everything he ingested, hot or cold, sweet or sour, shrieked against his nerve endings. He also knew that once he was there, when his mother kissed him dryly on the cheek and welcomed him in, when his father came out of his study and stretched both his hands toward him, the toothache would disappear. It was only in the phase of anticipation, if you could call it that, that his dental symptoms kept him awake at night.

"I will be back at nine tonight," he told his housekeeper, Madame Arnaud, entirely unnecessarily, since he always came home at nine in the evening after these Sundays, but she just nodded and handed him his hat, cane, and gloves.

He walked there. It rarely took him more than an hour, and in principle he could therefore visit his childhood home much more frequently. But the pattern of monthly visits had been set when he lived in Jena, and all parties had maintained the model without discussion even now when he lived on Rue Faubourg, less than an hour's walk from the old gray house behind the cast-iron fence on Boulevard Saint-Augustine. If he had made use of the new streetcar, he could have been there in fifteen minutes.

A light drizzle speckled his gray overcoat but without penetrating the worsted fabric to the layers underneath. He held his cane under his arm; he was not the kind of man who felt a need to swing it and thus take up about twice as much room on the sidewalk as necessary. At the corner of Place d'Armistice and Rue

Concorde, he ran into Oreste Gervaise from the Botanical Institute, who was out walking with his wife. Though he did not actually care for the man, he stopped for a moment and exchanged a few words with him. One should avoid rudeness; it would inevitably damage one's chances in the constant and frequently acrimonious interdepartmental squabbles. Madame Gervaise was a large, bony woman without a trace of charm, but it was said that she had money, and that this was the reason Gervaise himself was so blithe and cocksure in the debates about the future of the university. He could always, it was said, purchase his own institute if he felt like it.

Adrian smiled politely at both Monsieur and Madame and was not at all jealous of Gervaise. One could pay too high a price . . .

The brief intermezzo had cost him five minutes, and he therefore picked up his pace a little. And it was while he was thus hastening along the promenade that Mademoiselle Karno's likeness appeared before his inner eye.

Two pictures of her fought for his attention. One was the grainy newspaper photograph under the unbelievably vulgar headline "Mademoiselle Death." How did these journalists come up with their peculiar ideas? The other one was sharper and more fascinating, in spite of the fact that it was plucked from the dubious records of memory. Her profile, bent over the entrails of the rabbit, concentrated, competent, free of any feminine feeling, delicacy, and distaste.

Interesting.

Yes, that was exactly the word. There was no doubt that she was the most interesting woman he had met in a very long time. A pity, really, that she was, as the article noted, engaged to the Foghorn of Heidelberg, the unbearably self-absorbed Professor Dreyfuss.

He realized that while he had been thinking of Madeleine

Karno, his toothache had disappeared. Should he consider this a sign?

Engaged to Dreyfuss. But the insufferable Dreyfuss was not invulnerable. Far from it. He had an Achilles' heel so glaringly obvious that it practically hurt one's eyes.

Adrian smiled and found himself actually swinging his cane a little. Tonight when he got home, he would write a letter. No, wait—perhaps even two.

He began to whistle quietly. The toothache had entirely disappeared and did not return.

Intermezzo: Ari and Alice

It was in October 1887. The death masks were not selling as well as before, said his father. People did not appreciate the craftsmanship anymore, and many preferred instead to have a photograph taken. That was the future, but cameras were expensive and the development process was complicated, and though Ari had attempted to obtain an apprentice position, he had not succeeded. But instead there was work at the new Hôpital Marine des Hyères that had been built a bit south of the city, below Costebelle and—naturally—in proximity to the sea.

Two English doctors, Dr. Madden and Dr. Griffin, ran and owned the place. Dr. Madden was the older and had had a practice in Hyères for some time; he spoke French, albeit with an almost incomprehensible accent. Dr. Griffin had arrived only recently, from the English city of Birmingham, it was said, and it seemed he had brought along half of Birmingham's population, or at least half of its invalids—Hyères was teeming with cloth manufacturers and merchants, and to an even greater extent their wool-wrapped wives and daughters, who strolled along the newly constructed palm-lined Boulevard Victoria, or took their afternoon tea on the hotel terraces along the promenade.

What the English doctors were looking for was "bath assistants." Since a significant part of the treatment of their English patients consisted of daily immersion in the sea, they had ordered the construction of a number of bath machines so that even the weakest could benefit from the healing effect of the seawater. A cabin on tall wheels was pulled out into the water by a horse. While this was happening, the patient changed into a bathing costume inside the cabin, and when the horse was unhitched, the bather could descend directly from the cabin and into the waves, with the assistance of what the English clientele, in spite of Doctors Madden and Griffin's nomenclature, simply and plainly called "dippers."

"We educate our assistants," Dr. Madden said seriously at Ari's hiring interview. "They are far more than just robust individuals who can hold reluctant bathers underwater. If we decide to hire you, monsieur, you will undertake a course that will enable you to understand the range and effect of the treatments, and to engage with our patients with poise and propriety. You will likewise learn enough English to provide the necessary instructions and understand the most common phrases of politeness. Do you know how to swim?"

Ari said yes. It was actually a dog paddle from his childhood, but he thought that would be fully sufficient for the purpose.

The hardest thing about the job, it turned out, was neither the English phrases nor the detailed charts that had to be memorized. He actually enjoyed the language classes and quickly discovered he had a certain talent for it, and he had always had a good memory. Nor was it the many hours he had to stand in the cold water, summer as well as winter, though his legs would grow entirely numb and senseless toward the end of the workday, prior to burning like the fires of hell when they came back to life.

No, the most difficult thing was, without question, Alice.

Alice was actually called Miss Anderson, and it was in fact wrong of him to think of her as anything else. That was part of the problem.

She—Miss Anderson—had hair of a particular cinnamon shade somewhere between blond and brown. It was so smooth that one might think she ironed it as other women iron shirts. Her mouth—which he ought not to notice at all—was small but with plump lips, so that the word "rosebud" had a tendency to force its way into his thoughts when he saw her. She was, like most of the English, very fair skinned and had to constantly shield herself from the sun because even the tiniest exposure resulted in a scalded blush.

Her petite, slender form emitted, it seemed to him, a quivering nervous energy, and it was in fact weak nerves and constant headaches that brought her and her mother to Hyères that winter.

"Last year, we were in Menton," explained Mrs. Anderson helpfully to Dr. Griffin. "But poor Alice could not sleep at all, it was that awful wind, what is it they call it—the monsoon?"

"The mistral," Dr. Griffin corrected her kindly.

"Yes. That one . . . Everything *rattled*. I myself had trouble sleeping, though I am luckily much more robust than poor Alice."

It seemed as if Mrs. Anderson never used her daughter's first name without apposing the word "poor."

"I hope, Mrs. Anderson, that both you and your daughter will have a more peaceful stay here. Unfortunately, the mistral blows everywhere, but we are somewhat better sheltered here. In addition, the sea baths have a wonderful effect on the nervous system, so I am sure that poor"—the doctor corrected himself at the last minute—"that the young lady will soon experience an improvement. I feel confident in giving you my medical guarantee."

"Ohhh, the sea baths, yes. If you say so, but . . . poor Alice is terribly afraid of water."

"I can assure you that it is completely safe. Aristide here is one of our most experienced bathing assistants."

Mrs. Anderson considered Ari doubtfully, as he automatically straightened up and attempted to inspire confidence.

"He is a man," Mrs. Anderson pointed out.

"Most of our assistants are," said Dr. Griffin. "Some of our weakest patients need the support that only the more rugged strength of the male physique can provide, and that is often true for the more anxious as well. But if you and your daughter wish, I will of course find a female assistant for you."

"No," said Mrs. Anderson. "If you think that this is the right choice . . ."

It was a golden and blue October day, and the light fell with a creamy golden mildness on the beach and the bathers, both the ones using the machines and those who—more boldly—waded into the waves without assistance. Miss Anderson's bathing costume was navy blue, with blue and white ruffles that somehow made her look even younger and childish, perhaps because it was vaguely reminiscent of a sailor's suit. She stood on the wagon's uppermost step and looked, as her mother had predicted, entirely petrified.

"Please descend," said Ari with one of his carefully memorized phrases. "There is no need to be alarmed."

She turned toward him and looked straight into his eyes.

"I am going to die," she said. "I know it." And the fear of death did indeed shine from her velvet brown eyes.

"No," he said. "I will not let you die. You have my word."

The protocol prescribed other vaguer assurances: "There is absolutely no risk," "You will be entirely safe," and "The sea is completely calm today. There is no reason for fear." But he sensed instinctively that she needed him to conjure up the spectacle of death and, all in the same sentence, dispel it with his words.

She grabbed hold of him, not his outstretched hand but his arm. Her fingers dug clawlike into his biceps, quite painfully, but he did not let it show. She took the first shaky step down the stairs and then the next one. He could both see and feel the trembling that went through her when the water clasped her legs and lower body.

"Ohhhh . . ." A drawn-out, plaintive gasp.

"Do come, mademoiselle. I will not let go."

And then she was down. Her bare feet touched the bottom just like his. Her pupils expanded abruptly so that her hazel eyes looked almost black. She clung to both his arms, and at first he could not get her to hang on to only one, so he could support her back with the other.

"All the way?" she said with a shaking voice. "Must I really go all the way under the water?"

"Yes, mademoiselle. But only for a few seconds. And only three times, at least today."

She closed her eyes and abandoned herself to the mercy of God. He could actually see the inner prayer move her lips.

"Now," she said. "While I dare."

He wrested one arm free of her grip.

"You should hold on here," he said, and more or less established the correct submerging position. When he began to tilt her backward, she panicked, and she fought against him with all her might. But he placed one hand over her nose and mouth to protect her against the insistent water and forced her down under the surface for the prescribed ten seconds. A few cramp-like jerks passed through her body. Her one knee hammered repeatedly against his thigh, and he would later note that she had made ten precise blue marks on his forearm.

Then he brought her back to the surface.

"There you are," he said with an unfamiliar hoarseness in his voice. "It is not the least bit dangerous."

She slowly opened her eyes. A deep blush spread across her neck and face, until now gray with terror, and she looked around as if he had re-created the whole world for her and brought her back from the dead.

"Ohhh," she said. "Oh. I did not know . . . Dear God, I did not know . . ."

"Should we try again?" he asked. "If you close your mouth yourself and hold your nose, then I will not need to."

She shook her head. "I dare not. It must . . . You must . . . please do it exactly like the first time."

So he held her in the same way, with his right hand over her nose and mouth and his left around her waist, when he dunked her the second and third time.

Later, after they were married and had learned to make love, he occasionally saw precisely the same expression in her eyes when she tilted her neck back and opened her mouth in the involuntary silent scream that was her climax. This helpless and transported gaze, I want and yet do not want, as in the duet from *Don Giovanni* that she loved so much, "*Vorrei e non vorrei*." He never understood the darkness in her, no matter how familiar everything else became.

"There you are," he said again, when the third dunking had been carried out. "You survived."

"Barely," she said, her pupils still huge and dark. "Only barely . . ."

But the next day, Mrs. Anderson looked at him with greater confidence and reported that Poor Alice had eaten a substantial dinner and had slept like a log all night.

The physiologist is no ordinary man. He is a learned man, a man possessed and absorbed by a scientific idea. He does not hear the animals' cries of pain. He is blind to the blood that flows. He sees nothing but his idea, and organisms which conceal from him the secrets he is resolved to discover.

—CLAUDE BERNARD, *INTRODUCTION À L'ÉTUDE DE LA MÉDECINE EXPÉRIMENTALE*, 1865

August 16, 1894

Early in the morning, Sante Geronimo Caserio was executed outside the prison in Lyon. According to the *Varbourg Gazette*, which had replaced *Varonne Soir* on the salon table now that we no longer subscribed to that offending publication, the blade of the guillotine had fallen at precisely five o'clock, a few seconds after Caserio had yelled his last words: "*Coraggio, cugini! Evviva l'anarchia!*"

I have to admit that I was personally less occupied with the fate of that young man and the political situation than I perhaps ought to have been, because this day—the day Caserio did not live to experience—was my first day as a student at the University of Varbourg.

It had rained during the night and in the early hours, but now the sun was shining again, and in Réunion Square the air was full of rain-drenched scents—wet dirt, wet chestnut leaves, the sweetness from ripe peaches and grapes of the fruit stalls and, it must be admitted, the penetrating smell of formerly dried-up horse dung that had now been resoftened by the rain.

Mindful of Professor Künzli's concerns, I had tried to dress in as undistracting a manner as possible, so as not to unduly disturb the flower of Varbourg's youth. My high-necked white blouse had only modest trimming across the chest, which served more to veil than to emphasize, sleeves and cuffs hid both wrists, the skirt was light brown and without frills, and Elise had helped me let down the hem a few centimeters so it did not, when I sat down, slide up to the point where one might glimpse my ankles. I wore pale thin gloves, and my hat was extremely plain, a small flat boater with a ribbon in the same light brown color as the skirt. Proper and serious, that was the impression I wished to make.

There were more gendarmes in the street than usual, I noted, and they appeared more alert. No taking a moment to smoke a pipe in the shelter of the side streets or stopping to exchange a few words with the stall keepers. Those who were supposed to keep guard kept guard—especially in front of the new government building that housed Varonne's chamber of commerce—and the ones who were on patrol, patrolled. It was feared that the execution would stoke the anger of other anarchists, as had happened in several other European countries during similar events.

I was exceedingly prompt this time, so instead of changing to the No. 7 streetcar, I decided to walk the last bit. It would most likely take me less than ten minutes, and perhaps it would have a beneficial effect on my nerve endings, the excited state of which had made it impossible for me to eat breakfast.

The last hundred meters, I found myself walking behind a somewhat familiar-looking young man. He was tall, broad shouldered, and very blond, and there was a cockiness about his stride that reminded me of someone. Perhaps it was one of the young medical students my father occasionally took under his wing? He strode up the impressive steps with an assuredness as if they had been built just for him. I myself had to reduce my speed considerably, and I lost sight of him somewhere among the pillars of the colonnade and did not give it any further thought, being rather more preoccupied with finding the correct lecture hall.

I had barely crossed the threshold before a sarcastic voice hit me from behind. "Well, well, Fräulein. So we meet again."

He spoke French with a considerable German accent, which in itself was a useful clue. But when I turned around and saw him face-to-face, I recognized him instantly in any case. The straw blond hair and fair beard, the muscular neck, the gaze that was as blue and chilly as ice crystals on a windowpane.

I did not know his name. August and I had spoken of him only once, that day in April when I agreed to our engagement.

He was my future husband's previous lover. And thus more or less the last person I wanted to meet here.

"What are you doing here?" I blurted, even though it might not have been the wisest way of handling the situation.

"What am I doing here?" he asked, eyebrows sarcastically raised. "I am a student. This is an institute of higher learning. There is nothing odd about my presence. I ought rather to ask you. What do you think *you* are doing here, Fräulein?"

The room fell silent around us. The chatter that had filled the room before I entered had been instantly silenced. Without looking around, I sensed the presence of at least thirty young men, standing or perched on benches and tables around us, with their attention focused on one sole person: me.

"The same as you, I imagine," I said as neutrally as possible. "I am a student."

He fired off a short burst of vulgar laughter.

"Really? Listen, Fräulein, I have not been in Varbourg for long, but I have learned one thing: *Étudienne* is just another word for whore."

I stood stock-still and felt my jaw stiffen so that for a few seconds it was entirely impossible for me to close my mouth. At first, I was not sure I had heard him correctly, but from several loud gasps around me I understood that there was nothing wrong with my hearing.

"Come, come . . . ," said one of the others, clearly embarrassed. "You are speaking to a lady."

"Am I?" drawled the young German. "Then I don't know what a lady is. But if she insists on remaining, I shall leave. And I suggest every honorable man here should do the same."

One or two took a few hesitant steps—whether it was to follow him never became clear because at that moment Dr. Althauser came into the room. How little or how much he had heard I did not know. My cheeks burned at the thought that he might have heard it all. He did not look at me but at my adversary.

"Herr Falchenberg? How have you hit upon the idea that it is up to you to decide who is to be taught here?"

The young Falchenberg looked surprised for a brief moment.

"Herr Docent—" he began.

Althauser interrupted him. "If you do not wish to attend the lecture, then that is naturally your choice. But I would appreciate it if you did not otherwise interfere with the composition of this class."

Falchenberg said no more but disappeared into the hall with a respectful bow that was so tightly executed that he managed to signal contempt at the same time. He did not look excessively guilt ridden.

Althauser ignored both him and me and continued to the front of the room, and in his wake the rest of the students settled in a long, chair-scraping wave. I myself fell into the closest seat on offer.

Throughout the roll call I sat with flaming cheeks and tried to fight back my anger and humiliation so that neither would be allowed to turn into tears. The worst thing was that Falchenberg was right, linguistically speaking—the ladies of loose morals with whom some students kept company were colloquially called *étudiennes*, student girls. And there was no other word for female students.

Not yet, I whispered to myself. But one day . . . soon. When reality changed, surely language had to follow?

Unfortunately, Falchenberg had achieved one thing with his harassment. Though he had left the room, he had made me so agitated that for the next fifteen minutes I barely took in a word of what was being said at my life's first official university lecture.

In the course of the next hours, my wounded vanity began to heal, and my intellect stirred. While Althauser skillfully introduced his field of study, I wrote furiously in my newly purchased notebook, and somewhere between "methodology" and "practical exercises," a footnote snuck in that did not have much to do with physiology: "Falchenberg: Why?"

It was hard to believe that it was a coincidence. In spite of the department's excellent new building, it had to be admitted that Heidelberg far exceeded Varbourg in terms of facilities, faculty, and reputation. There was unlikely to be anything here that Falchenberg could not learn better and more quickly where he came from.

The thought that he might have come to Varbourg because of me—or rather because of August and me—was cause for concern. It might have been naïve of me, but I had imagined that the engagement settled the matter. Whatever Falchenberg and August had done together, it was the past now that he and I were getting married. I was sure that August was of the same opinion, and I had not thought any further than that. Would I have reacted differently if the relationship August had ended for my sake had been with a woman?

I had tried to read about the subject in my father's copy of Krafft-Ebing's *Psychopathia Sexualis: Eine Klinisch-Forensische Studie*. Krafft-Ebing was of the opinion that any type of sexuality directed at the same sex instead of at the opposite was a biological aberration that occurred in the womb—a sort of brain damage that resulted in "sexual inversion." I found it difficult to regard August as brain damaged, but the fact remained that the fetus could be damaged or infected with illnesses in the womb—pox, typhoid, tuberculosis, and syphilis, for example. My father was similarly of the opinion that a mother who drank heavily during her pregnancy could harm the fetus or even kill it, and he attempted—mostly without luck—to convince the women he cared for at Saint Bernardine to stop drinking while they were carrying an innocent child.

On the other hand, Krafft-Ebing also believed that the "woman, if physically and mentally normal, and properly educated, has but little sensual desire. If it were otherwise, marriage and family life would be empty words. As yet the man who avoids women, and the woman who seeks out men are sheer anomalies." Perhaps I was, with my undeniable "sensual desire," just as abnormal as August?

I should perhaps have asked August himself, but I had not yet dared to do that. He had assured me that he was just as interested in women as he was in men, that he found me exceedingly desirable, and that he would do his best to be faithful to me.

He had never hid the fact that it had gradually become more and more important for him to be married. It was expected of a man in his position, and it would protect him to some extent from gossip. For my part, beyond the physical attraction I felt, August possessed another attractive trait—he found my intellect at least as interesting as my appearance, and he encouraged me to develop it. He had promised me two things: that he would treat me in every respect as a person, not just as a woman, and that he would never lie to me. In my marriage to him, I believed I would find a freedom I had hardly dared hope for. Assuming we did not have children. Married, impregnated, conquered—no, I would not let it happen. Not now. Perhaps not ever . . .

That this would be a sensible and convenient marriage for us both, undertaken under certain rational premises, did not, however, mean that it was to be a loveless marriage of convenience. Not at all.

I had to tell him that Falchenberg was in Varbourg, I decided. I glanced at the clock on the wall behind Althauser. August would be on the train right now, somewhere south of Strasbourg. He had swapped lectures with a colleague in order to be able to invite me and Papa out to dinner tonight to celebrate my first day at university. If I went directly to the lodging he used when he was here, I would have time to speak with him there. This was a conversation I preferred to have out of my father's hearing.

The house in Carmelite Street was so cramped that we had little room for overnight guests unless they felt like being quartered on the chaise longue in the salon or among the beakers and test tubes in the laboratory. In fact, August would probably not have minded the latter, but Madame Vogler would never have survived it. A professor from Heidelberg! On a bench in the laboratory! Never in her live-long days . . . !

Consequently, August had rented lodgings from a widow who ran a small pension not far from Réunion Square. I think he discovered it was a temperance establishment only after he had moved into two nice rooms overlooking the street. It hardly suited his at times quite Latin temperament, but it did make the whole arrangement all the more respectable. It also meant there was an excellent tearoom where I could wait for him.

Madame Guille recognized me and greeted me politely when I arrived.

"Bonjour, mademoiselle. Does this mean that we may expect the professor before too long?"

"I hope so," I said, and ordered a pot of orange pekoe.

The salon had a large bow front protruding into the little square at the end of Rue Fevre, but the sun was so fierce that I chose a table at the back of the room, shaded even further by a tall rubber tree in a tub. I did not need to keep an eye out for August after all; Madame Guille would tell him I was here. I borrowed yesterday's edition of *Varonne Soir* from the newspaper rack. Despite the fact that there had been no decisive development in the investigation of Rosalba Lombardi's death—or perhaps precisely *because* of that fact—interest in the case had dwindled.

Today, Caserio's execution took up most of the front page, and of Rosalba, Eugénie Colombe, or Jack the Ripper there was no mention. Mademoiselle Death was equally absent from the headlines, I noted with a deep-felt gratitude. Christophe had devoted his efforts to a more rewarding subject and was trying to make his readers so afraid of "vengeful actions from Caserio's anarchist coconspirators" that they hardly dared venture into the streets. As usual, it was impossible to tell if Christophe was a first name, a last name, or just a nom de plume.

In the midst of my reading, I suddenly became aware of a German-speaking voice. Varonne is a border province, and many of Varbourg's inhabitants are bilingual, even though the Third Republic is reluctant to acknowledge this fact. But I did not know many who were capable of expressing themselves in so articulate and precise a Hochdeutsch. I was already halfway out of my chair, with a spontaneous smile, when I realized that my fiancé was not alone.

He was standing in the street outside in intense conversation with Falchenberg. He had placed a hand on Falchenberg's arm, as if he wanted to prevent him from leaving, but had now lowered his voice so that I was able to pick up only a word here and there.

I sat back down abruptly.

I caught "unpleasant" . . . "emotional" . . . "can't go on."

The conversation went on for interminable minutes. Then Falchenberg tore himself loose with a violence that made passersby turn around for a second look. I had no trouble catching the word he threw in August's face.

"Coward!" he shouted, and stormed off with long, ill-tempered strides.

If Madame Guille had not intervened, I would probably have remained in the cover of my rubber tree while August walked by and would then have fled home to my father. Waves of extreme emotions shot through me. Indignation, anxiety, a nauseating uncertainty—but stronger than all these was an intense urge to smash, tear, kick, slash that pompous Teutonic fool. If only he would get run over, if only large horse hooves would stomp on his ridiculously broad German chest, if only a wagon wheel would roll across his blond head and . . .

My entire body was shaking, and I only slowly realized that this entirely unfamiliar wave of destructive urges and homicidal hatred was what other people called jealousy.

"Monsieur le Professeur," I heard Madame Guille exclaim outside in the vestibule, "your fiancée is waiting for you."

Her unintentional warning gave me a moment to collect myself and try to control this unhelpful emotional phenomenon. I rose when August entered.

"I came to tell you that Erich Falchenberg is in town," I said with as little emotion as possible. "But I can see that you already know that."

He threw me a long look. Then he turned to Madame Guille.

"I think my fiancée and I will take our tea upstairs," he said. "In my drawing room."

"But of course," answered Madame Guille with a quick little dip in her knees—there is something about August that makes even full-grown women curtsey.

"August!"

"Not here, Madeleine!" he said quietly. "Come upstairs."

He took my arm, and unless I was prepared to entertain the present café guests with yet another scene, there was nothing to do but to follow him.

I had visited August's lodgings before but had never been alone with him there. He hesitated for a moment, on the verge of leaving the door ajar in the name of propriety, but then apparently decided that our topic of conversation required a more complete privacy.

Though he stayed here for only a few days a month, the "drawing room" was already looking more like an office. There was no bookshelf, so books were piled on the dresser, on the desk he had installed himself, and even on the window ledges, thus severely hampering Madame Guille's efforts to maintain the décor in a simple modern style dominated by black, white, and charcoal gray. I hope he tipped the maid generously, because he did not make her work easy. There was not quite the same debris of sports equipment that characterized his office in Heidelberg, but to compensate there were several glass jars displaying organs I suspected were riddled with parasites—I recognized a sheep's brain and something I thought must be a segment of a bovine rumen. He collected interesting pathologies with the intention of adding them to the Heidelberg collection wherever he had the opportunity.

"You saw me with Erich," said August. "Did you hear what we were talking about?"

"No," I said. "I did not think you were still seeing him!"

"I am not, at least not in the way that you mean," he declared. "In Heidelberg, there is no way to avoid occasionally bumping into each other."

"But what is he doing here, then? And why did he seek *me* out?"

"Has he done so?" August asked sharply. "When?"

"Today. At the university." The skin on my neck and face burned with the thought of the way he had behaved, the words he had used. I was not going to repeat them to August.

"He is very young," said August with an apologetic tone that did not lessen my indignation. "He thinks everything in life is either black or white, all or nothing."

"Excellent. Then he will have no difficulty understanding that you and he are nothing from now on."

"Madeleine . . ."

"I will not share you with him. Ever. Not in . . . in any way."

"I would never do that to—"

He did not have the chance to complete his sentence, because I had a bizarre sense that my body had been taken over by someone else. My hands grabbed hold of the nape of his neck and forced his face down to kissing height, my mouth opened so abruptly and totally that he must have thought I was planning to devour him, and perhaps I was. I had never before experienced so thorough and unstoppable an urge to possess someone or something. *Mine*, screamed my rebellious body. *No one else's! Mine.*

I think he tried to say something, but the words were lost inside my open mouth. I felt them as an odd mutual breath, a moist gulp of air that emanated from him and died against my tongue, as a vibration in my jaw when our teeth collided. His arms closed around me. I could not feel his hands as anything but a general pressure against the back of my corset, and I was so impatient that tears burned against my eyelids. I wanted to feel his long strong fingers directly against my skin, I wanted to own him, consume him, make him so fully and completely mine that there was no way back. But in this first moment I had already used up my modest practical experience. Why couldn't Madame Aubrey have given us just a few concrete directions about how to get to the "happy duty" part?

"Madeleine . . . Wait."

This time the words could be heard. I still clutched his neck so hard that he could not quite straighten up, and he had to pronounce them in the vicinity of the corner of my mouth. But I heard them.

"I want you to show me," I said. "I want to know if we can!"

He laughed quietly and warmly against my cheek.

"Oh, I wouldn't worry too much . . . ," he said teasingly.

I was not ready to be teased. "Krafft-Ebing calls it brain damage," I lectured him.

121

"What?" he asked, though I was pretty convinced he knew exactly to what I was referring.

"To be drawn to one's own sex. It happens in utero, he says . . . and what if it is irreversible?"

"Herr Krafft-Ebing is an idiot," he said hoarsely.

"He is a professor!"

"As am I, my sweet."

"Of parasitology," I protested. "It is not the same thing!"

"No, but I do happen to know what I am talking about. In practice, so to speak."

"Then show me how to do it!"

His breathing changed abruptly. It became deeper and more audible. And his hands pressed even harder against my back.

"Are you sure?" he said, with a voice that I would not have recognized if I had not been staring at his lips while he said it.

Somewhere in the deepest nooks and crannies of my brain, I heard Erich Falchenberg's contemptuous whisper: "*Étudienne* is just another word for whore." But I did not care. Or rather, it just made me more eager. At that moment, it seemed to me the only thing I could do to exorcise his towheaded ghost. I pulled August's head closer to mine and kissed him again.

"I think I must tell Madame Guille that we do not want tea after all," he said. But in the end he just locked the door.

It was astounding. Astounding to be undressed by a man. Astounding to stand before him without feeling the least bit of shame. A certain self-consciousness, perhaps, but no shame. Astounding to discover that his gaze was caress enough, just to be seen and enjoyed was enough for my muscles to contract, for my blood vessels to expand, and the nerve endings of my skin to send electric waves through my body.

I wanted so badly to reciprocate and began to open his shirt, button by difficult button. The shirt had presumably been clean and freshly ironed when he put it on in the morning in Heidelberg, and I could still smell the soap even though there were now sweat stains under the arms and on the back. He wrenched it off and let it fall on the floor with the unconscious indifference of a man who has had someone to pick up after him his entire life. He was surprisingly tanned and even more muscular than I had imagined—I later discovered that he quite often rowed in his vest or even completely shirtless.

I think he was waiting to see if I would lose my nerve. He made no move to continue the undressing. But I was determined enough to press on, despite the shyness burning in my cheeks.

He kissed me passionately and deeply, and finally I could feel each single one of his fingers, spread out in a fan against my back, one hand between my shoulder blades, the other somewhat lower. I could *feel* the nakedness, his and mine. The warmth that was generated where skin touched skin. His sex that rose between us, foreign and yet already familiar. So what if I had never done this before? My body already knew his, had exchanged thousands of unheard messages during the past months. While he and I had conversed, all proper and rationally sensible, those two, his body and mine, had secretly been discussing entirely different matters.

Suddenly it was very quick. I don't think it was his intention. I think he was taken by surprise, overwhelmed by the covert understanding between our bodies. Nothing was measured and considerate any longer. He abruptly pressed his knee between my legs, and I fell—let myself fall—back against the bed. I did not quite make it, sliding down onto the floor in an avalanche of pillows and sheets, and with a single jerk of pain and desire he was inside me, and I had him where I wanted him, *mine*, and Professor Krafft-Ebing and Erich Falchenberg could take each other by the hand and jump into the sea, because neither of them could touch what was happening now. Neither of them knew *this* precise rhythm, *this* pulse, *this* sweet salty desire and the dark explosions that occurred behind my closed eyes with each surge, with each thrust.

The afternoon sun fell in through the windows and burned against my eyelids. The sound of the traffic on Rue Fevre came and went as if I could turn it off and on at will. The infinite became finite again, and time picked up its ticktock pace. I felt a fold in the blanket beneath me, a tiny, insignificant discomfort. A soreness inside, a stiffness in unfamiliar muscles. It was terrible that it was over. I wanted to go back. I did not want to lie here and register all these details as if it was information I needed to record in one of my notebooks. As if they were symptoms.

"What's wrong?" he asked, and stroked me along my neck with gentle fingers. "Are you having regrets?"

"No," I whispered. "I just wish that it was not already over."

Again, his intimate and quiet laughter.

"When you say yes, you certainly say yes," he said. "But, Madeleine . . . It isn't over. This is just the beginning of what you and I will have together."

"Yes, of course," I said, trying to smile. It was ridiculous and meaningless, this pitch-black sense of loss, missing him even while I was still lying in his arms and was with him, skin to skin. But it was nonetheless what I felt.

August 27, 1894

"It was kind of you to come."

Marie Mercier opened the door herself. In fact I suppose I should think of her as Madame le Commissaire, but although I had been present at the quiet wedding at city hall, I still found it difficult.

"Not at all," I said politely, though in truth it was quite a journey to get here. The Commissioner had bought a house in La Valle, an old village that had not yet quite completed its transformation into a suburb. The plan to expand the streetcar line was still only a plan, and I had been forced to hire a hansom.

"No, I know it is a long way to come," she insisted. "And that you really have no reason to take the trouble for my sake. I am grateful to you."

"Where is Louis?" I asked.

"In school. Everything is a bit strange for him still, but his teachers say he is making good progress." Her smile was apologetic, but the maternal pride beneath the surface was unmistakable. "That was one of the reasons we moved out here. I think it is a good place for a child to grow up."

For Louis, the street urchin who was used to boasting that he was named after two kings and an emperor, it was certainly a new life, I thought.

The house was not quite new—until recently it had belonged to the little town's doctor—and it was definitely not modern either. It had more the air of a country house than an elegant villa, and the large conservatory facing the garden paradoxically strengthened this impression. If one ignored the glass panes, it was precisely on such verandas that Sunday lunches were served in the summer on the farms of the region, in the shadow cast by grapevines and ivy. Tea, however, was an immaculately bourgeois affair, presented on the Limoges set that I myself had chosen as a wedding gift to the couple from Papa and me.

Also at the tea table was Fleur Petit.

Even though I was aware that they knew each other, it was still a minor shock to see her there. It would have been entirely understandable if Marie had tried to distance herself from her former life, but apparently she was not someone who forgot old friends just because her own circumstances had improved.

"Mademoiselle Petit," I said.

"Just call me Fleur." She rose and greeted me, and her alert, dark gaze swept across me from my not especially fashionable flat boater to the new canvas sporting boots August had given me because he thought they would make it easier for me to bicycle. I was still quite uncertain in the saddle and was not convinced that I would ever come to like it, but I had not told him that. I so much wanted not to disappoint him. Besides, the boots were considerably more comfortable in the late-summer heat than my old black button boots.

"As you can see, we are delighted with the Limoges," said Marie—slightly strained, it seemed to me. "Won't you sit down?"

By then, I had realized that Marie's invitation had a purpose beyond tea and cake and a courteous, if somewhat belated, "thank you for the present." The real reason for the visit sat across from me now, incarnated in Fleur's slight schoolgirl figure. The initial polite phrases glanced right off her, like drops of water that scatter and evaporate in a hot pan, and in fact it did not take long before she cut right through Marie's attempts at light conversation.

"They haven't found him," she said.

There were shadows under the alert eyes and a fragility to her features, which made me wonder if she was able to sleep at night.

"No," I answered. "I heard as much." Rosalba Lombardi might have left the professional jurisdiction of Papa and the Commissioner long ago and now belonged under Inspector Marot's, but I still followed the case as well as I was able. After more than two months, there was still no decisive lead in the hunt for Rosalba's killer.

"I think they've given up trying."

"I shouldn't think so. Inspector Marot is a very determined man."

Fleur made a dismissive gesture. Her hand was no larger than a child's, I thought. Though she was clearly in her adult persona today, there was still a youthfulness about her that spontaneously provoked a desire to protect her, even in me.

"I found this." She placed a pink envelope on the table. "Rosalba had stuck it to the bottom of a drawer, and they did not discover it when they searched her room." She pushed the envelope toward me. "It seemed as if they were more interested in making a mess than in actually *searching*. As if it was just supposed to *look* as if they were thorough."

I sighed and opened the envelope. The hourly wage that Varbourg was able to pay its constables was not high. At times their commitment to their work matched it.

Inside, separated by thin sheets of tissue paper, lay six postcard-size photographs. Four of them were hand tinted, the last two black and white. They were all of Rosalba Lombardi, and she was not wearing much in the way of clothes.

The first four, the tinted ones, were playful and piquant, in a way almost childish, in spite of their erotic character. Rosalba posed up against a column, naked except for boots and a hat. She promenaded wearing only stockings and a corset in front of a backdrop with a not especially well-executed landscape painting, accompanied by a small white poodle. She sat on a picnic blanket, entirely undressed, and held a filled wineglass up toward the beholder. In a close-up, she hugged a huge basket full of grapes that only half hid her breasts, and bit playfully at a bunch she was holding up in the air. It made her neck look so impossibly soft and graceful that a swan would have cause for envy.

The two final pictures were different, and not just because of the unadorned black and white. For one thing, Rosalba was clearly pregnant—further along, it seemed to me, than the four months we had guessed. Furthermore, she was not alone.

She had been placed in a bathtub and equipped with a large sponge, with which she was pretending to wash herself. But whereas in the tinted pictures she had been coquettish and clearly comfortable in her state of undress, she now sat in one end of the tub and attempted to pull her knees up to her chest, despite her pregnant stomach. She held the sponge against her bosom as if she was trying to hide it. Her gaze did not flirt with the camera—instead it was fixed rigidly on the figure observing her from an armchair at the end of the tub. It was a man—which was about all you could tell with any degree of accuracy. He was elegantly dressed in top hat and cape, and sat balancing a silver-headed cane across his knees. But between the collar of the cape and the brim of the hat there was no face, no head, just a white sack with gaping dark eye sockets and a grotesquely painted charcoal smile that looked more like the mouth children might give a snowman than any human expression I had ever seen.

I looked up and met Fleur's intense gaze.

"Why are you showing me this?" I asked.

"Because it's him."

"Him?"

"Yes. I am convinced. Can't you see how afraid she is?"

I looked at the two black-and-white pictures again.

"Have you shown these to the police?"

"Yes."

"But . . . why have they not been added to the evidence file, then? Didn't they want them?"

"Oh yes." Fleur smiled bitterly. "Very much. But it was not to . . . what did you call it? . . . add them to the evidence file."

I blushed. It was only now that I grew truly uncomfortable with the pictures, now that Fleur's sarcasm made it crystal clear what men used such things for.

"I would not let them take them," she said. "I could see . . . that they would just make the rounds among the men. She is dead. Murdered. I could not bear the thought of all those knowing grins, the vulgar remarks, their grasping fingers, and all their moaning and grunting. She had enough of that when she was alive, didn't she? Can't you understand that?"

I folded my hands in my lap and observed the pearl buttons on my gloves as if I had just discovered that they were there. I could not make myself look directly at this wary, knowledgeable woman-child who had experienced so much more of life's darker side than I had.

"Yes," I mumbled. "I understand. But why not the Commissioner, then? I know you are familiar with his character. He would not . . . grunt."

"I asked. Or rather, Marie asked on my behalf. He referred me to Marot. Mademoiselle Karno, I know you found Marie's little Louis and helped to save his life. Can you not also find . . . *him*?" She pointed with a sharp chopping movement at the man with the snowman's grin. "Tear that *wicked* mask off him. Make sure that he is punished. The guillotine is too good for a man like that!"

I did not know what to say. In her voice churned not only the hatred she felt but also her despair and sorrow. She probably did not understand what unrealistic demands she was making, how much she overestimated my abilities and options. Even if I did by some miracle manage to find this man, he might have nothing at all to do with Rosalba's death. Fleur had no logical evidence, only her own stubborn conviction and her interpretation of a facial expression in a photograph. There was, I feared, no relief to be had even if we were to tear off the mask of the voyeur in the obscene picture. I took a deep breath and told her more than I should have.

"Do you know that both the fetus and the placenta were removed?" I asked. "And that it most likely was this, and not the subsequent lesions, that killed your friend?"

She was silent for so long that I inadvertently looked up. Her face was pallid.

"No," she whispered. "They didn't say anything about that."

"Fleur, you said yourself that Rosalba was very worried about the future," I said. "Is it possible . . . could you imagine that she had found a person who was willing to carry out this extremely risky operation for her—and that it simply went wrong? That this was a tragic accident, and that the awful circumstance under which she was found was just a clumsy attempt to confuse the police?"

Fleur began to cry in her uniquely silent, sobless way, like a child who knows she will be scolded if she "whines" and therefore has taught herself to let the tears flow without a sound.

"No," she said. "She would not have done that. She had felt life, don't you understand? It would have been a deadly sin. She would burn in hell forever. Burn in hell! No. She did not do that. He was the one! He was the one who killed her!"

But I could tell from the very fervor of her denials that she was no longer as certain as she had been.

"You must find him," she said. "Will you promise me that?"

She was so small. So furious. In such despair. I discovered that I did not have the power to leave her without giving her some vestige of hope.

"I promise you that I will search," I said. "I cannot promise you that I will find him. In return, you must also promise me something."

"Anything," she said simply.

"*If* I find him, then you must be content with whatever retribution the police and the justice system can provide you with. Even if the verdict is not murder."

"He killed her!"

"But perhaps not intentionally."

"But . . ."

"If you will not give me your word, then I cannot help you."

She stared angrily at me, but she was no longer as pale as before.

"Fine," she said, lifting her small stubborn chin. "You have my word. And you can keep the pictures for the time being. I expect to hear from you as soon as you have news!"

"*If* there is any news, how do I reach you?"

"Leave a message with the caretaker in Rue Vernier. Or ask Marie—she usually knows where I am."

They exchanged a tender, complicit look. Marie extended a porcelain dish full of tiny meringues toward me.

"Cake?" she asked.

August 28, 1894

"*Onykia ingens*, gentlemen," Dr. Althauser said, and tapped the large, beautifully colored poster a few times with the tip of the pointer. "Discovered and named in 1881 by Edgar Albert Smith from the British Museum during an expedition to the Straits of Magellan with the good ship *Alert*. Also known as *the greater hooked squid* in English. In French it does not yet have a name beyond the Latin. What can we say about this organism, gentlemen?"

Dr. Althauser professed to teach by the Socratic method and conducted his classes more like cross-examinations than lectures. But I had quickly discovered that there was no doubt as to who possessed the correct answers.

I did not complain—at least not about that. For me it was a victory just to be here.

This was my third lecture with Althauser, and though his dismissal of Erich Falchenberg had affirmed my right to be in the class, he still had not looked at me once. One might argue that he could not gaze with equal intensity and interest at all the more than forty students who followed his lectures, but as the only woman, I stuck out like a white duck in a flock of crows, and it must take conscious effort not to glance at me now and again. In spite of his Socratic leanings, he had not addressed me once—possibly because that would require looking at me—and in a way I was no more visibly present than back in the days when I used to hide in the highest gallery of the operating theaters at Saint Bernardine in order to observe the surgical procedures.

Althauser tapped the poster once more.

"Janvier. Yes, you. What do you observe?"

"A . . . squid," Janvier said hesitantly.

Althauser tilted his head and considered his victim. "A squid. Yes, verily. Describe it."

"It has . . . tentacles."

"Like every squid, yes. In this case ten. Or to be more precise, eight arms and two tentacles. What more?"

"Fins."

"How do they look?"

Janvier was perspiring. "Almost a bit . . . triangular."

"No, Janvier, they are not triangular. They are joined to form a perfect parallelogram with equal sides, or in other words, a rhombus. Unlike, for example, the *sagittate fins* more common among cephalopods. So: rhomboid fins. What else? Malleau? Would you continue?"

Malleau stood up. "Head, beak, arms, and gills protrude from a funnel-shaped mantle. The skin of the mantle looks as if it is covered in spots, as with the common European squid, *Loligo vulgaris*, but these appear more . . . prominent. Warts?"

"Correct, Malleau."

"In addition, it looks as if the tentacles are equipped with claws or hooks . . ."

"Likewise correct."

"If the professor permits . . . How large is it?"

"About half a meter long. Excellent. We have now described the animal's exterior, and that is of course critical to categorizing and identifying it correctly. But as physiologists there is something far more vital that interests us." With a practiced flick of his pointer, Althauser turned the poster over to display an illustration of a partly dissected specimen. "As you can see, the mantle has been opened, and the gills, the digestive system, and the reproductive organs are visible. Villeneuve, would you be so kind as to identify them?"

Villeneuve walked helpfully up to the board and took over the pointer.

"Beak, oral cavity, intestines . . ." He stopped.

"The reproductive organs, Villeneuve?"

Villeneuve looked. Suddenly someone in the class began to snicker. He whispered briefly to his neighbor, who likewise had to repress his laughter.

"Perhaps it is helpful to learn that it is a male squid, Villeneuve?"

Villeneuve kept searching. I too had noticed the condition that was the cause of all the merriment, but Villeneuve had not. Perhaps he mistook the organ in question for a tentacle and had not realized, in the nervous fervor of his predicament, that the creature in that case now sported eleven arms, and that the eleventh "arm" was significantly longer than the others, was, in fact, longer than the entirety of the body.

The merriment spread, and Villeneuve began to blush but still had not seen the light, so to speak.

Finally, Althauser took the pointer from him. "The creature's penis, Villeneuve." He jabbed at the eleventh arm with a certain firmness. But it was not Villeneuve he was looking at now, it was me. After having ignored me entirely through the three previous lectures, he now regarded me with an intense gravity that actually made the snickering cease.

"In its erect state, this penis is, as you can see, longer than any other part on the animal, in fact, longer than the animal itself. Sixty-seven centimeters, gentlemen. That makes *Onykia ingens* unique. Relative to its body size, it has the longest penis of any animal we know."

During this entire speech he kept his eyes stiffly focused on me. I did not understand why. Did he think that if he pronounced the word "penis" enough times, I would disappear?

I endured his gaze as calmly as I could. I did not look away, I did not show the discomfort I felt. I am even fairly sure that I did not blush.

"Is there anyone present who can explain why the *Onykia* has such an unusual reproductive organ?" he asked. "What about you, Mademoiselle Karno? Can you give us an explanation?"

I took as deep a breath as my corset permitted.

"No doubt there is an evolutionary advantage. It permits fertilization to happen deep inside the female's body, whereby as little reproductive material as possible is lost."

I knew nothing whatsoever about squids, but the thing had to have some kind of purpose.

Malleau could not quite stop giggling. Especially not when I used the word "fertilization." Althauser ignored him.

"Excellent, mademoiselle," he said with a small nod, as if I had passed an exam. I exhaled.

"Gentlemen, in the aquarium in the adjoining room you will find twenty-five squids. Perfectly common European squids, I regret to say, but you may learn something even from such ordinary creatures. I want you to undertake a thorough vivisection of the animals, do detailed measurements, descriptions, and drawings of all the critical physical organs. Afterward you should perform whatever tests you consider pertinent. Let us hope that will be sufficient to solve this week's assignment, which I will present to you once our time in the laboratory is up."

How he perceived me now, I was not yet certain—but it was apparently a step in the right direction. He looked at me, he spoke to me. Apparently one of the criteria for my continued presence here was that I could hear the word "penis" without making a feminine fuss. A somewhat peculiar key to the world of learning, and yet again . . . perhaps most fitting.

Vivisection requires that one cuts into something living. I understood that perfectly well, yet still it took an act of will when this living being stared back at me in concrete form. I looked down at the squid that I and Villeneuve—my partner for this exercise—had managed to pin to a varnished wooden board. A dark maroon flush shot across the animal's leatherlike mantle, and even without a fevered imagination, it was tempting to conclude that this play of colors expressed something very like feelings—fear, anger, aggression. The lower half of the board, Villeneuve's left hand, and part of his sleeve bore witness to the defensive powers of squid ink. Several of the ten arms shook and writhed and grabbed at everything in their vicinity.

"Can't we kill it first?" I whispered to Villeneuve.

He did not look as if he thought the task of opening up the live animal was any more appealing than I did. He was very young, more or less redheaded, with an accent that suggested he came from a rural background. After a momentary blush when he discovered with whom he had to share his squid, he had shown neither hostility nor excessive curiosity toward me, and it did not seem as if he held me responsible for his somewhat embarrassing incident earlier in the day.

"If it is dead, we cannot observe the processes," he said. "Janvier claims we need to study its circulation. He also said that we needed to find its . . . that is . . . um . . . scrotum, but I think he was just teasing . . ."

I glanced at the workbench next to ours. Malleau and his partner had already cut open the mantle on their squid and had pulled it aside so that the internal organs were displayed. Malleau was sharp—in every way. His features were narrow and intense, his profile pointed and almost birdlike. From the very first day it had been clear that he assumed he was the most intelligent student in the entire class, and he might be right.

I was on the verge of offering Villeneuve the scalpel and asking whether he wanted to make the first incision when I became aware that Dr. Althauser was standing a few meters away, studying me.

"Do you find it difficult, mademoiselle?" he asked, with a gentleness that was somehow also a warning. This was how one would address a young lady, not a student. If I ever manage to get him to stop calling me "mademoiselle," I thought, then I will have won. The day he calls me by my last name like the others . . . only then will we be on an equal footing.

"Difficult?" I asked, as if I could not imagine what he meant. "What should I find difficult?"

"To cut into the living flesh."

"Of course not," I lied, and reminded myself that I had after all taken part in operations on living people, even if they had most often been anesthetized. With a flowing and precise movement, I stuck the scalpel through the animal's mantle and cut it open. This is not much different from gutting fish, I told myself.

"You noticed, of course, the mantle's change of color," said Althauser. "How do you think it occurs, and what is its function?"

I could feel small drops of sweat trickle forth along my hairline, and I had to make an effort to steady the faint trembling of my hands.

"It could be connected to the animal's blood circulation," I said, at about the same moment that I discovered that the blood that colored the scalpel and my hands was not red but greenish. "I should think it functions as a signal in relation to the fellow members of its species. Villeneuve, we will need to take samples of that blood."

"Blood?" said Villeneuve. "Where?"

Apparently he did not have the ability to imagine that a liquid that was not red could be blood. Perhaps he thought it was ink, just of another color.

"Everywhere," I said. "It is green."

At last he understood and filled a couple of small test tubes.

Together we spread the mantle and pinned it to the board so the squid looked more or less like a living version of the poster Althauser had shown us earlier that morning.

More or less, because these were no thin diagram-like lines on a white background. Everything glistened, undulated, trembled, contracted. The entrails were exposed now, the heart pumped, the flesh quivered. No matter how much I tried, I could not see the animal as anything but a living, suffering creature. I felt a faint crisp ringing in my ears and grabbed with one hand, discreetly, I thought, at the edge of the table. But Althauser had seen it.

"Are you feeling unwell, Mademoiselle Karno?"

"No," I said curtly. To faint like the weak female creature he no doubt thought I was . . . not if I could help it!

"Do you know Claude Bernard, mademoiselle?" asked Althauser.

"Of course," I said. Bernard was France's leading physiologist. One could not be interested in the subject and not have heard of him.

"Then perhaps you will recognize these words: 'The physiologist is no ordinary man. He is a learned man, a man possessed and absorbed by a scientific idea. He does not hear the animals' cries of pain. He is blind to the blood that flows. He sees nothing but his idea, and organisms which conceal from him the secrets he is resolved to discover.'"

One could tell that it was far from the first time he had quoted Bernard's words to a student—they had an almost liturgical ring. I nodded and tried to concentrate on what I wanted to know. Circulation. We were supposed to study the circulation. I focused on the heart and carefully removed the membranes that surrounded it. Why was the creature's blood green? The difference was unlikely to be in the mechanical form and function of the heart.

Behind me there was a loud crash and a sequence of softer bumps. Villeneuve had fainted, bringing a couple of steel trays down with him as he fell.

I went directly to the laboratory when I got home. With me I had my drawings of the organs of the squid and a series of corresponding test notes, some vials of its various body fluids—including the ink—and last but by no means least, three test tubes full of the peculiar green blood. The assignment Althauser had eventually given us was precisely that—to determine why the blood had this color, and what function it might serve.

I knew that human blood was red because of the oxygen bound by the iron molecules in the red blood cells. To examine whether the amount of iron in the cephalopod's blood differed from that of humans and other red-blooded creatures seemed an obvious place to start, and I quickly determined that this was the case. But if oxygen wasn't bound and transported by iron, what, then, did a squid do instead?

It used copper, it transpired—multiple experiments and several hours later. For some reason, the squid found it practical to use copper rather than iron as a transporter of oxygen. And whereas iron became red—rust-red, to be specific—copper, when it oxidized, turned green. Verdigris, in fact, like the spires and copper-plated roofs of Varbourg's churches. So simple. So beautiful.

My new knowledge rested inside me like a pearl in an oyster. It had been won through suffering and discomfort—the suffering and death of the squid, my continued discomfort—but it was mine now, and I could not help but take pleasure in it.

The experiment of the day involved a woman who, according to the case notes, was twenty-four years old and registered as a *fille*

isolée. She was physically a fine specimen, 163 centimeters tall, weighing 62 kilograms, without any visible defects. Her diet had been good, there were no signs of either head lice or scabies, and she had an appealing head shape, domed and regular, with a high forehead. A lucky find, in other words.

But they had not washed her.

His nose registered the fact immediately—not so much because she had an unpleasant body odor, even though there was a certain amount of nervous sweat, but because he instantly caught the absence of the scent of soap.

He tried to control himself, though it was difficult.

"She has not been washed according to the protocol," he stated.

"But . . . she is not dirty," said one of the policemen who accompanied her. He was new, and apparently the others had not warned him. A young whelp, probably no more than nineteen or twenty, still with signs of adolescent acne on his cheeks, and his attempt to combine mustache and sideburns had not been entirely successful—the sideburns frizzled and curled as luxuriously as his auburn hair, but his mustache was a pathetic affair that led one to think of the whiskers of a smaller mammal of the rodent variety, a mouse perhaps, or, at most, a rat.

"Monsieur. Are you, or are you not, familiar with the instructions?"

The young constable still had not grasped the gravity of the situation.

"Yes, but . . . the baths were occupied, and—"

"If you cannot follow a simple protocol such as this, we will have to transfer you to other work. Take her back to the custody cells."

"But . . ."

"Did you not hear what I said?"

"Yes, but . . ."

"Afterward, you may go to the duty officer to receive instructions on your future employment."

The enormity of his blunder finally sank in.

"I'm sorry," the youth stammered. "It will not happen again. I'm sorry, I did not know . . . Can't you do it anyway? Or . . . can I bring her back later?"

She was so suitable that he had to consider it. If he did not maintain the frequency, he would have to remove her entirely from this series, and he hated to do that. It was not easy to find suitable specimens with the material at his disposal. Perhaps he could still . . .

A wave of nausea welled up from his stomach into his throat, and released a swallowing reflex he could not control. He had to remind himself how important this was, how much was at stake.

"Spray the table with carbolic acid," he said. Perhaps that comforting antibacterial odor would help him.

He regarded the woman, first out of the corner of his eye, then more directly. She stood with her head bowed and her arms gathered protectively across her chest. According to the files, it was the eighth time she had been here, so she knew the procedure. There was neither protest nor true resignation in her, just a silent and passive resistance that he had seen in so many of them by now. It was preferable, at least, to the ones who yelled and screamed.

"Lie down," he said. "It will only take a moment." The latter was said as much to calm his own anxieties as to soothe hers.

The constable had to lead her to the examination table. She did not resist, not directly, but every movement had to be initiated by others.

He breathed deeply. It was a mistake, because once again his nose told him with unwanted clarity what was missing.

She was lying on the table now, strapped down according to the regulations. At least the constable had mastered that part of the protocol. The whelp also readily—a bit too readily—pulled

146

up the woman's skirts. She would have been made to remove her undergarments in advance, and there was therefore now an unobstructed view of the area he needed to examine.

He tried not to take in too many details. The blue veins that were visible under the skin on the inside of her thighs, the frizzy hair that suddenly reminded him of the constable's ill-conceived facial hair, the folds and cavities of her sex.

Had he been able to delegate this task to others, he would have. But he despised most of the people he was forced to work with. So few of them—if any at all—understood the overwhelming necessity of what they were doing. How many did not succumb to base thoughts and unhealthy fascination? He had noticed, for example, a marked change in the young constable's breathing.

No, it was no good.

Unable to speak, he turned abruptly and left the room. He did not know how long they waited for him in there before they realized that he would not return, and he did not care. On his way out of the building, he made good his threat to fire the moronic young constable. One really could not hope to achieve anything in science surrounded by people so lacking in discipline and protocol.

It was just as well, he thought, that Mademoiselle Karno—in addition to her other estimable qualities—possessed an excellent understanding of the importance of personal hygiene. He even thought he had caught, on several occasions, the scent of lavender soap.

September 17, 1894

My studies continued to be a source of both knowledge and discomfort. Professor Künzli had been correct when he warned me that Althauser was not a patient teacher—he relentlessly pushed us, and especially me, to perform new experiments, new assignments, new tests. Most of them involved vivisection, and I grew accustomed to fighting back nausea and tremors every time I stepped into the dissecting room. Althauser watched me as an owl watches a mouse: "Do you feel unwell, mademoiselle? Do say if you wish to break off the experiment." My answer was always no, even though there were times when everything in me screamed yes—yes, I want to stop. Yes, this suffering has to end. I often wondered what kind of human being Claude Bernard must have been, that he had been able to stop seeing the animal's pain. I could not. Was I betrayed by my femininity? This was clearly Althauser's belief, and I fought not to prove him right. Once in a while I wished in my weakness that I could return to the anonymity of the first days, back when he had not yet wanted to look at me. Now I felt myself just as observed, and at times just as dissected, as the poor creatures we slit open and studied.

I preferred theory—here there was no nausea, no shaky hands. I eagerly devoured all the knowledge Althauser gave me, and he was excellent. His insight was deep and without compromise, his intellect as sharp as a well-polished, sterile instrument. It was intoxicating to speak on an equal footing with the other students, to be challenged in the same way. During the questions hailed down on us—"On what do you base that assumption?" "Can you support that claim?" "Facts, mademoiselle, what are the facts?"—I discovered that I could not only hold my own in the thrust and parry of that duel, but also manage an offensive strike to win a point now and again. It was intoxicating, and this joy was the reward awaiting me when I had made it through yet another vivisection without fainting or fleeing.

This battle between knowledge and nausea occupied me to such an extent that at times it threatened to exclude everything else. There were days when I felt distracted and forgetful in the work I still carried out for my father, days where I did not think once of my relationship with August. I had not entirely forgotten my promise to Fleur, but to my shame I have to confess that more than three weeks passed before I followed the only clue I had: the photograph itself.

"You must have a very low opinion of me," said Gilbert, slowly swirling the absinthe around in his glass, as if he were aerating the finest of cognacs. His deliberations on other sources of intoxication had apparently not yet borne fruit. "But I suppose that is understandable."

"So you did not take these pictures?"

"No." He looked up at me with an odd, calculating look. "May I ask how they came into your possession? Did Marot send you?"

"No. Why on earth would he do that?"

"I don't know. It just seems as if . . . is that not the unfortunate woman from the coal merchant's yard?"

I nodded and could see why he thought it must be a police matter, however unlikely it was that Marot would choose me as a go-between. Perhaps I was more sensitive than usual, but it seemed to me that melancholy hung so heavily in that room that it was difficult to think anything but dismal thoughts. The potted palm looked, if possible, even sadder than last time. The windows facing the yard were so grimy that the light took on a fuzzy character, and Aristide Gilbert's clothes looked as if he had slept in them.

"Do you ever take photographs like that?" I asked.

"No."

"Do you know of anyone who does?"

He emptied his glass in a single gulp.

"What could you possibly want in that world?" he asked. "Some of us are doomed to live in this darkness, in the land of shadows. But you . . . You who are young—engaged to be married, I hear—why don't you stay in the light where you belong?"

In the light. It was an enchanting thought. But I too was, in my own way, a creature of the shadows, raised as I was in a home where the dead were just as important as the living.

"Please just answer me if you can," I said. "As you will recall, you owe me a favor."

He sighed deeply and audibly. "As you wish. I cannot be completely sure, but . . . I think Gaston LaCour took them. The poodle belongs to his wife."

"Thank you!" I said, surprised at making such progress so soon. Perhaps it would be possible for me to keep my promise to Fleur after all. "Do you know where he lives?"

It was growing dark when I reached Palais Blanc. It was quite windy, and for the first time one felt that fall was on its way, perhaps not today or tomorrow, but soon. I got off the omnibus at the main entrance to the estate, but Gilbert had instructed me to follow the wall around to the left until I reached a row of former workers' cottages on tiny plots, all built as quarters for the farmhands and gardeners when the estate had still been run as a farm. Sure enough—the name LaCour had been painted in a neat black script on a board nailed to the white picket fence. There was a deep sweet scent of ripe grapes in the air, and a smallish dog—a poodle, perhaps?—barked sharply and hysterically inside the gardener's cottage. According to Gilbert, Gaston LaCour both lived and worked here, though he certainly did not support himself by gardening, and it did indeed look as if there was a light on behind the shutters.

The garden gate shrieked hair-raisingly when I opened it, and the poodle barked even more shrilly. The gravel path leading up to the front door was damp. It seemed someone had just watered the low lavender hedges that bordered it.

Although I was convinced that the inhabitants of the house must have noticed me the moment I walked up the garden path, it took quite a while for the door to be opened. To my surprise, a woman greeted me. Her hair was combed tightly back from a center parting into old-fashioned bunches of sausage curls on either side of her head, and she was dressed in a pearl-gray crinoline dress that had probably been the latest fashion when it was purchased. Unfortunately, that was more than forty years ago. Still, the woman was not as old as her hairstyle and couture suggested. In her late thirties, I thought, with a face that was more tired than actually wrinkled. The poodle, a thin little lapdog trimmed like a living topiary, sat in the crook of her arm and continued its monotonous yapping. It looked like the dog in the picture.

"Yes?" she snapped through the poodle racket.

"Madame LaCour?"

She nodded grimly.

"I would like to speak with your husband," I said. "My name is—"

But apparently she did not care about such details.

"Downstairs," she said. "Be so kind as to use the back door when you leave." Then she turned and yelled down the stairs: "Gaston! There's another one!"

The photographer himself sat hunched over some contact prints with a magnifying glass, and he did not look up when I came down the stairs. There was a strong camphor-like odor in the room, vaguely reminiscent of a pharmacy, but I knew that it was the celluloid. That same smell hung in the air at Gilbert's when it was not overpowered by that of absinthe.

"You may undress behind the screen," said LaCour, still without looking up. "There is a robe you may use between sessions."

I cleared my throat in acute embarrassment. "Oh . . . no. I . . . That is not why I . . ."

He looked up. His gaze swept across me, probably taking note of certain signals in my dress and posture. Then he shook his head.

"If that is not why, mademoiselle, may I ask what on earth you are doing here?"

I laid out the postcard photographs on the table, like a kind of bizarre solitaire.

"Monsieur, you are the one who took these pictures, correct?"

It was better to pretend that I knew rather than guessed, I had decided. And the poodle did provide convincing evidence.

"How do you know?" he asked.

"That is not important. I have no interest in what you do here except in this one matter: Who is the man in the mask?"

He did not answer at once. Instead he asked, "Do you know that she is dead?"

"Yes. That is why I am here."

"She was unusually photogenic," he continued, with a touch of sadness. "She liked to perform, had a talent for it . . . many of them need direction, and even then it is often no good. But her . . . It is odd, because she always felt guilty afterward. I have seen her several times standing with her rosary and offering one prayer after another while she waited for the omnibus. Still she came back and seemed happy and comfortable while the game was on. But then she had to go and get herself in the family way, and . . . well, that is not really something the gentlemen want to look at, is it?"

"Except for him." I pointed to the masked man. "He did, it seems?"

"Yes." He looked up at me quickly. "You see, the others . . . That was just a bit of fun. Frivolous, yes, but not . . . I am not forcing the girls to do anything, you understand, for them it is easy money compared to other modeling work or . . . well, you know. Or—I am sorry. Of course I do not know what you know."

"But these two are different."

"Yes. She did not really want to. She did not like that he was there, and when he wanted her to . . . She really did not want to."

"Why did she do it, then?"

"I think she needed the money. Like I said, with that belly getting bigger every day—it was not easy for her."

"You took the pictures," I said. "Even though you knew that she did not want to do it." It sounded more accusatory than I had meant it to, but I could not quite hold back my contempt.

"Listen, mademoiselle. We all need to make a living. She, I— perhaps even you."

"She is no longer living," I could not help pointing out.

"No, and that is a great shame, because she was . . . lovely. So you can take your well-bred disapproval and go on home where you belong."

"Not before you tell me who he is."

"Why do you think he is wearing a mask? He doesn't want anyone knowing who he is—and that includes you, I have no doubt."

"But *you* know?"

"No. Not really."

There was a glint of something . . . off, a hint of falsity that told me that his surprising candor had run out.

"You do know something," I pressed him. "How did he find you? Where did he come from?"

"He came with her. She brought him. He paid me to take some pictures, I took them. That was all. So no, there is nothing I can tell you."

"You must have seen him without the mask?"

"Not very clearly. He was wearing a scarf around the lower part of his face when they came in."

"What did he sound like? How tall was he? Can you describe his hair and beard, his posture, his gait?"

"Mademoiselle, have I not made myself clear? I have nothing further to say."

"Perhaps you prefer to speak to Inspector Marot about it?"

He cast another calculating gaze at me, this time deliberately unpleasant. "Do you know, you would be quite good yourself. Very suitable. All that straitlaced respectability, and yet . . . one can sense the vixen under the frock. You are not so prissy as you like to pretend, are you now?"

He wanted me to leave. This was just a strategy to intimidate me, I told myself. He wanted me to be so embarrassed that I simply fled. It was not because he knew . . . he could not know. What August and I . . . no. It was *not* visible. That was not why.

"You have a choice," I said coolly. "You can tell me what you know, or you can have that conversation with the police. I have heard that the préfecture could do with a showcase or two, to demonstrate how serious they are about upholding the public decency laws."

For a moment, he seemed to be considering a counterattack, but then he resigned himself.

"He was a gentleman," he said. "Cultured, well spoken. Dark hair, I think, though I did not see much of his face or his beard. There was nothing unusual about the way he carried himself. I have told you everything I know. Except . . . there was something I heard them say. He and Rosalba."

"Yes? What?"

"I think . . . I think she believed he had a responsibility—that perhaps he was the child's father."

"Can you prove that?" I said, like an unwilling echo of Dr. Althauser.

"Why else would she think he would help her?"

"With . . ."

"Yes. With the child."

"But he rebuffed her?"

"No, he agreed. On the condition that she let herself be photographed as . . . well, as you saw."

"So it was not for money that she did it?"

"No. It was the other thing."

I inspected the black-and-white photographs once more. If he had agreed to help her, why was she still in such anguish? The more I looked, the more convinced I was that these were pictures of a human being who was poised on the edge of complete perdition—and knew it.

"When did all this take place?" I asked.

"I don't recall," he said evasively.

"Surely you write down your appointments," I said. "A diary, ledgers, accounts . . . even you surely cannot run your business without a certain amount of clerking."

"My wife does all that."

"Then we will ask her."

That obviously did not appeal. I had to threaten him a third time with Marot and the decency laws before he relented.

"Wait here," he said.

But I would not. I insisted on following him upstairs.

"My wife . . . ," he objected. "She is not used to . . . She expects me to . . ."

"Your wife expects you to be currently busy photographing a young woman en déshabillé. She is unlikely to come to any major harm from seeing me fully dressed instead."

She did not even look up when we came in.

"You know that I prefer that it only happens by appointment," she said sharply. "How else am I supposed to impose any sort of order on your muddled affairs?"

She sat at a small escritoire, hunched over a ledger. There was only a single lamp in the room, the one on the desk, and its wick was turned almost all the way down, which was perhaps the reason she had to hunch as much as she did.

The salon was quite possibly of a respectable size, but it was so cluttered that I hardly dared breathe for fear of knocking into something. There were dolls everywhere—on shelves along the walls, in two large vitrines, on the divan, and on chairs and dressers; no matter where I looked, I was met by unmoving porcelain faces and glass eyes, by crinolines and corkscrew curl wigs, bonnets, skirts, and ruffled pantalets. The way she dressed herself found a bizarre resonance here, so that for a dizzying moment I perceived her not as a human being but as a bizarrely lifelike, speaking, and moving crinoline doll.

"Daphne," said LaCour apologetically, "the young lady would like to see the appointments for June."

Her head came up with a jerk. "*What is she doing here?*"

"As I said—"

"Get her out! I will not have them upstairs!"

"Daphne, Mademoiselle Karno is not—"

"Out, I said!"

"Madame," I attempted, "I shall leave at once if you will only permit me to—"

But she would not allow herself to be calmed. In a hiss of petticoats, she was on her feet. She held the pen like one would a knife or a spear and thrust it toward me so that I instinctively took a step backward.

"Be gone!"

"Please leave," begged LaCour. "You can see . . . Wait outside and I will bring you what you wish to see. Daphne, dearest, sit down, Mademoiselle Karno is leaving now."

I am ashamed to admit it, but I allowed myself to be chased from the scene by a disturbed woman armed only with a pen and an insane temper. Outside on the lavender-edged path, as I attempted to collect my scattered wits, I felt a moment's pity, not for her but for her besieged husband.

Fortunately, he kept his word. I had been standing there for only a few minutes, surrounded again by the warm scent of grapes, when he emerged with a small notebook.

"Here," he said. "R.L. and companion. Twenty-second of June 1894, at six o'clock in the evening."

The date of Rosalba's death was etched in my memory, possibly because it was the same as that of the president's murder: They had both left this world on the night between the 24th and 25th of June. In other words, the photographs had been taken just two days before she died.

By the time I reached Carmelite Street, eight o'clock had come and gone. Elise had turned on the lights, I could see, so Papa must be home from the hospital.

This time there was no Paul Tessier to warn me. Out of the corner of my eye, I simply saw a tall figure step out of the shadows by the gable.

"I hear that you do not like the sight of blood, Fräulein," he said, and it was only then that I recognized Erich Falchenberg. He brandished an object that I did not have time to identify before it hit me.

Something soft, heavy, and wet exploded in my face. The stench was overwhelming. When I gulped for air, a thick fluid filled my nose and mouth, and I was left snorting, coughing, trying to wipe off the sticky mess. His words should have warned me, but I was still shocked when I saw the clotted smears on my gloves and realized it was blood. A half-choked yelp escaped me.

"What do you do when it pours out of your crotch every month?" he said in an almost clinical tone. "One would think that you would be used to such filth. Stick to your own kind, Fräulein, and leave August in peace!"

"It is unlikely to be human in origin," said my father. "Pig's blood, I suspect. The bladder is definitely a pig's bladder."

At that point, I did not care where the putrid blood came from, I just wanted it *off*.

"I am going to report him," I said furiously. "Send for Marot. I refuse to tolerate this!"

"So you know who the attacker is?" said my father, astonished.

That made me hesitate. Did I really want the whole world—or at least Marot and the rest of Varbourg officialdom—to know that my fiancé's previous lover had attacked me with an inflated pig's bladder full of blood?

"No," I lied. "It was dark. I didn't see him clearly."

"Do you have any sense of the motive for this . . . peculiar attack?"

"Perhaps there is someone who does not like female students," I said, which was not too far from the truth.

"Maddie! Do you really believe that?"

"I don't know. Elise—is that bath not ready yet?"

The house was so old that it did not contain an actual bathroom, but not long ago we had knocked a door through from the laboratory to the laundry shed, had a tub set up, and arranged it so that the former laundry copper could be heated with the aid of a gas burner. We had not yet established the pipe system for the water, so for the moment one still had to fill it by hand. It was nevertheless considerably faster than before, when the bathwater had to be carried all the way up to the second floor.

"It's still only lukewarm," said Elise. "Why don't I take the dress? If we soak it in cold water, we might be able to save it."

"Try," I said grimly. If I could not report Herr Falchenberg, then what could I do about him? Tattle to August, of course, but would that be wise? Perhaps that was actually what the towheaded idiot wanted. If August were to do anything, then they would have to meet, and then . . . I tried to stop myself, but my imagination ran away with me. Two naked bodies in close embrace, slick with sweat and other bodily fluids . . . No. The less August *thought* about Falchenberg, the better. It pained me that they would occasionally be in the same town, never mind the same room. How on earth could August ever have fallen for that . . . that oversize infantile *oaf?*

"Lukewarm or not, I'm getting into the tub now," I decided. "We can heat more water as we go along."

It took almost an hour and a half before I felt sufficiently clean. Elise, bless her, ladled and ladled without complaint even though it was now completely dark outside and her mother would be waiting for her to come home. At last, I thanked her and sent her off but remained sitting in the tub for a while, pondering what I should do about Erich Falchenberg.

The petroleum lamp began to flicker and smoke. I repressed an unladylike utterance and reached for the towel, but before I had time to get up, the flame went out.

The unconscious mind is odd. The eye does not always see what is there but sometimes what is not. In the sudden darkness, he stood at the foot of the tub. Clad in black, at one with the shadows, so that only the white hood with its grotesque black grin shone toward me and made my heart pound so hard in my chest that I felt faint. And though I knew two things—that I was entirely alone in the laundry shed, and that Erich Falchenberg was, in any case, both too tall and too broad to be the man in the mask—there was nonetheless a moment when my entire body seized up because it thought he was there.

September 25, 1894

"But ... what about God, then?"

The question shot out with an explosive power, an outburst it was clear that Janvier had been holding back as long as he was able. Now it was no longer possible.

The lecture hall fell completely silent. Docent Althauser let the words hang in the air for a long time. I was beginning to suspect that he possessed a certain flair for the theatrical, and the length of the pause supported that hypothesis.

"What about God? Is that your question?"

Janvier already looked as if he regretted having opened his mouth, but he held his ground nonetheless. Janvier was a country boy, the son of a wine grower with ambitions. He was here to learn biology and chemistry, he had told us, so that he and his scientific training could help his father develop improved methods for the vinery. The introductory course in physiology was for him a necessary evil, and he was definitely not among Althauser's favorites.

"If the scientist, as you say, is supposed to not simply observe nature but to raise himself above it and ... and ... You said that man can now create new life-forms."

"That is correct. Two years ago, for example, my honored colleague Jacques Loeb succeeded in creating *Tubularia* with two heads, one at each end."

"But isn't that against God's will?"

"Young man, if it is theology you wish to study, you are in the wrong place."

There was a malevolent snicker, led by Malleau. The back of Janvier's broad neck flamed bright red from ear to ear, a phenomenon I was well placed to observe as I was seated almost directly behind him.

"Perhaps you also believe that Pasteur's vaccines are an offense to the laws of God? If Our Lord has sent us pox, rabies, and cholera, who are we to attempt to eradicate these diseases? Is that not also to place ourselves above nature? Should we perhaps reject M'sieur Darwin's theories because the Bible informs us that the world was created in six days?"

"No, I just think—"

"Sir, as far as I am concerned, you can believe in everything from Virgin Birth to the miracle of the Ascension, and why not include the Easter bunny and Saint Nicholas while you are at it—provided you do so on Sundays. When you step into this room, you are first and foremost a scientist. Or at least I hope to transform you into one. And for the scientist, there is no belief—only facts. We register and observe, but we also *act*. As far back as 1780, Spallanzani was able to copy the Holy Spirit and impregnated a dog with no sexual contact other than that created by a pipette—and he was a priest, sir. Only ten years later, John Hunter reported the first known case of artificial insemination in humans. And three years ago, Walter Heape in Edinburgh succeeded in transplanting a fertilized egg from an Angora rabbit doe to a Belgian rabbit doe, and the Belgian gave birth to the loveliest little Angora bunnies. These are the times we are living in, gentlemen, a time that is not satisfied with dull reproduction of the dogmas of the past, a time that demands courage, vision, and creative genius from those of you who are privileged enough to possess the ability and the will to act. And if you do not understand that, m'sieur, then you are better served by going back home to your cows and your chickens and your precious vines."

The contempt in the last words was sulfuric, and Janvier shrank in his seat.

Perhaps Althauser realized he had gone too far. Janvier was no longer the only one who looked uncomfortable, and as a former seminary—theology remained one of the largest departments—it was not general policy of the university to encourage firebrand attacks against religion. He concluded the lecture with a few more conventional platitudes about due diligence and meticulous attention to detail, and sent us home to read Heape's description of the rabbit experiment for Monday's lecture. Or rather, he sent the others home.

"Mademoiselle Karno, do you have a moment?"

I stopped in the middle of my final hurried notes and looked at him with surprise.

"Of course, Monsieur le Professeur. What is this regarding?"

"If you would come with me—it will only take a few minutes."

He led me across the hall to the small room at the back of the laboratory that he used as his private office. When I saw who was waiting, I instinctively took a step backward, but Althauser did not seem to notice.

"So, you are here," he said. "Good."

Erich Falchenberg and I stared at each other behind Althauser's back while he unlocked the door. It would have been hard to determine which of us detested the other more.

"Sit down please, mademoiselle," instructed Althauser. "Monsieur Falchenberg, if you would please begin?"

Monsieur Falchenberg looked as if he would prefer to bite off a finger at the root. Still, he cleared his throat and declared, "Mademoiselle Karno, I have come to give you my unreserved apology."

That was the last thing I had expected.

"Eh . . . thank you," I said.

"My behavior toward you has been entirely unacceptable, not to say criminal. I deeply regret it. I have no expectation that you will pardon me, because I do not deserve it, but I wish to assure you that you have nothing further to fear from me. You and I are fellow students at this university, and in the future I will make every effort to treat you with the respect you have the right to expect."

That was probably the most suavely worded apology I had

ever received. As for its sincerity, I did not believe it for a minute.

"That is kind of you," I said in a carefully neutral tone.

Althauser rubbed his palms together. "Excellent. That should clear things up. Good-bye for now, M'sieur Falchenberg."

My towheaded rival clicked his heels together with an audible snap and bowed briefly to both of us. His face was expressionless. Despite my lack of belief in his good intentions, I reciprocated with a nod because anything else would have been unaccommodating to the point of rudeness.

Althauser waited until Falchenberg's steps had receded in the corridor.

"Mademoiselle Karno, if you are exposed to any form of harassment from this young gentleman in the future, you will immediately come to see me. Is that understood?"

"Yes, Monsieur le Professeur."

"I can inform you that his continued presence at this university depends on his behavior being flawless from now on. I can also report that he is no longer a student at Heidelberg and is unlikely to be so in the future. I expect you to treat this information with discretion, but since I know how deeply he has offended you, I think you have the right to know the truth."

Had Althauser heard about the assault with the pig's bladder? If so, how? Had Falchenberg actually boasted to the others about it? The thought was unpleasant.

"Starting on Monday, M'sieur Falchenberg will attend lectures here, and I will keep an eye on his behavior. As I said, if you experience any unpleasantness from his side, you must tell me. I will honestly admit that I was, myself, initially skeptical of your own commitment and aptitude, but you have put my doubts to shame. You and Malleau are without a doubt the most promising intellects in the class."

I attempted—unfortunately, without success—not to blush like a schoolgirl.

"Thank you," I said as calmly as I could. "Your opinion matters a great deal to me."

He actually smiled—a small measured smile that made his eyes look slightly less like those of a bulldog.

"Well, then. Good-bye, Karno. I will see you on Monday."

I left with a bubbling sensation in my chest that I could barely contain. He had put Falchenberg effectively in his place. He had praised my work and my intellect. And as if that was not enough, he had finally left off the odious "mademoiselle" and addressed me on equal footing with my fellow male students, as simply "Karno." My soul, what more could you desire?

When I emerged from the colonnade, I saw Falchenberg's tall, broad-shouldered figure disappear into Réunion Square. He walked with rapid explosive steps and did not look happy. I did not care. Whatever he tried, I would be ready for it. Today, I could handle both him and the rest of the world.

I had decided to go by Fleur's lodgings on the way home. Ironically, my high spirits almost made me change my mind, because it was hard not to be depressed by the world she lived in. What was it Aristide Gilbert had called it? The land of shadows. *Stay in the light where you belong.* For once, it actually felt as if I had a right to a place in the daylight. I was "an intellect." I could see a future for myself, a useful and industrious one—discoveries I could make, knowledge I could contribute. When I then thought of Fleur and Rosalba, of Madame LaCour and her dollhouse, of that sordid basement studio and what had occurred there, of Rosalba's desperation . . . then it was as if I was dragged down into a morass of fleshliness and degradation. I wanted to prolong my golden afternoon, I wanted to be on top of the world for a little bit longer.

But when I was waiting for the streetcar in Réunion Square, it was the Number 4 that arrived first; its route would take me directly to Rue Vernier, where Fleur lived. I got on.

She had only just risen. I could glimpse the unmade bed in the room behind her, and she had simply thrown on a loose morning dress that did not require a corset. Her hair hung down her back in a thick braid, and her face was without makeup. There was a sour, unwashed odor in the apartment, and I was seized with the desire to open a window and let in some air.

"Have you found him?" she asked as soon as she saw me.

"No."

"But you have news?"

"Possibly. I have found the photographer who took the pictures." I shared what Gaston LaCour had told me about the man with the mask. "He thinks that the man might be the child's father . . ."

Fleur let out a snort. "Oh, really?"

"I don't understand . . . ?"

"Mademoiselle, think about it. The children of women like us have no fathers. Or many, if you will. How would Rosalba know which of them got her into trouble?"

"I assume you use . . . certain preventive methods?"

"You mean condoms. Yes. When we can. They are not very effective, and there are many men who do not like to put on a piece of sheep's bladder just to please a whore they have bought and paid for. It is a bit better with the new rubber ones, but they are hard to get hold of and extremely expensive."

"So it was not possible for Rosalba to determine who . . ."

"No. Mademoiselle, that is a professional risk. Prostitutes have children. That is the way it is. Rosalba knew that, and I don't understand why she . . . We would have managed. I would have taken care of her. I would never have . . . if that wasn't what she wanted."

"Fleur, what are you talking about?" Something was surfacing in this conversation, something I had previously sensed without quite pinpointing it. Fleur was not just grieving—she was also feeling guilty. The question was, about what?

She did not meet my gaze. She sat picking at the end of her braid, like a schoolgirl caught whispering to her neighbor. But when one looked more closely, there was an awful bottomless depth to the guilt that no schoolgirl could have felt.

"What are you thinking?" I asked as gently as I could.

The silence stretched on.

"If you don't tell me everything you know," I said at last, "how will I be able to discover what happened to Rosalba?"

When she finally began to speak, her voice was cracked and frail.

"There is a place . . . ," she began. "A place we had heard of. Prostitutes have children, unmarried women have children. That's just the way it is. Most cannot have the children with them, and not everyone has a grandmother willing to make the sacrifice, or money to have them fostered in the country. And it is better, surely, than leaving them with an angel maker!"

"Of course," I said, though I only partially understood what she was talking about. "And you suggested to Rosalba . . . ?"

"Worse than that," she said, and looked up for the first time. Her eyes were dark and red rimmed like gunshot wounds. "I brought her there . . . I don't know what happened to her in that place, they would not let me stay with her for the admission interview. I only know that when she came home, she was inconsolable. And afraid. She was terrified, but she wouldn't tell me why."

"When was that?"

"Four days before she . . . was murdered."

"Who was present during the interview, do you know?"

"The director, Madame Palantine, and some doctor, I think."

"A doctor?" I said. "Why?"

Fleur's braid had fallen forward over one shoulder. She threw it back with an unconscious gesture that suddenly made her look like a schoolgirl again.

"It is . . . a very clean place. Like a hospital. You can give birth there if they let you."

She lowered her head again.

"Get dressed," I said. "You need to show me this place."

She was reluctant, to say the least, but I insisted. I would probably have been able to find the place myself, but I wanted to get her outside, into daylight and crowded streets, into a world that still had some life in it.

I should have left her alone. It was safer there, in that airless, grief-choked room, even for a soul as anguished as Fleur's. But I had no way of knowing that.

INSTITUTE OF CHILD CARE AND NURSING it said on the enameled plaque on the brick gatepost. INQUIRIES AT THE GATE. VISITORS WITHOUT APPOINTMENT BETWEEN 5 AND 6 IN THE EVENING ONLY. Below, there was a somewhat more makeshift, painted board announcing that the institute also undertook to provide HEALTHY AND RESPONSIBLE WET NURSES AND NANNIES.

It did not look terrible, I thought: a large square ivy-covered building set among lawned grounds, like a scaled-down version of Saint Bernardine, where my father often worked. I don't know quite what Fleur's despair had led me to imagine, but certainly something much less orderly and hygienic. There was something comforting about the plaque, the cast-iron fence, the well-trimmed lawn.

Fleur stood mute and unresponsive next to me. Her resistance was still palpable, and only repeated references to the ultimate goal—to discover what had happened to Rosalba—had goaded her into coming with me this far.

It occurred to me that in the short time I had known her, she had undergone a change of such enormity that it seemed quite beyond reason. She was still small of stature, of course, but what there had been of softness and sweetness in her had been worn away by grief and fury. Her features had sharpened—I think she had lost several kilos that she could not afford to lose—and her eyes now seemed unnaturally large in her pale, thin face. Her hair seemed lifeless and greasy, her clothes uncared for, her entire presence was one of fierce determination and complete indifference to appearances. If a scientist, according to Althauser and his idol Claude Bernard, was a person so caught up in and absorbed by an idea that there was no room for other considerations, then Fleur was fairly close to that ideal now. Only one thing absorbed and motivated her, and where I had initially been concerned about what she might do to the masked man if I found him, I was now more anxious about what might happen to Fleur herself. If one took away this all-consuming purpose, what was left? Would she be able to hold herself upright? Would she be able to live at all?

"Visiting hours will be over in ten minutes," the gatekeeper informed us in a discouraging tone.

"I am aware of that," I said. "We are here on a different errand. I understand that one may hire a wet nurse here? Sadly, it is a matter of some urgency."

"In that case, you will need to speak with Madame Palantine. Through the main entrance, first door on the left."

Fleur threw me a sidelong glance but did not say anything until we had passed through the gate and were on our way up the gravel drive toward the central building.

"A wet nurse?" she said. "Why did you say that?"

"To get us in, naturally."

"Yes, I understood that. But why a wet nurse?"

"Didn't you see the sign? Wet nurses and nannies for hire, or whatever it said. If anyone asks, my cousin is unfortunately too ill to nurse her newborn. Also, we are lost."

A smile briefly illuminated the sharpened features.

"Mademoiselle Karno," she said with a small, appreciative nod. "Your poor cousin . . ."

I felt a flush heat my cheeks. Had I perhaps become a little too good at lying and dissembling to receive such ironic praise from a practiced professional of that art?

"There are only ten minutes left of visiting hours," I said defensively. "And who were we supposed to claim we were visiting anyway?"

"Most of the children are infants," said Fleur. "They probably don't care who 'visits' them."

Inside the main entrance, we discovered a long, deep foyer that went up three stories, to judge by the metal stairs that clung to the sidewalls. Our steps resonated against dark, hard-fired tiles, and it smelled comfortingly of carbolic acid and floor soap. INFANT HALL AND WET NURSE OFFICE it said on the first door to the left, and it turned out to be an entirely correct nomenclature.

We entered a glass-walled corridor overlooking the hall in question. It stretched back for the entire length of the building—at the farthest end, the evening sun shone through the windows, muted by thin white muslin hangings. The infants lay in long straight rows, placed on broad shelves like ribbons and buttons and bolts of cloth in a draper's shop. Even the cribs with their simple square wooden frames looked more like packaging than baby cots. Some of the children were crying, but the sound reached us only mutedly through the glass. Others lay quietly, apparently sound asleep. Between the rows walked two women dressed in black, with white aprons, their hair hidden under starched white caps, but they did not stop by the children who were crying, just went on patrolling, guards rather than nurses, or so it seemed to me. "Why don't they pick them up?" I whispered to Fleur without actually expecting an answer. But she had been here before, after all.

"It is a part of the regimen," she said. "They are fed at the same time, they are changed at the same time, they are expected to sleep at the same time. We were told that they quickly adjust to the rhythm."

"I see." At least it sounded like a logical and planned approach to child rearing. I really knew nothing about infants, I realized. I had no siblings and no small cousins nearby that I had been expected to take care of.

At the end of the glass corridor, a group of young women had gathered, some in uniform blue dresses and caps and aprons similar to those of the patrolling guardians, others in a mottle of more civilian garments. A few spoke together quietly; the rest waited in silence. One had separated from the group and stood at the glass window staring at the rows of children on the other side.

I noticed that some of the girls, especially those closest to the door, had the slightly absent expression of someone concentrating on listening. There were voices coming from inside, very loud voices. One violent outburst especially penetrated the closed door.

"You can't do that! How am I supposed to live?"

A less audible voice answered: "... thought of ... *before* you ..."

"You sanctimonious old *cow!*"

Bang. The door flew open, and a young woman came marching out. She snatched off first the cap and then the apron and threw both on the floor. Her still childishly rounded face puckered with anger and outrage.

"She is giving me the boot," she said to the waiting girls. "It was just beer! Beer isn't alcohol. *Everyone* drinks beer."

"Not Madame Palantine," one of the others said.

"There are many things that Madame Palantine doesn't do," said the girl. "Including . . ." She made an unmistakably vulgar movement with her right hand.

"Pauline!"

Pauline flung out her arms.

"What is she going to do? Fire me twice?" She pushed her way through the crowd of young girls and strode past us. We received only a brief disinterested glare on the way—she clearly had other things to think about.

"Fleur," I said quickly and quietly, "follow her. Convince her to wait outside. Here, give her this. Tell her we'll pay to speak with her . . ." I gave her what I had of change, observing with some dismay that my purse now held only a franc and a half. Hardly enough to bribe a clerk or a matron, or whatever Madame Palantine was, but might it tempt an unemployed wet nurse with nothing to lose?

Fleur looked skeptical but turned and followed the girl. I was consequently alone when I introduced myself to Madame Palantine a few moments later, once again trotting out the story of my "poor cousin."

"I understand that you might be able to help me a engage a wet nurse?" I concluded.

Madame Palantine was a stout red-haired woman with a complexion the color of buttermilk. A pince-nez perched on her nose, but the lenses were so greasy that they were unlikely to be of much use. She was dressed in a garment reminiscent of that of the matrons at Saint Bernardine, high-necked black dress with a white collar and white cuffs, and her cap was a tall monstrosity of a cone that stuck up like a Spanish mantilla with a multitude of streamers falling like a bridal veil down her back and shoulders.

She glanced at a pocket watch that was mounted on her considerable bosom with the twelve facing downward, so that it could more easily be read by the wearer.

"If you would wait here for a moment," she said. "We start the evening nursing at precisely six ten, and unfortunately I need to redistribute the nurses."

"Of course," I said.

With queasy fascination, I learned that after Pauline's departure, some of the young women were expected to nurse seven of the wailing infants, and the remaining, six. I was amazed that it was even possible to nurse more than two or perhaps three in an emergency, but most of the girls accepted the extra burden with a shrug.

"And Evangeline, remember to wipe between feeds!" admonished Madame Palantine. "First carbolic acid, then hot water. *Every* time."

"But, madame . . . it stings so." The young girl, apparently Evangeline, touched her breasts and made a face.

"Would you rather spread disease down the entire line? No, thank you. We will have no epidemics here. If you cannot abide by the rules, we will have to find someone else. Is that understood?"

The girl curtseyed anxiously. "Yes, madame!"

"Good. Off you go, then. You too, Lise-Marie." The latter was directed to the solitary girl who stood still, gazing at the children through the glass.

"Madame . . . ? If I promise not to say anything?" she whispered.

"No, girlie. It is better this way. If you knew which child was yours, the temptation to treat them differently would be too great. Here, it is the same for everyone. No special cases."

"Madame, I beg you . . ."

"Absolutely not. Besides, it would only cause you unnecessary pain. Believe me, it is better this way! It is six ten, mademoiselle!"

"Yes." Lise-Marie curtseyed and hurried into the infant hall. Madame Palantine pulled a bell cord and a crisp peal broke out in the hall. Each girl promptly picked up a child and placed it at her breast. There was a symmetry to it that was at once aesthetic and yet oddly off-putting. I could not quite identify the source of my discomfort. It was well organized, meticulously planned, and very hygienic, and why should nursing and child care not be systematized?

"As you can see, all our wet nurses are healthy young women, and we place a great emphasis on clean and healthy habits. Plenty of rest, regular walks at a calm pace, a good diet, no alcohol or other sources of intoxication, no unnecessary excitement or bodily overexertion. It is one of the institute's fundamental tenets that the constitution and viability of a child are deeply influenced by its earliest conditions, beginning in the womb, even. If your cousin is infirm, you would be wise to find a robust and conscientious wet nurse."

"Where do you get your wet nurses?"

"Most of them have given birth here at the institute. A few we hire from the outside."

"Are they all . . . unwed?"

Madame Palantine's plump mouth became considerably narrower. "Some. But I can assure you that there is no indecency once they come to us." She glanced at the watch on her bosom.

"I am sorry to take up your time," I said.

"No, I am the one who is sorry," she said, not very apologetically. "But we must maintain the schedule."

"Which is?"

"Fifteen minutes for each shift, including our hygienic measures."

"How frequently are the children nursed?"

"Six times a day during the first month, later we reduce it to five."

My brain could not help doing the math. That meant that each of the young girls had a child at her breast for nine hours or more a day. No wonder Evangeline had complained that it stung . . .

"How can they possibly nurse so many children . . . ?"

"Not everyone can. Those who cannot, we typically send on to infirm mothers like your cousin. Most grow accustomed, though. Lactation adjusts to the demands that are placed on it. We have even had the occasional girl who nursed eight and nine without difficulty."

It was a dizzying thought. Suddenly, I realized the source of my discomfort. The symmetry made me think of cows in long rows, ready to be milked. The female body transformed into a lactating organism, the children into entirely interchangeable milkers, with no relation beyond that of giving or receiving suck.

I felt an urge to object to this unemotional factory-like suckling. How strange. I ought to applaud this more scientific and rational approach to child rearing, and yet I had to hold back a protest and remind myself I was not here to discuss nursing.

"I am here on a different errand as well . . . ," I said hesitantly.

The effect was surprising. Madame Palantine's entire demeanor changed, as if she was setting aside one mask and putting on another. Her courteous manner slipped, and raw calculation appeared in her gaze.

"I see," she said. "And when is it due?"

"I beg your pardon?"

"The happy event." Her voice was cold with sarcasm.

My blush must have been positively crimson—it certainly felt that way.

"Madame! I am not . . ." But the painful realization hit me before I could finish my sentence. I could not, in fact, know for certain that I was not pregnant. August and I had . . . it was possible that . . .

Confusion robbed me of intelligent reply.

"May I tell you something, mademoiselle? Young ladies are hardly ever sent here to engage a wet nurse. If you had been forty or fifty instead of closer to twenty, then I would have been more likely to believe you."

Really, I ought to seize upon her misunderstanding with

gratitude. It was the perfect way to learn how Rosalba had been received when she came here. But I could not make myself do it.

Instead I got up.

"I am sorry to have inconvenienced you . . . ," I stammered, and fled out the door.

"As you like," she said indifferently. "You know where to find us if you should change your mind." She glanced at the watch on her bosom and tugged at the bell cord. Like automatons, the girls in the hall plucked the infants from their breast, held them over one shoulder for burping, then replaced them in their boxlike cribs, before proceeding to the next small scrap of living humanity. Everyone, even Evangeline, remembered to wipe off the nipple she had used, first with carbolic acid and then with hot water.

I hurried down the corridor and back to the foyer. I hoped Fleur had prevailed upon . . . what was her name again, the rebellious wet nurse? Pauline. I hoped Fleur had persuaded Pauline to wait so we could question her. But Pauline had not been present during the interview with Rosalba. There had been only Madame Palantine, from whom I had fled like a coward, and "some doctor."

I stopped. It was too shameful, I thought, to flee with my tail between my legs in this way. There were four other doors besides the infant hall. One of them was marked ARCHIVES, another ADOPTION OFFICE, and a third PRO PATRIA: PERINATAL with a hand-scribbled note below: UNAUTHORIZED ACCESS PROHIBITED. I hesitated between the archives and perinatal. But if Rosalba had been refused admittance, she would probably not figure in the archives. A conscientious doctor, on the other hand, might well be in the maternity ward even after six o'clock in the evening.

I carefully opened the door. The room was much smaller than the infant hall, and thick curtains muted the light to a cave-like dimness. There were no box cribs here either. Instead there was what at first glance looked to be ten large kitchen sinks connected by a system of pipes. There was a gentle gurgling, and somewhere the low hissing of a gas flame. Five of the sinks were covered by glass lids partially draped with sterile-looking white sheets. The rest were empty.

If it had not been for the sign on the door, I probably would not have guessed what this was, at least not immediately. But even though my career had, until now, brought me into more frequent contact with the other end of the life cycle, I had heard of the famous obstetrician Étienne Stéphane Tarnier and his so-called *couveuse*. It had been developed with funding from the French state because of a particular anxiety that had gripped the leaders of our republic since the ignominious defeat to Germany in '71 and the loss of Alsace and Lorraine. The birthrate in France was plummeting while nations around us continued to increase, not least in the Kaiser's newly militarized German Empire, and anything that helped more children survive childbirth was seen as a matter of national importance. In just three years, Dr. Tarnier had reduced infant mortality among the newborns at Paris Maternité by almost a third, due to this peculiar apparatus inspired by the incubators some farmers used for hatching eggs. Or if not with this particular apparatus—I did not recall having seen a picture of anything that looked *precisely* like this—then with something built for the same purpose: that of keeping precariously premature infants warm and protected while their little bodies fought to adjust to life outside the womb.

As I bent to examine one of the incubators, a door was opened at the far end of the room and a figure appeared in the doorway.

"Out!" If you can shout quietly, then that is what he did. "Get out of here right now, you idiot woman!" He took a couple of angry steps toward me, and in confusion I backed through the still open door behind me into the front hall. He followed. But it was not until he entered the hall's far stronger light that I recognized him, and he me.

"Mademoiselle Karno," he said. "What are you doing here— beyond compromising the sterility of my perinatal ward?"

It was Docent Althauser.

"I didn't know you were an obstetrician," I stammered.

"I am not," he said. "I am connected to Pro Patria in my capacity as physiologist. Among other things, I have developed a more efficient incubator on the basis of the Tarnier-Auvard design. But it continues to be necessary, mademoiselle, to keep the risk of infection at a minimum. Only I and my personnel have access to the incubator room."

"I am so sorry," I said. "But would it not be safer to simply lock the door?"

"I suppose we shall have to from now on," he said acerbically. "Until you came along, the sign was deemed sufficient to keep out intruders. And you haven't answered my question, mademoiselle. What are you doing here?"

Oh no. Would he reach the same assumption as Madame Palantine? I had solemnly promised Professor Künzli that I was a model of chastity and the least distracting woman in Varbourg. If he thought I was pregnant, I would be out on my ear in about the time it would take him to say "permanently dismissed."

"I have a relative who has just given birth and is considering engaging a wet nurse," I mumbled. The ruse rang hollow and false even in my own ears now that it had been so easily discredited by Madame Palantine. But what could I do except repeat it? He might well ask the rest of the staff once I had left.

"I see," he said. Whatever assumptions he made, he kept them to himself at least. "Are you interested in perinatal treatment, Karno?"

Relief washed through me. He had stopped calling me mademoiselle and I was once again his student, liberated from gender because of what he had referred to as my promising intellect. That I did not *feel* especially promising right now was another matter.

"I'm considering specializing in obstetrics," I said. While not actually true, it would *sound* right, I thought. What field could be a more natural choice for a female physician?

The heavy folds around his eyes crinkled, and the same was true for at least one corner of his mouth. It was not much of a smile, but there was a surprising warmth to it.

"Since it is you, I would be happy to offer a tour," he said. "On the strict condition, of course, that you follow the appropriate hygienic rules—and promise not to touch anything."

Ordinary newborns seem frighteningly small and fragile. But the child I saw now was so tiny that every rapid flutter of breath seemed to me almost unnatural. The head was larger than the slight torso, the eyelids thin and blue tinged so that I had the thought that the chick-like creature down there under the glass lid could see us, or at least sense us, right through the barrier of the skin. A quick, flickering heartbeat pulsated visibly through the minuscule chest, a moth wing beating against a window.

"How old . . . ?" I whispered.

"Since birth? A week and a half. But it is probably more relevant to calculate the age of these tiny scientific miracles from the moment of conception. Counted like that, he is just over eight months old. So there is actually still another month to go before he should have been born under normal circumstances."

The little boy was naked except for a cap that covered his head. The rest of his frail body was covered by a thick yellowish-white coating that could surely not be fetal fat a week and a half after birth. Goose fat, perhaps? The incubator was about half filled with slowly circulating warm water—as constantly at 37°C as was possible, Althauser explained—and a tiny harness ensured that the infant kept his head above water.

"We have re-created the primal sea," said Althauser. "Is it not miraculous that the environment in which we grow to term to this day precisely mirrors the sea wherein evolution began? Mild, warm fluid with a saline percentage of point nine. It is almost the same for him as it was in his mother's womb. Or in his case, actually better."

"And will he survive?"

"It looks that way. In spite of all that his so-called mother has done to attempt to kill him."

"Kill him?"

"Yes. After several failed attempts at poisoning with various quack remedies, she finally tried using a knitting needle. She was bleeding like a stuck pig when she arrived, and had she not come here, they would probably both have died. Believe me, however exposed his life is here in the incubator, he is safer than in his mother's womb, and he is receiving significantly more care."

I was not used to seeing Althauser's normally heavy and passive features express emotion, and certainly not of this kind—care, tenderness, protectiveness. It jarred with his normal pretense to be, like Claude Bernard, exclusively focused on the scientific idea. Certainly there was a scientific project—to improve the incubator and hence the premature child's chances of survival—but unless my eyes were entirely deceiving me, there was also a real passion here, an emotion that included the little human creature whom he properly ought to register only as the object of the experiment.

I do not know if this made him a less worthy scientist. It definitely made him a more interesting person, I decided.

"Why did you call the project Pro Patria?" I asked.

"Because we are making a great and vitally necessary effort for the fatherland," he said. "You will be aware, I am sure, of the birthrate crisis?"

I nodded. "I understand that it is causing concern in military circles."

"Not only there, Mademoiselle Karno. Not only there. I am, in fact, speaking at a gathering this Friday evening—a series of lectures that address precisely this problem. If you are interested in attending, I can introduce you to some of the project's supporters after the event. I am sure you would make a good impression on them, which might be useful to you in your future endeavors."

He looked as if he would actually like me to come. It flattered me, and I thanked him for the invitation and promised to be there.

Fleur stood at the edge of the lawn and pretended to admire a bed of perennials. With her slim, gloved hands, she tilted the flower heads one by one, as if this was the only way she could fully appreciate the colorful presentation of asters and chrysanthemums. Somehow it did not look entirely convincing.

"She didn't want to wait," she said when she saw me. "But she agreed to meet you later . . ."

That had to be better than nothing.

"Where?" I asked. "And when?"

"At Le Crapaud," Fleur said hesitantly. "In Rue Vanasse. It is . . . a tavern. Not very appropriate for someone like you, I'm afraid. But she'll be there between eight and nine tonight, if you want to speak with her. I promised her two francs."

"Fleur, won't you come too?" I said in a rush of mild panic. "Please?"

"If you wish . . ."

"I think it would be better if there are two of us," I said, knowing perfectly well that the only thing it was "better" for was my delicate nerves. Rue Vanasse was rather less than salubrious, from what I had heard. I had never been there myself.

Footsteps crunched on the gravel path behind us. I half turned and to my surprise saw Docent Althauser hurrying toward the gate, wearing his overcoat and hat and carrying his cane. He hesitated for a moment and threw us both a probing look. Then he raised his cane in greeting, tipped his hat, and strode on.

Fleur stood, surrounded by the scarlet, lemon, and fiery orange splendor of the asters, observing his departure with sparrow-bright eyes.

"Who was that?"

"One of my teachers from the university," I said. "Apparently he works here as well."

Her eyes had become narrow slits. There was a small juicy snap when the flower head she was holding separated from its stem.

"What is his name?"

"Althauser."

"Does he always carry that cane?"

"Fairly often. Why?"

"No reason. I just think I've seen him before."

"Here? When you were here with Rosalba?"

She hesitated. Looked down at the flower head in her hand as if she was wondering what it was doing there. It was one of the red ones, dark and liverish like venous blood.

"It must have been," she said.

Having stood outside Le Crapaud for fifteen minutes, it began to dawn on me that Fleur was not going to turn up. I was already intensely uncomfortable. I had fielded several calculating looks, two awkward attempts at conversation—"So, mad'moiselle? How's it going?"—and a single, definitively insulting offer, in spite of the fact that I had put on my least distracting university garb. Other than my face—and even that was half hidden by my veil—not a centimeter of my skin was exposed.

The same could not be said about the other gentlemen and ladies out for the evening. Several men strolled about with rolled-up sleeves and open-necked shirts and their hats pushed back on their heads, some with their jackets slung over their shoulder, others apparently entirely devoid of such an article. And as for the ladies—well, "ladies" might not be quite the right word.

Inside Le Crapaud someone was subjecting the most popular melodies of the day to accordion and violin, and I could hear singing and loud conversation. The front of the building had been decorated with a mural of sorts, a garish and very warty toad with an anatomically improbable tongue arching above the door and a couple of the windows to capture what at first glance looked like a fly but on closer inspection turned out to be a scantily clad fly-winged nymph. She had the toad's pink tongue looped several times around her waist and did not appear to appreciate it. I completely understood how she felt.

If only August had been with me . . .

I took a deep breath, or as deep as my corset permitted, and entered the den of the toad.

The smoke from the men's pipes and cigars hung heavy and blue above the tables, and I even saw a few women smoking. A middle-aged, broad-bosomed woman in a black wig—it sat crooked on her head—puffed on a long skinny chalk pipe, and a somewhat younger woman with bright red lipstick held a cigarette rolled in pink paper in her black-gloved hand. Between the tables, three or four couples were milling around to a cheerful polka tune. One of the men had unbuttoned his shirt to the point where we could all see his somewhat soiled undershirt. Sweating and red cheeked, he swung his partner in the dance, and I suddenly felt a completely unexpected stab of envy.

They were enjoying themselves. They did not care what it looked like, what *they* looked like. Sweating and laughing and hollering along to the refrain, he grabbed his girl around the waist with both broad hands and raised her high into the air, and she flung her head back, laughing uproariously. Some might call it loose manners and reckless abandon, but this was exactly what I envied: their ability to abandon expectations and conventions and demands for propriety. I had never had even a moment's freedom like that, at least not in public. The memory of what I had done with August in private returned and warmed not just my cheeks but also several other parts of my body. Compared to that, the dancing here suddenly looked quite innocent.

The girl Pauline sat at one of the tables closest to the accordion player and the violin. She was not alone. A young man in waistcoat and shirtsleeves sat with his arm around her waist, occasionally pinching her side so that she shrieked and wriggled and slapped his arm lightly. As she sat there, leaning against his chest, she did not look like the desperate young woman who had yelled at Madame Palantine. *How am I supposed to live?* I could not tell from her demeanor whether her distress had been less deep-rooted than it had first seemed, or if it still lurked somewhere beneath this wholehearted attempt to forget about tomorrow.

"Pauline?"

She sat up a bit straighter.

"Oh, there you are," she said. "Where are my two francs?"

One of the gentlemen at the table had apparently picked up a few manners at some point; he rose unsteadily to his feet and offered me his place. Repressing an urge to wipe the seat first, I sat down.

"Thank you."

He touched the brim of his hat with two fingers and mumbled something about "a call of nature" before he disappeared.

I took the requested sum from my purse and placed the coins on the table between the wine puddles and glasses, but kept my hand on them for now.

"Tell me how you came into contact with the institute," I said.

She glared at me—whether her hostility was due to my question or to my unwillingness to pay in advance I could not tell.

"What do you think?" she said.

"You were expecting a child?"

"Of course. Otherwise the dairy don't work, now, does it?"

"And then you went to see Madame Palantine?"

She nodded. "Mean old vulture. But at the beginning she didn't seem that bad. She was ever so concerned, asked if I was engaged—she could see I wasn't married, but I said yes, I was engaged . . ."

She looked up at her companion. He gave her a squeeze and a kiss on the neck.

"'Course," he said. "And you are, aren't you?"

"His mother doesn't like me," Pauline said bitterly. "But we're going to get married anyway, right? Soon!"

"'Course."

"But I worked at the cotton mill, and they don't let you have kids running around, so . . ."

"What precisely does the institute offer?"

"If they take you," she corrected me. "They examine you from top to . . . well, all over. The vulture and the professor. You have to be ever so healthy and strong and proper. If they take you, then they let you have it at their hospital, and that's a damn sight better than lying in Ma's filthy old bed, screaming my head off, I can tell you. There's a midwife and doctor and everything, and it's all really clean and nice. Then they take the little one. You don't know which one it is, even though you go there every day and let them nurse until you're about to keel over. But I thought, five solid meals a day and a clean bed to sleep in, plus four francs a week . . . that's got to be better than coughing cotton dust for twelve hours and then staggering home to try and sleep with eight snotty brats underfoot and constantly howling, and all Ma ever does anymore is bitch and complain. So I gave notice at the factory and told Ma that she'd need to find someone else to help with the brats. They aren't even all hers, two of them are my sister's, and then there are the three she takes care of for next door 'cause *she* cleans at the factory at night."

"Did you ever see this woman at the institute?" I took one of the tinted photographs from my bag and placed it on the table. It was the close-up with the grapes, which I had carefully masked with cardboard so no nudity was on display. Rosalba's expression was still unbelievably coquettish, and the way she was nibbling at the grapes was anything but decent, but it was the picture that showed her face most clearly.

Pauline looked at the photograph for a while. "Who is she?" she asked.

I did not answer.

"Have you seen her?" I repeated.

"I might have."

"Do you remember when?"

She shook her head. "Not exactly. It must have been a few months ago."

"When did you yourself give birth?"

She made a face. "In May. The twentieth."

"Had you just given birth when you saw her?"

"No. It was four or five weeks after that, I'm pretty sure."

That would make it the week before Rosalba was killed, which again might mean that Pauline had merely seen her during the visit with Fleur that I already knew about.

"Was she alone?"

"No," Pauline said without hesitation. "She was talking to the professor. And she was crying. That was why I noticed her, be-cause that's something we are all told—he does not care for what Madame Palantine calls 'emotional displays,' so we are supposed to 'comport ourselves with dignity' when he is examining us."

"What were they talking about?"

"I couldn't hear them."

"And when you say the professor, you mean . . ."

"That man Althauser. Who else?"

She reached for the two francs, and this time I let her take them.

I may have been a little too eager to leave Le Crapaud. In any case, I was returning the photograph to my bag while heading for the door, and noticed too late that a man sitting at the table closest to the door chose that same moment to rise. We did not quite knock each other over, but there was a significant and most unwelcome moment of bodily contact.

"Mademoiselle Karno! You do get around."

Felt hat, red paisley scarf worn casually with a velvet-collared jacket in a somewhat foppish style. It was my tabloid nemesis, the semi-nameless Monsieur Christophe.

"Are you following me?" I asked indignantly.

"Not at all. I am merely observing the nightlife of our fair city. I am quite astonished to find that you are part of it."

When did one grow out of blushing? Soon, I hoped.

"May I ask what you are doing here, mademoiselle?"

"Charity," I snapped, which was probably stupid, but it was the only excuse I could think of.

"I see," he said. "Of what kind?"

"That is really none of your business. Good evening, m'sieur."

He stepped aside and let me pass. But about halfway down Rue Vanasse, I realized I was no longer holding the envelope with Rosalba's picture in my left hand. It was not in the bag either. I must have dropped it in our collision.

I turned to go back, only to find that Christophe was heading my way, with the envelope in one hand and the masked photograph in the other.

"You dropped something," he said.

"Thank you," I felt obliged to say.

"Are you really still pursuing the case?" he asked.

"What case?"

"That poor girl. Months ago now." There was a casual indifference in his tone of voice that provoked me unreasonably.

"I truly regret that we were not able to solve the killing before your deadline," I said. "But not all victims are thoughtful enough to write 'X did it' with their last remaining strength."

"Now you are being sarcastic."

"Oh, really?"

I reached out for the picture, but he withheld it in a way that reminded me unpleasantly of my own strategy with Pauline.

"Do you know something I don't?" he asked.

"Undoubtedly quite a lot," I said. "But nothing that is relevant to your readers."

"If there was a new development," he said, "then there might be another article in it."

"There isn't," I answered shortly. "Give me that picture. You cannot print it anyway." The mask had slipped and the erotic nature of the photograph could no longer be denied. He smiled crookedly.

"No," he said. "We probably cannot. But if you discover anything I may print, mademoiselle . . . then come to me. I will make sure you do not regret it."

The conceit of the man was monumental. Did he really imagine I would ever seek him out voluntarily, after what he had written before?

194

September 26, 1894

When I came down the next morning to head for the university, Erich Falchenberg was standing in a doorway on the other side of the street, somewhat stooped, and trying to look as if he belonged there. He did not succeed. A whole passel of kids had surrounded him, discussing loudly in French how you might get money out of the "foreign gentleman." I considered ignoring both him and the scene but decided to confront him instead. I did not want him to think I was afraid.

"How may I be of assistance?" I said coolly.

He sighed and straightened up to his normal height.

"You can't. Fräulein." There was a noticeable pause between the first and second part of his statement, as if he had had to remind himself to be polite.

"Why then are you standing here watching my front door?"

He looked as if he had been there for a while. His eyes were bloodshot, and his flaxen hair stuck greasily to his skull. He did not look at all well.

"I . . . just wanted to speak with August," he mumbled.

"He isn't here."

"Perhaps not. But he will come."

I shook my head. "Not until Saturday night. I hope you are not planning on remaining here until then?" There was something about his demeanor that prevented the use of more forceful expressions, such as "Go away!" or "Keep your hands off *my* fiancé!" He was simply too . . . sorry looking. Though he was technically still upright, it would be too much like kicking a man when he was down. "Why don't you go home?" I suggested mildly.

He looked at the ground.

"I cannot," he said. "And neither can he."

"What on earth do you mean?"

He looked at me for less than a second before lowering his head once more.

"I'm sorry. It . . . it was not supposed to turn out this way." Then he abruptly tore himself away from the doorway and down the street, rapidly but with uncertain steps. His urchin tormentors followed suit, at least until I yelled at them.

"Hey! Philippe. Roland. Luc-Luc. Find someone else to tease."

"Oh, Maddiiieee . . . ," Luc-Luc protested.

"Do it, or you won't see so much as a cracker next time I go to the bakery!"

They stopped and let their prey escape. He rounded the corner at Rue Perrault and disappeared from sight, and I noted with surprise that I felt a tiny spark of compassion.

Docent Althauser had to mark Erich Falchenberg absent that day. It did not really surprise me—he had not looked like a conscientious student, eagerly hastening toward the halls of learning—but it was distracting all the same because it made me wonder what was wrong with the man.

"Are you bored, mademoiselle?" Althauser asked pointedly.

"No, Monsieur le Professeur," I said quickly. Apparently it wasn't possible to show even the tiniest lack of focus without him noticing. There was something decidedly unnatural about the scrutiny to which he subjected his students.

In truth, today's exercise was not the most interesting he had asked us to complete. Armed with several large tubs of various kinds of mussel specimens—the smell of brackish water and half-rotten seaweed was pronounced—our task was to determine which were hermaphrodites and which were single sex. Since I knew at least a part of the answer already—fingernail clams and scallops were hermaphrodites—it was not quite as exciting to search for the mollusks' sexual characteristics as it might otherwise have been.

"What on earth is this?" asked Villeneuve with disgust, pointing at a wobbling, slimy, pale red creature that looked most of all like a long oblong balloon with two openings. "That must have fallen in accidentally . . ."

"It is definitely not a mussel," I said.

"Excellent observation," said Althauser right behind us. Villeneuve jumped at least ten centimeters, and I was hardly less startled. "It is a sea squirt. Now, see if you can determine the sex of *that*."

Sea squirt . . . Something emerged from the most distant regions of my cerebral cortex. Spurred on by Althauser's predilection for the dissection of marine life-forms, I had recently acquired several handbooks on the subject—among them was a somewhat ragged edition of Louis Agassiz's *Études critiques sur les mollusques fossiles*.

"It can assume both masculine and feminine sexual characteristics," I said. "Simultaneously or sequentially. And like sea anemones, it reproduces through gemmation. A highly versatile species." I looked down at the tunicate with renewed interest. It looked no more beautiful than before, but definitely more fascinating.

"You've done the reading, Karno, I'll give you that," said Althauser. "But we are not here to repeat the knowledge others have recorded. Experiment. Examine. Control."

But I never had the chance to personally observe the sea squirt's sexual versatility. One of the university porters had entered the room.

"Is there a"—he had to look down at his note an extra time—"a Mademoiselle Karno present? A gentleman wishes to speak with you. He says it is important."

August stood in the middle of the room, as if he did not want to risk touching the walls. His back was so straight that it approached rigidity, and he held his hands behind his back in an extremely controlled manner. There would be no gesticulating, emotional outbursts were banned.

"I have come to tell you that I have resigned my position in Heidelberg, effective immediately," he said, "and that I completely understand if you wish to break off our engagement."

I was still wearing my laboratory gown, and my hands stank of fish or, rather, of mollusks and brine and a lone sea squirt. Althauser, not normally a man to tolerate interruptions, had shown himself to be surprisingly considerate and had offered us his office.

"You are going to have to explain yourself a bit more clearly," I said carefully, and tried to calm the twisting feeling of dread in my stomach. "What has happened?"

He considered me for several long moments.

"I came as quickly as I could," he said. "I thought you would have heard. But apparently not even this kind of smut spreads that quickly. Thank goodness the railroad is still faster than the gossip."

"August . . ."

"I had been warned, but I thought—"

"August!"

"Yes. To be brief, I was given a summons by the city court in Heidelberg this morning for having violated the German Criminal Code's paragraph 175. Naturally, the university could not countenance my continued tenure, and they had heard—someone made sure that they heard very quickly—but I would have turned in my resignation anyway. The zeal of the tattler was entirely unnecessary."

"Paragraph . . ."

"My beloved Madeleine. What you and Krafft-Ebing call brain damage is a crime in the empire of the German Kaiser."

I felt slow and stupid. Even now the message was only gradually penetrating my thick brain. August had been fired. No, worse than that, he had been given a summons . . . charged with . . .

"Are you planning to show up in court?" I asked.

He looked at me with a wounded gaze that made him seem younger, almost as if we were the same age.

"They have Erich's testimony. The dean told me. How can I stand in front of a judge and deny it? But if I don't appear . . . Madeleine, that is the same as a confession. I would never be able to return to Germany."

"But here . . . ?"

"Here it is not illegal. But my name, my reputation . . . I would be a marked man. I do not know if I would be able to obtain an academic position again, or indeed *any* position. I have no idea what sort of life I can offer you."

Some nights ago, I had dreamed that I was on the streetcar on the way to the university, making hurried notations in my notebook. Right across from me sat Docent Althauser. His gaze rested sternly on me. "Mademoiselle," he said after some minutes of observation, "would you be kind enough to get off. You are improperly dressed!" Only when he said it did I discover that I was naked.

The feeling from the dream was creeping into me again, despite the fact that I was as properly dressed as one could reasonably expect of a woman who had just spent most of an hour dissecting mollusks. I should undoubtedly have thrown myself into August's arms with an "All of that means nothing—I love you." But I hesitated. It was weak, it was despicable, but I could not help thinking about what other people would say. What my *father* would say when he heard. It was one thing that I had accepted August's nature when I decided to become engaged to him—more or less, anyway. It was a private matter, I felt, something that was now in the past and did not concern anyone but the two of us. But this private matter had now become a very public court case, or would become one, whether August appeared or not.

My body had quickly formed its own opinion—it was shortsightedly and selfishly rejoicing in the fact that August was here and would have to stay here. No longer those hasty meetings every two weeks, no, *every* day, and who knows, before long perhaps even every *night* as well. Perhaps I would then be able to rid myself of that terrible black sense of loss and longing that seized me even when he was still present?

"Say something," he begged. "Madeleine, I . . ."

I did not say a word, not then. I let my body make the decision and clung to him so tightly that it would be difficult to insert a scalpel between us, kissing him on the neck, on an earlobe, on the chin, on the mouth.

"We'll get married," I said. "As soon as possible. That should silence some of the gossip."

"Don't be so sure of that," he said. "I'm afraid we run the risk that soon your reputation will be no better than mine."

That did matter. I could not pretend that it meant nothing. We would both find it more difficult to obtain a respectable livelihood, and to gain recognition and financing for the work we did, and the research I dreamed we would do. If August was to be exiled and outlawed by his own country . . .

"We have to speak to my father," I said, and that thought put a damper on even my body's jubilation.

There was a discreet cough from the door. For the third time that day, Docent Althauser had succeeded in sneaking up behind me without my noticing.

"Mademoiselle Karno. M'sieur Dreyfuss, I'm sorry, but . . ."

He did not look especially sorry. In fact, it seemed as if he found it offensive that we were embracing like this in his office. Or was it simply that he needed to use it himself?

"Of course," I said quickly. "We were just leaving. Weren't we, August?"

It seemed to me that the two men glared at each other with an unusual hostility. It was not very courteous of Althauser to call August simply "m'sieur" when he knew very well that August was a professor. Or . . . had been . . .

Perhaps it was only then that I realized I was no longer engaged to Professor Dreyfuss, the eminent parasitologist from Heidelberg.

"Please do not forget my little speech on Friday, mademoiselle," said Althauser. "You were planning to do me the honor . . . ?"

"Of course," I avowed, though truthfully I had not actually decided until then.

September 28, 1894

The Pro Patria event was not exactly packed, but the hall was more than half full. By far the majority of the attendees were men, clearly of the more well-heeled variety, but a few women had also dared to enter this evening. We were in the palatial headquarters of the Brotherhood of Freedom, a society rarely open to the general public, and still more rarely to the female half. Above us arched a ceiling decorated with oak leaves and grapevines and gold leaf, framing the coat of arms of the brotherhood: a crucifix and a sword crossed on a field of scarlet—or gules, as they would probably insist it was called. I had a faint memory of having been here as a little girl for some kind of Christmas gathering. I must have been five or six, Mama was still alive, and I remember that I loudly informed Saint Nicholas that he did not exist, or so Papa had said. That made several of the other children cry, and we were not invited the following year.

"Let me start with some simple facts. At the beginning of this century, France was Europe's most populous nation. That is no longer the case. It took a mere seventy years for both Germany and Russia to pass us, and soon England and Italy will be able to muster greater forces than we in every field of life. The birthrate of our nation is plunging, and as an unavoidable consequence we are on our way to becoming a lesser power. Every year more potential scientists, inventors, visionary businessmen, and generals are born in Germany. More artisans, more laborers, more soldiers. If this development is allowed to continue, in seventeen or eighteen years the Germans will be so superior to us in every military sense, that we are most unlikely to win a war against them. It is that simple, gentlemen. There is a direct link between these cold facts and the tragic defeat in 1871, a defeat that led in turn to a whole generation of young men and women from Alsace and Lorraine growing up under German rule these past twenty-three years. I cannot emphasize this too strongly: That way lies submission, weakness, and ruin."

Althauser was no demagogue. He spoke to this audience precisely as he spoke to his students, dryly and factually and without any attempt to move them emotionally with his presentation, in spite of the doomsday language.

"Furthermore, those among us who bear the most children are by no means the ones best suited to parenthood. It is the lowest class of people—those whose offspring have the slimmest chance of growing up to a good and useful adult existence for the benefit of our nation, those who expose the coming generation to degenerate influences even in the womb. I speak of alcoholism, unhealthy habits, diseases, and the consequences of vice and promiscuity. Were they horses or hounds, no one here would allow them to breed. Yet it is on this poor strain that we base the future of Varonne, and of France. Gentlemen, it cannot be!"

"Hear, hear!" shouted a member of the audience, but without triggering the applause for which he had probably been angling. Most people merely looked thoughtful.

"How has it come to this? Why do Frenchwomen of class and breeding no longer have as many children as before? We can place part of the blame on Madame Thomas, Madame Floury, and their ilk—and make no mistake, Varbourg has her own share of these monsters. These infamous Parisian abortionists have been found guilty of terminating more than ten thousand pregnancies. Ten thousand! And since the two angel makers charged well for their criminal services, we can draw the conclusion that it was not women of more modest means who thus murdered the next generation. These women, who could easily feed and raise children, are choosing instead to kill them before they are born. Apparently motherhood is not sacred to them, the child is not a gift. Their husbands—for some of them are married, and the rest must perforce have some kind of relationship to the child's father—their husbands, I say, have through weakness and convenience allowed the crime to occur. They have permitted their seed to fall barren to the ground, so that the stock they should have left instead has come to naught on the blade of an abortionist's knife. It is convenience too when men of means, pillars of our society, accede to the wish of their wives not to give birth to more than a single child or two. They ought instead to encourage, advise, and if necessary demand that the woman return to what is, after all, her vital task in life and in society. Failing to insist in this area is misconceived kindness—weakness, even—a weakness that costs our nation dearly."

He might as well have hit me.

I had encountered such words before, but I had not expected to hear them from his mouth.

My father sat very straight on the bench next to me, and his face had taken on a disapproving cast.

"*This* is your teacher?" he asked.

A rhetorical question, of course.

It went on. And on. And still I sat there. My skin felt full of pins and needles as if the words were having a physical effect. I think my face was frozen in a grimace of forced politeness. If this was how Althauser really perceived a woman's "vital task," why on earth had he agreed to have me for a student? For more than two months, I had tried to live up to everything this man demanded of me—through initial humiliations when he scorned even to look at me, through the nausea and nightmare of vivisection and the ceaseless testing and probing he subjected me to. I had fought to earn his approval and had—or so I thought—finally won it. Time after time he had challenged me to "rise above my sex." I could certainly understand that, because it was obvious that his view of women in general would have placed me only slightly above the status of a good broodmare.

How I wished that August were here. I deeply missed his intelligence, his ironic wit, the respect he always showed me as both a person and a woman. But he had crossed the border while he was still able, to explain himself to his grandmother in Heeringen and ask for her understanding. Papa was loyal, but in spite of his bold scientific outlook terribly old-fashioned when it came to me. If he thought Althauser was insulting me, he would no doubt feel the need to defend my honor, but he would never think to leave that defense to me, nor have faith in my ability to carry it out.

"Should we go?" my father asked.

I shook my head. "People will stare."

Althauser would definitely have noticed if we left, and he was still the only lecturer at the University of Varbourg who was willing to instruct a woman in natural sciences. I had fought so hard for that opportunity. I was not sure if I could bear it if it slipped from my grasp. I did not have to agree with the man's political ideas, I told myself. His professional skill was indisputable; I could still learn from him. But the feeling of having been deeply betrayed would not leave me.

Althauser was demonstrating the defects that an "unsuitable maternal subject" could pass on to her unborn child. He had a series of large posters—"based on photographic records, which you may examine afterward, gentlemen"—showing examples of children who had been born with physical or mental defects.

"As you can see, degeneration is obvious in the facial features," he said, and rapped the poster with the quick little smack of his pointer that I knew so well from university lectures. "The mother is an alcoholic, undernourished, and infected with syphilis. I have had the child photographed every month through its first four years, and in spite of good nourishment and care after birth, the defects are clear. The child is witless, it is often ill, both sight and hearing are reduced. At the age of four it is still incapable of speech, cannot dress itself or feed itself with a fork or spoon, and has no control over its bowel movements. Is this how we wish France's next generation to look?"

Papa shifted uneasily.

"He is right as far as the alcohol is concerned," he whispered to me. "I am convinced that there is a connection between birth defects and the mother's excessive consumption. And unfortunately we also all too often see the damage done by syphilis."

He clearly said it only because he felt obliged to "give the man credit," but I still took umbrage.

"So you agree that women should serve as broodmares for the good of the Republic?" I asked, more loudly than I had intended. Several listeners in the row in front of us turned and shushed me.

My father waited until they had turned away again. "Of course not," he said quietly. "But . . ."

"Shhh," I said. I sensed that this was not a subject I could bear to discuss with him right now.

I meant to leave as quickly as I might without causing undue notice or offense, but there was a congestion at the door, and my attempt at a timely exit did not succeed.

"Mademoiselle Karno!" Althauser came rushing down the central aisle. "How good of you to come! And I see you have brought your father. Monsieur le Docteur, you are a highly respected man in university circles. I am so pleased to meet you."

Papa stopped as well, of course. I could sense how he stiffened with reserve, and I gave his arm a quick little invisible squeeze. Even though I felt no desire to praise Althauser's great plan for saving the Fatherland, I did not want Papa to provoke a scene.

"Sir. The pleasure is entirely mine," said my father politely, without that pleasure being particularly evident in his features or tone of voice.

"But your fiancé is not doing me the honor?" Althauser continued.

"No," I said. "Unfortunately, he was prevented from coming."

"What a shame." Althauser performed a quick duck of his head, but there was something in his manner that seemed rather more triumphant than regretful.

An elderly gentleman, resplendent in white tie and tailcoat, headed toward us through the crowd.

"So this is the young lady you have spoken about," he said, and clapped Althauser approvingly on the shoulder. "Excellent, excellent. Mademoiselle, my admiration!" He bowed with a precision that would not have been out of place in the officers' mess, nor indeed in the ballroom, and kissed the air a few centimeters above my right glove. His hair was completely white yet still thick except for a few shiny glimpses of scalp at the crown. His mustache and beard were a few shades darker and the eyebrows still almost black.

Althauser introduced us.

"Mademoiselle Karno, this is Vice Marshall Delafontaine. He is one of Pro Patria's most prominent supporters."

"Not at all, not at all. Mademoiselle, there are some modest refreshments in the adjoining rooms. May I have the honor?"

He offered me his arm, and I felt compelled to curtsey and allow myself to be escorted. I thought my father and Althauser would follow us, but when I looked back, I discovered that Althauser was busy showing Papa the "photographic records" his posters were based on.

The "adjoining rooms" were smaller than the actual lecture hall but hardly more humble. Gold leaf glittered on ceiling and walls, scarlet silk tapestries flamed in the light from the crystal chandelier, and the floor was covered by the largest and most exquisite Bokhara rug I had ever seen. Champagne flutes awaited on white tablecloths, and small delicate canapés were thickly clustered on tiered porcelain stands.

"Do you like champagne, mademoiselle?"

"On special occasions," I said.

"Then you must definitely have a glass now, because this is a *very* special occasion. We have so looked forward to meeting you."

"Really?" I did not quite understand the enthusiasm.

"The professor has not told you as much?" He wrinkled his striking black eyebrows.

At first, I thought he meant August, but how would the two of them have been acquainted? I was just about to ask before I realized that he meant Althauser.

"You are a true pioneer among women," he continued, undaunted. "The first of your kind. It is brave of you to forge a completely new path, but I am sure that many of your sisters will soon follow in your footsteps."

"I hope so," I answered, and tried to look modest even as a small ember of pride rekindled itself and made my heart beat a little faster. What he was saying was of course more or less true—I *was* the first of my kind, at least in Varbourg. But I had not expected a man with his background and high position and a declared sympathy for the Pro Patria project to look at it this way.

"Excellent. Excellent. And the professor has assured me that it will occur without any . . . er . . . discomfort for you. Clean, sterile, and without . . . er, unnecessary intimacy." He smiled avuncularly and patted me on the hand. "One could almost say that you have been chosen to be visited not by the Holy Spirit but by the very Spirit of Science."

The doors behind us opened, and ten or eleven gentlemen of similar avoirdupois entered in amorphous chatting, cigar-smoking groups. While I was still trying to work out what he had meant by his spiritual reference, he turned with an expansive gesture to the newcomers.

"Gentlemen, gentlemen. Here she is at last! Intelligence, beauty, strength—and above all, a sound and rational consciousness in a healthy, young body. A worthy foremother of the nation's future elite!"

There must be some misunderstanding. That was the only rational thought in my head. Through the open door, I could see Papa and Althauser approach. Applause and bravas had erupted from the swarm of men around me, several had taken up champagne glasses and raised them toward me, and at least one of them, one of the few young men in the gathering, could no longer look at me without blushing. The air was so thick with masculine approval that it seemed to me that the temperature in the room must objectively have gone up several degrees.

"There must be . . . there must be some misunderstanding," I stammered, and tried to find a place to set aside the champagne glass. "I am no . . . foremother. To anyone!" Perhaps I had spoken too softly. Only those in closest proximity lowered their glasses and looked puzzled. I took a deep breath and spoke as loudly as was possible without shouting. "This is a misunderstanding. I am not planning to have children at all!"

Now they heard me.

"Pardon . . . ?" said the vice marshall. "But the professor said . . ."

Althauser forced himself through the crowd.

"Gentlemen, I am sorry. I think that what I said was that I had finally found a suitable candidate. I am afraid I had not yet fully discussed our future dream with Mademoiselle Karno."

He was clearly ill at ease, and more than that. His eyes glared at me with an only partially controlled rage that I had never expected to find in my tight-lipped lecturer, usually so clinically detached.

I still did not quite understand the details of this "future dream," but one thing was painfully obvious. What the circle of men had applauded was not my intellect, my so-called courage, or my academic ambitions. The only thing that really interested them was my potential ability to pass on a healthy physique and a certain minimum of intelligence to my offspring.

I could not reach the table. In the end, I simply handed my glass to the shy young man, who took it nervously.

"Gentlemen," I said with what shreds of dignity I could muster. "Please excuse me. Good evening."

I held my head high as I marched from that room, not just for the sake of my bearing, but to keep my humiliated tears from brimming over and becoming visible to the entire world.

My father hurried after me as quickly as his injured leg permitted, but I could not slow my pace even for his sake. I do not know if Althauser tried to follow me. He did not, at any rate, succeed in catching up with us before we reached the street. Luckily, a hansom cab was passing by just then, and I ignored every propriety and hailed it myself instead of waiting for Papa to do so.

"Madeleine!"

I tore open the door and got in. As soon as I was more or less hidden from public gaze, the tears came pouring out, and I could not even control the loud sobs that made the driver half turn in his seat.

"Carmelite Street," my father said to him.

"Is that all right with you, ma'mselle?"

"Yes," I managed.

The carriage springs groaned, and my father let himself drop clumsily into the seat across from me. He slammed the door shut, knocked on the roof with the cane he was still forced to use, and the hansom set off.

"Madeleine, what is all this about?"

I was reminded of how proud I had been, just a few hours ago, when I dressed for the evening. How I had imagined that Papa and Althauser would meet and talk. In my innermost thoughts I had hoped that Althauser would repeat his praise of my intellect to Papa. That they would both have looked at me with the approval I was only now realizing I so badly craved.

Instead . . . no, I could not bear the thought. I would never drink champagne again, never. That grotesque salute, the blushing young man, the Holy Spirit and the Spirit of Science . . . I still did not understand that reference, but right now it was humiliatingly obvious that Althauser had been intending to show me off to these men as a "candidate" for some form of Pro Patria breeding program that was to save the nation from being overrun by Germans and degenerates. What if that is what he had wanted all along? Perhaps his willingness to instruct female students sprang exclusively from the need to examine the field for "candidates" of a certain intelligence?

"Maddie, say something!"

I looked up. My father's long, ascetic face—Mama used to tease him that he looked like a prophet who had wandered in the desert for forty days—lay half in shadow, but I could still sense his concern. It was extremely rare nowadays that I cried while he could see and hear it.

"I don't think I can attend the university any longer," I said at last.

"Why not?"

"Because I was accepted . . . under false assumptions."

"What do you mean by that? You were completely honest in your application—I saw it myself."

"My assumptions were not false," I said. "Theirs were. His. He took me on not because he thought I was intelligent, but because . . . he hoped that . . . I could be *useful*."

"Are you referring to all that foolishness about degeneration and motherhood?"

"Yes. I think so."

"The man is clearly deranged. He is not the right person to be in charge of your continuing education."

"But, Papa . . . He is the only one. The *only* one who wanted me."

"Nonsense! There must be other and far more worthy educators. And otherwise there is the Sorbonne." He lifted his chin as if ready for battle. "Madeleine, you are going to get the education that your intellect deserves!"

Oh, how I loved him in that moment. Until now it had been August more than Papa who had supported me in my ambition to receive a formal education. Papa had not opposed it, certainly, but I think he ultimately imagined that my future lay in my role as my husband's assistant, just as I had for the past many years been his. He never acknowledged my abilities to strangers and apparently believed it was unnecessary to praise them to me. It was the first time ever that I had heard him use the word "intellect" about me.

The Sorbonne was an impossible dream. We simply could not afford it, especially not now when August's livelihood was in doubt, and when we did not know if his family could and would support him economically in his exile. But I loved Papa for having suggested it.

He would have given almost anything to be able to believe in preformation rather than epigenesis. It was such a beautiful thought that everything was already present in the vigorous little spermatozoa, that they did not require anything but a fruitful medium in which to grow in order to develop from microscopic homunculi to fully developed sons. But he was a scientist. He had to accept the evidence, and the proof of epigenesis was irrefutable. It was therefore all the more catastrophic when the female sex betrayed its role in the reproductive process.

His rage was affecting all but a few of his internal organs. He felt the acid content of his stomach rise and burn, there was a painful mutter in the region of his liver, his heart and vascular circulation strained to the point where he could hear his pulse pounding in his ears. He ought to have foreseen it, knowing what he did about her and her sex, yet it still took him by surprise—this defeat, this shameful treachery. He had come so close to falling as so many others had fallen before him!

It had taken almost an hour to convince Delafontaine that Mademoiselle Karno's peculiar reaction was not a serious hindrance to the completion of the project. It had even been necessary to mention certain information he had obtained about the vice marshall's unfortunate handling of public funds in connection with the Panama scandal. Delafontaine was an excellent figurehead for Pro Patria and also their only access so far to funding from the Republic, but he was a man sadly lacking in systematic thought, in spite of his military background. A great deal was left half done because this admirably respected man did not possess the ability to pursue a pure thought all the way to its logical realization. It was, therefore, useful not only to rely on carrots but also to have a stick; the danger was that it might break if used too often.

It had all been extremely uncomfortable, and when he arrived home, he had to ask Madame Arnaud to bring him two slices of dry bread, a glass of water, and the jar of sodium bicarbonate along with his chamomile tea. He dissolved the two teaspoons of bicarbonate in the water and drank it slowly, accompanied by small mouthfuls of white bread. Only then did his agitated innards begin to calm down.

It had been a couple of upsetting days altogether, and he could not help but feel that the world was against him. He had not believed in God since that awful day when he lost his simple childhood faith and more or less found his path in life, but there were moments when it seemed to him that the universe was sentient and seemed to lurk, waiting to punish his every single, insignificant mistake.

He suddenly realized that Madame Arnaud was standing in the doorway and had been for a while.

"What do you want?" he asked unkindly, mostly because he did not like to be observed without knowing it.

Several seconds passed before she answered. "May I go there now?"

He looked at the clock. It was past eleven; that ought to be sufficient even for his incompetent photographer. And yet . . .

"Wait an hour," he said.

He returned his attention to the chamomile tea, but the woman remained in the doorway instead of leaving.

"She misses me," she said.

His soured stomach produced another painful half belch. He had originally hired the woman because she was reliable and withdrawn. He was free of any unnecessary talk, and since she had an invalid husband and could not afford to lose her position, she carried out the relative few duties he assigned to her in a timely manner and without objections. Or that was how it had once been.

"Madame," he said, mustering all the patience he possessed at the moment, "women are a true wonder. They are able to attach feelings to anything—a lapdog, a book, a view, yes, even a hat. Only when you begin to believe that these feelings are reciprocated is there reason to fear for your compos mentis. Compose yourself. And wait until twelve o'clock."

Again long seconds passed—so many that he wondered whether he would need to replace her in spite of all the fuss it would require. Then, thankfully, the silly woman curtseyed, said, "Yes, m'sieur," and left.

He rested his head on the armchair's antimacassar and closed his eyes. Oh, to be a sea anemone. To reproduce by simple gemmation seemed to him nature's highest ideal. To bud, and pass oneself on, unchanged and undiluted, to the next generation— that was a beautiful form of immortality. But alas, sexual reproduction drew mankind down into filth, disease, senility, and ruin. Where woman was, there was also death.

September 29–October 1, 1894

I woke up confused and exhausted and with a nagging head-
ache. My bedroom felt as if it had shrunk during the night,
and the air was musty and thick. I was grateful that I did not
immediately have to decide, with yesterday's humiliation still so
raw, if I should attend the lecture and confront Althauser or just
make it easier for all involved and refrain from showing up. It was
Saturday, and my plans were simply to study at home and assist
my father in the morgue with the autopsy of an elderly woman
whose neighbors suspected her son of having "done away with
her for the sake of the money." The Commissioner had shaken
his head at this.

"She owned a sideboard, a bowl and pitcher set, a mantel clock,
twelve fish forks in silver plate, various other items of dubious value,
and a cash sum of thirty-two francs, which she had saved from her
widow's pension. I really hope the neighbors are wrong. I would
so prefer not to believe that any son would cause his mother's un-
timely end because of thirty-two francs and a bit of silver."

"People have been murdered for less," said my father.

"I know. I would just prefer not to believe it . . ."

To my surprise, the Commissioner himself was already in
the salon when I came down. The autopsy was not scheduled to
begin until past noon, when my father had completed his rounds
at Saint Bernardine.

"Good morning, Madeleine," he said. There was a light drizzle
outside, and drops of rain sat like pearl buttons on the new tweed
cape that had replaced his worn overcoat after Marie had entered
the picture. He had taken off neither hat nor gloves. "I am sorry
to disturb you so early in the day, but . . . well, Marie sent me. It is
regarding a young lady named Fleur."

"The one who identified Rosalba Lombardi," I explained.

"Apparently my wife had an appointment with her two days ago. They knew each other from . . . well, from before. But the young lady did not show up. This caused Marie sufficient concern that she went to inquire at Fleur's address. The concierge said she had not been home since Tuesday."

Tuesday. That was the day she and I had visited the Institute for Child Care and Nursing.

"She and I were together on Tuesday," I confessed. I had not told either my father or the Commissioner about this visit, but had simply made it seem as if I was at the university those afternoons and evenings that I had actually devoted to the investigation of Rosalba's death.

"I see. Then Marie is right that you and this Fleur are . . . er, acquainted?"

Tuesday evening was also the night Fleur had not shown up at Le Crapaud. Certain nerve endings in my stomach and along my spine began to send chilled signals to my brain. I remembered how exhausted she had seemed that day, how guilt ridden and despairing. I would have to tell the Commissioner most of what we had done together, I realized.

"Fleur showed me some photographs of Rosalba, which . . . well, I understand that you have seen them." I had no desire whatsoever to go into detail and was not sure how I should continue.

"Please go on," said the Commissioner when the pause grew longer. He had not moved a muscle.

"Fleur was convinced that some of the pictures had a . . . connection to what happened later. She felt that I could perhaps help her to unravel events."

"Dear Madeleine, do I really need to tell you that police investigations are best handled by the police?"

"Fleur does not have a great deal of confidence in men, especially not in policemen. I was merely trying to help!"

"But you were not with her yesterday or the day before?"

"No. I have not seen her since Tuesday either."

"It worries me that you may have exposed both yourself and the young lady to danger."

I shook my head.

"I don't think so. The only thing we did together was visit an institute for child care . . ." A couple of disjointed visual memories flittered through my head. Long rows of infants. Pauline's rebellious face. The judgmental pince-nez gaze of Madame Palantine. I remembered the stuffy, unhealthy smell in Fleur's bedroom, her bottomless sorrow. Was it strong enough that she might . . . choose to end it?

Then another and perhaps less dramatic explanation occurred to me.

"Could she have been arrested?" I asked. *Three months . . . for buying a pint of milk in the wrong place*, she had said. That sounded like a personal experience.

The Commissioner shook his head.

"That was also among the first things Marie asked, but I have investigated the matter. She has not been jailed. In fact, she has never been arrested—remarkable when one considers her . . . means of support."

Perhaps it was Rosalba who had bought that pint of milk. Or it might just be a random example, though I did not really think so. It was too specific.

"The hospitals?" In addition to Saint Bernardine there were two, both smaller and—according to Papa, anyway—less professional.

"No. And Marie has asked several . . . mutual friends. That is why I am here. We have exhausted the most plausible possibilities, and Marie thought that you might . . ."

"No. I don't know anything."

"Well, then, I apologize for the inconvenience. I suppose we will just have to wait for her to show up."

I felt an uneasy helplessness, mixed with guilt.

"Is there perhaps some family?"

The Commissioner shook his head. "Marie says that there isn't. She seems quite alone in the world, our Fleur."

That did not lessen my guilt or my unease.

We found her at last. Or perhaps it would be more accurate to say that she found us.

She was lying on the muddy bank of the River Var, in the shadow of the Arsenal Bridge.

"At first I think it is a child," said the young English engineer who had reported it. "But then I could see that she isn't." He spoke French in his own manner, fast and with an excellent vocabulary, but with somewhat patchy grammar. "We examine the bridge pilings, and there she is. Tiny. The poor little thing."

It was daybreak, more or less, but the fog was so thick that it was difficult to differentiate the faint glow of dawn from the fuzzy symmetrical points of light emanating from the streetlamps along the promenade. Somewhere farther down the river, a pontoon bridge was rubbing against its moorings with a repetitive screeching, as if someone were plucking a live goose.

Fleur lay on her back, with wide-open eyes. If there had been any truth to that tale, we would have been able to photograph her killer because, unlike Rosalba, she had fought and scratched and had not gone gently and dreamily to her death. Almost all her fingernails were frayed or broken, and she had vivid bruises on her arms and wrists where someone had tried to hold her or pin her down.

She was sodden. Her clothes, her hair . . . everything was dank and dark from the river. The yellow silt that collected in the bends of the Var daubed the skirts of her dress and clung to her legs, shoulders, and neck. Around her mouth there were traces of foam, as one may often observe in the drowned.

Aristide Gilbert set up his tripod and camera as well as it was possible in the mud and mumbled apologetically about the quality of the light and hence of the photographs.

"Too diffuse," he said. "Not enough contrast." The absinthe on his breath was overpowering, and his movements so uncertain that the Commissioner raised an eyebrow. If Gilbert did not watch his step, I thought, he could lose his commission from the police even if no one else ever discovered that he had been selling his material to the overzealous Monsieur Christophe.

"Homicide?" asked the Commissioner.

"If not, she was definitely in a fight before she drowned," my father said, and indicated the nails and the blue spots.

"It's murder," I said, and squatted next to the corpse. "Look at her dress."

The mud had camouflaged it at first glance, but when you looked more closely there were two tears in the skirt, and I was certain we would find corresponding lacerations when we undressed her.

"It is less brutal than was the case with the Italian and Eugénie Colombe," said my father.

"And made through the skirt. He did not wish to expose her abdomen," I pointed out.

Gilbert turned abruptly from the camera and let the cloth fall. Without a word he staggered ten to twelve paces toward the steps leading back up to the quay and began to vomit. Whether it was the effects of the absinthe or the subject he was being forced to photograph was impossible to determine. We all three looked at him—Papa, the Commissioner, and I—and then, as if by mutual agreement, ignored his suffering.

The Commissioner greeted my announcement with a slow, disbelieving shake of his head.

"Does this mean we cannot even be sure it is the same assailant?" he said.

"We cannot tell with certainty," acknowledged my father. "Madeleine is right. There are similarities but also differences."

"This is madness," said the Commissioner. "That one man should perpetrate such a horror is bad enough, but—"

"I don't think it is madness," I said, feeling an unfamiliar cold rage collect somewhere in the region of my solar plexus. "I think it is very deliberate and carefully planned."

My father glanced at me.

"First the facts, Maddie," he said quietly, "then the conclusions. Never the other way around."

I nodded curtly. Fleur's little-girl face was blank and dead. The lively eyes were dark and empty, the energetic body now nothing more than a collection of bones and decomposing tissue. The engineer's description, *the poor little thing*, was only too precise. That was all she was now—an object. And perhaps all she had been to the killer while she was still alive.

I got up, perhaps a little too abruptly. That was why, I assured myself later. That was sufficient explanation.

A wave of dizziness robbed me of all strength in my legs and the ability to hold myself upright. Neither my father nor the Commissioner had time to react before I collapsed on the riverbank in the mud next to Fleur's dead body.

Marie Mercier's shoulders were shaking, and she cried quietly.

We had been forced to ask her to formally identify the body, because we had no one else. She bore it with dignity, but there was no doubt she was deeply shocked. Briefly and in a quiet voice, she answered the necessary questions, so cold and factual, and signed the documents with her new married name. The Commissioner placed both hands on the trembling shoulders and kissed her on the hair, and the tenderness that existed between them was unmistakable. A jab of longing went through me, and I had to remind myself that August would be coming home from Heeringen later today.

"Madeleine," said the Commissioner, "would you take Marie home? I think she would appreciate your company."

"Yes, why don't you do that, Maddie," my father seconded him.

I knew that this did not just concern Marie. It was about getting both of the frail women out of the way. My idiotic fainting fit had left its marks not just on my clothes and in the form of a painful crick in my neck—it had also ruined much of the professional respect I had worked so hard to attain. My father wished to perform Fleur's autopsy without my assistance. I hated my body's weakness in that moment, but I could see that it would do no good to protest.

"Of course," I mumbled.

A hansom was hired. During most of the drive, Marie sat completely still and upright and stared down at her hands and the pocket handkerchief they were gripping. Only once did she break the silence.

"She liked you," she said.

I felt a lump in my throat.

"It was mutual."

"She was . . . so *alive*."

"Yes." I had experienced Fleur only in shock and sorrow, and now in death, yet I knew exactly what Marie meant.

The sun had gradually burned off the fog, and there was a golden haze across the gardens and the trees along the road, summery rather than autumnal despite the date. Where Varbourg had been busy and loud in the midst of the day, La Valle still dozed deeply. A dog barked at us from one of the gardens, a maid in a doorway was shaking out a tablecloth and looked up as we passed. Other than that, we saw not a soul.

"It is so peaceful here," I said at last.

"Yes," said Marie with a fragile little smile. "It reminds me of the village where my grandmother lived. She often looked after me when I was a child."

Marie's own newly hired maid, Adele, received us and served tea and brioches in the dining room. I discovered that I was actually hungry in spite of the emotional upheavals. Marie picked a little at her roll but did not seem to manage more than a few crumbs.

"The Commissioner said that you did not think Fleur had any relatives?" I said.

She shook her head.

"I think she was quite alone in the world, except for Rosalba. She didn't say a word to me about a home, or relatives. In fact, she never talked about her background at all, but I had a feeling it was grim. Possibly an orphanage?"

"And you don't know whether Petit was her real last name?"

"No. But I have never heard her use anything else."

"How long have you known her?"

"It must be . . . six or seven years." She stretched and got up restlessly. "You know what they call girls like her, don't you?"

"*Filles isolées*. She used the term herself."

"Yes. And it was true in more ways than one. She and Rosalba looked after each other. They created their own little island and only rarely allowed anyone else into their private world. I was one of the lucky few who were permitted to visit once in a while. She was tough as nails and ready to defend herself against all comers, but with Rosalba . . . when they were together, one could see a different Fleur, quick to laugh and vulnerably open, happy and loving and full of the best kind of silliness. Madeleine, you have no idea what she lost when Rosalba was killed. After that, there was only hard-as-nails Fleur left, and even she was mortally wounded."

"The Commissioner said you and she had an appointment. Where were you going?"

"She had made me promise that I would go with her to the Commission for Public Health and Decency. I think she believed they would be more likely to listen to me than to her."

"What on earth did she want there?"

"Rosalba was taken into what they call custodial quarantine this spring. For three months, according to the new rules."

"For buying a pint of milk in the wrong place," I exclaimed.

Marie nodded tightly. "Yes. By some self-important busybody who knew who she was. Do you know what they do?"

"No."

"It is horrible. Humiliating and . . . horrible. You may think that women like us have no sense of modesty."

"No. I don't believe that."

"We do. It matters how they treat us! To be forced onto a table with two men to hold you down while some coldhearted *swine* of a doctor spreads your legs and . . . they call it a health test, but it is . . . horrible."

I felt a nauseating unease in my chest. Elegant, refined Marie, who now was my friend the Commissioner's wife and lived here in the villa in La Valle with a maid and a full set of Limoges china—she too had been subjected to the forced examinations the préfecture inflicted on what they called "public girls," *isolée* or otherwise.

"Rosalba was not sick," said Marie. "They found nothing because there was nothing to find. But the doctor still wrote that she was in the early stages of syphilis and sent her into custody."

I myself knew that Rosalba did not have syphilis. We would have discovered that during the autopsy.

"Fleur wanted to know who that doctor was," said Marie.

"Why?" I asked.

"I don't know. But she was very set on it."

"And did she find out?"

"No. I waited for over an hour, but . . . she did not show up. Madeleine, was she already dead at that point?"

"When had you arranged to meet?"

"Thursday afternoon. At two o'clock, when they reopen after lunch."

"No," I said. "She was still alive then." I did not know what Papa was recording right now about the time of death, but it could hardly be Thursday, or the decomposition would have been more advanced.

"But why didn't she come, then?"

"I don't know," I said. "But I am going to find out."

The Commission for Public Health and Decency was housed in a large, ugly redbrick monstrosity that looked exactly like what it really was: a prison. Only at street level did the building have proper windows facing Place Tertiaire; for the sake of symmetry, the architect had insisted on recesses and what looked like window cornices, but where there should have been glass, there was just more wall. If windows are the eyes of a house, then this house had had its eyes poked out.

I looked down at my only weapon against the massive defenses of the commission: a hastily written note from Inspector Marot asking its public servants to "aid Mademoiselle Karno in finding what she is seeking." I would have preferred to have the company of a police officer as a more visible and concrete proof of my claim, but the inspector had not been willing to stretch that far. He had seemed grumpy and overworked and had listened with only half an ear while I explained how critical it was to investigate what had happened while Rosalba was in custody.

"Fine, if you have nothing better to do," he said. "Though I do not entirely understand why you are so determined to chase that particular wild goose . . ."

So here I was, in front of the lion's den, hoping that this unimpressive piece of paper was enough. I strongly doubted that the commission would have allowed Fleur and Marie access to the archives out of politeness and the goodness of their hearts. Why had she asked Marie and not me? Perhaps she had lost confidence in my abilities as unofficial investigator. Perhaps she was right . . .

I stood still a moment longer to check if the anger was still there. It was. And if it could not be used for anything else, at least it made me march up the steps to the pompous entrance and across the outer foyer with decisive, authoritative steps.

I slammed Marot's note down in front of the young clerk who was posted behind the barred counter that was clearly meant to keep the general public at bay.

"As you can see, I require access to the archives of the commission. It regards the period from the first of January to the first of May this year."

He looked up at me in obvious consternation. "The archives?" he said.

"Yes. Everything regarding forced examinations and custodial quarantine during the time in question."

"And . . . um . . . who may I say you are?"

"In this errand, I am Police Inspector Marot's special assistant. As it says." I pointed down at the note.

"I'll see if that is possible," he said.

"No," I said. "You may announce that it must be possible and at once. The police inspector needs this information in an important case." At least I was convinced that he did even though he himself was not yet quite aware of it.

"Please understand, Monsieur Barbier does not permit . . ." he stammered. "I cannot myself . . . such a decision requires . . ."

"Of course," I said. "It is probably easiest if I accompany you and explain the case."

He looked at me with something like panic but then apparently decided that in fact it *was* simplest to pass the problem—me—on to the next level in the food chain.

"This way, mademoiselle," he said, and opened the counter's only gate.

We interrupted Monsieur Barbier at what was either a late breakfast or an early lunch. He sat behind his enormous mahogany desk, applying butter and orange marmalade to a second croissant—judging by the crumbs from the first—and looked up with irritation when we came in.

"What is it now, Pikeur? And who is this lady?"

"This is Mademoiselle Karno, she . . . she has been sent by Police Inspector Marot. She has . . . That is, she says . . ."

I decided to take over the explanations myself. "The inspector has asked me to collect certain information from the commission's archives. It is an urgent matter."

Barbier gave me a decidedly impolite once-over. There were crisp croissant crumbs in his beard, I noted.

"I see. Well, don't just stand there, Pikeur. Show the young lady what the inspector needs to see."

"Yes, m'sieur."

"And, Pikeur?"

"Yes, m'sieur?"

"I really cannot be expected to deal with every little thing myself. Show a little initiative!"

"Yes, m'sieur. Of course, m'sieur."

"And tell Madame Charles that the coffee is cold!"

The archives were situated in a library-like hall a bit farther down the corridor, with windows facing Place Tertiaire. Mahogany bookshelves ran from floor to ceiling, shelf after shelf of identical gray files and document boxes. Pikeur climbed up a ladder and fetched me QUARANTINE RECORDS JANUARY 1894 and its cousins FEBRUARY, MARCH, and APRIL.

"If you would permit . . . Here at the table perhaps?"

"Thank you, that will be fine."

"I must . . . you understand, the front desk is unmanned, and . . ."

"I shall manage. Thank you for your help, Monsieur Pikeur."

"You are welcome. Or . . . I am the one who . . . Tell me if there is more that I . . ."

He retreated, still without having completed a sentence, it seemed to me. I wondered fleetingly whether he always spoke like this or if I just brought out the worst—or in any case the least complete—in him.

The records were all arranged in the same way. In the column on the far left was the name of the woman, last name first. Then came "Date of Examination," "Case No.," a column without a heading that was meant for the examiner's signature, then a wider field for the description of the results, and finally one dedicated to the decision of the commission. There were apparently only three possibilities—"release," "1 month," or "3 months."

I found *Lombardi, Rosalba* on January 13. But next to her name, there was nothing except the date, case number, and two letters: PP. There was no signature and no description of the result. It did not even say "3 months," though I knew that was what she had been sentenced to, if "sentence" is the right word when no judge or court of law has been involved.

Frustrated, I leaned back in the chair. PP—that told me nothing. And why were the other areas blank?

I was just about to close the file when I discovered that Rosalba's name appeared more than once. She was also there on January 15, in exactly the same way: Lombardi, Rosalba. PP. Likewise the 17th. And the 19th. And the 21st.

She had been "examined" fifteen times—every other day for a month.

From a medical point of view it made no sense whatsoever. Syphilis lesions in the vagina did not sprout forth from one day to the next. To subject a woman to the invasion that Marie had simply called "horrible," so frequently, so systematically . . . It approached torture. I completely understood Fleur's anger, but I did not understand the purpose of this at all. Surely this careful, meticulously recorded sequence of events had to be more than random cruelty?

The record did not tell me enough. But I thought the archives here might be arranged similar to those of the morgue—the public records were only for quick reference, while the full report was stored elsewhere. I noted Rosalba's case number—94026—and went looking.

I guessed that the endless gray boxes would be the place to start, and after some searching found "94001–94100." But though there was a "94025" and a "94027," there was no file marked "94026." A quick perusal revealed that there were other gaps in the row of numbers. In theory, this might be because there simply *were* no documents or reports, but that seemed strange, not least because the record itself had seemed so lacking. Why register every single one of those awful examinations without noting their results? That would be even more meaningless.

After some consideration, I began to make note of the other gaps; I found seven. When I checked back in the records, I noted that they all, like Rosalba, had that enigmatic PP.

I looked at the endless shelves towering above me. Somewhere, I thought. Somewhere there is a gray box where those seven PP reports are collected. But where?

One's leg muscles can become very sore from climbing up and down a library ladder for an hour and a half. That is how long it took before I, highest up in one of the farthest bookcases, found the gray box that looked exactly like the other gray boxes, except for the fact that the spine was marked "PP 1894." Finally!

I climbed awkwardly down the ladder with the box tightly grasped under one arm. I was sweaty, dusty, sore . . . and triumphant.

Just as suspected, the box contained the seven missing reports, plus several more I hadn't found because they were from later months. All together there must have been about forty. I yanked Rosalba's from the pile and opened it greedily.

The first document was a general description of her, depressingly like the one I myself had noted in the autopsy report. Height, weight, hair color, body type, et cetera. Some more cryptic notations followed: "Cranial shape: A. Facial features: A2. Form and function of the limbs: 9. Deformities: None. Intelligence: Normal or above. Conclusion: Suited."

Suited for what?

This was not clarified in the next document, a slightly expanded report of the recorded fifteen "examinations." Next to most of them it just said "Completed. Nothing of note." But it did not stop there. Over the next two months, Rosalba had apparently been "seen" by the attending physician regularly once a week: "Seen. Nothing of note." But then, after one more week, there was finally a change: "Seen. Nausea." "Seen. Menses nil." And finally on March 19, about a week before Rosalba's release, one word, underlined with a thick black pen: "Gravida."

At this point I was not quite as shocked as I perhaps ought to have been to discover who had signed the certificate of her release: A. Althauser, Docent.

I left the building on Place Tertiaire with Rosalba's case file lodged between my shoulder blades and my corset. In my little notebook, I had carefully penned the names of all the other women in the PP box—thirty-six, it turned out, when I counted them carefully. Only eight of them had the final note "Gravida." I had written down the addresses these eight women had provided.

I assumed some of these would be false—they would not have wanted to leave the police a record of their whereabouts if they could help it—but I hoped to find at least one or two.

After four discouraging attempts—two "never heard of her," one "she doesn't live here anymore," and a house number that did not exist on the street in question—I now stood in a backyard behind Rue Carcassonne, knocking on a black-painted door to a tiny dwelling that had probably started life as a small laundry shed, or possibly even a byre. The yard was reasonably neat—the dustbins were lined up along the fence, the cobblestones had been carefully swept, and in front of the house's only window hung a wooden box in which various herbs were growing—in passing, I identified thyme and rosemary.

The door was opened by a girl of twelve or thirteen. Her black hair was braided so tightly that the parting shone white in the midst of the black, and her dark guarded gaze reminded me painfully of Fleur's. She stared at me as if I were a fairy or a witch or something equally foreign and unexpected.

"What do you want?" she asked, not with hostility or intentional discourtesy but as if she really wanted to know.

"I am looking for . . ." I had to consult my list, "Estelle Audran. She gave this address?"

"Mamaaa!" yelled the girl. "There's a lady here wants to see you!"

Greatly encouraged, I followed her into the tiny hallway. I had been prepared to come up with yet another blank in the address lottery, but here there was apparently a prize.

It was probably the smallest living room I had ever been in, not much more than a meter and a half one way and two the other. At a table by the window sat a woman putting together matchboxes. Her stubby fingers flew, folding and gluing and pasting the paper on both sides. She barely looked up.

"What do you want?" she said.

"I would . . . like to speak with you," I answered hesitantly. I realized that I had no desire whatsoever to mention the Commission for Public Health and Decency to this woman while her daughter was listening.

"About what? As you can see, we are busy." The daughter had already sat down on the other side of the table, and she too glued boxes at a pace that seemed to make her fingers blur in front of my eyes—she was even faster than her mother. "If it is the salvation of my soul that you are concerned about, then you may rest assured. I go to mass every Sunday just like other people do."

That was a natural assumption, I guess—religion and charity were about the only pursuits that regularly brought women like me into a working woman's home.

"I am sure, madame. That is not my errand. I just wanted to ask . . . Have you given birth recently?"

Her hands stopped.

"No," she said shortly. "How did you get that idea? Anette, we are about to run out of glue. Run over to the factory to get another pail."

"But we have enough for—"

Smack! The mother's hand shot out and slapped the daughter's cheek.

"Do as I say!"

From the girl's overwhelmed and hurt reaction, I could see that this was much harsher treatment than she was used to.

"Mama!"

"Go! Do I need to say everything twice?"

The girl got up, threw me a dark look that suggested that it was all my fault, and then did as she was told. She had to edge by me, and I caught a whiff of petroleum from her tightly combed hair—her mother's attempt to shield her from head lice, I thought.

"Well," said Estelle Audran as soon as the door had closed

behind the girl. "Get to the point. I need to deliver four hundred of these before six o'clock." In demonstration, she lifted the box that she was folding.

I cleared my throat. "I saw in the archives of Public Health and Decency that you were in custody for some months earlier this year."

"Ah, so that's it," she said flatly. "I knew you were here to preach!"

"No," I said. "I would just like to know . . . what happened to you during that time. Did you become pregnant?"

She looked up at me with a bitter gaze while her fingers still worked on as if they were independent organisms that did not require her attention to function.

"How could I have? Or are you suggesting that public servants of the préfecture are fucking the inmates?" She used the word coldly and deliberately, wanting to shock me. But by now I was willing to believe just about anything of the public servants of the préfecture—or at least about some of them.

"Madame," I said, "I just want to help. I know you were subjected to frequent health examinations while you were in custody."

"Every other damned day." Her voice shook a little.

"Would you describe to me what happened during these examinations?"

"No." The word fell bare, cold, and hard, without softening excuses.

"Why not?"

"Because it was bad enough while it was happening. I don't need wallow in it now."

"But . . . it is important."

"To you, perhaps."

"To everyone. So that horrible crimes may be solved and the guilty brought to justice."

She looked very directly at me with yet another hard, dark

gaze. Her heavy features somehow looked middle-aged already, though I knew from her file that she was no more than twenty-nine.

"You can take your big fine justice," she said hoarsely and deliberately, free of her initial attempts to "speak properly," "and you can stick it where your fiancé doesn't normally go. What's all that to me? You come into my home and you think . . . you say you want to help, but *you're* the one asking for help. Something for nothing, that's what you want. Do you think I can afford to give my time away? I lost my place at the tobacco factory, now we only have this, and you can barely pay the rent this way. I have to keep Anette home from school most of the time now. You think I'm going to stick my neck out without a centime for my trouble? Go back where you came from, little miss, and embroider this justice of yours on a pillow with gold thread and chubby little angels, because that's where it belongs. It has nothing to do with the real world."

"If I pay you, your testimony cannot be used in court," I tried to explain.

"Really? Seems to happen pretty often that Simon the Snitch gets five francs from the coppers for framing some poor sod that didn't even do it. But you needn't worry your head about that. I'm not going in any damn court, no matter what you pay me. You think I am telling some judge about what it's like to lie there naked and plucked like a roasting chicken and get their damn *medicine* sprayed right up your mossy? Medicine, *my ass*. They said it was against the whore's pox, but I wasn't sick."

"No. I don't believe you were."

"Stéphanie Margot, she was sick. But they didn't spray anything into her, she just got mercury pills."

She had started to cry. She had learned to do it in the same way as Fleur, it occurred to me—no sobbing, no noise, no attempts to ask for a consolation that would never come anyway. Her hard expression cracked, and she turned her face away.

"Get out," she said, without hostility this time, just with a heavy hopeless slump.

I got up. On the table among all the matchboxes I placed the few francs I had in my purse.

"I am sorry that is all I have," I said.

She did not answer. Her hands folded, glued, bent edges, pasted paper. She had had an abortion, I thought. Somehow she had scraped together enough money to have the unwelcome fetus removed. I found it hard to blame her.

I had three addresses left, but my feet were boiling, and I was fairly sure that I was developing at least two blisters. Besides, I still had the case folder uncomfortably lodged under my corset, simply because I had not found a place where I could fish it out with any degree of discretion. I decided to return home for rest and reconsideration before I went on. My head was buzzing with thoughts and theories, facts and hypotheses grinding against one another in a most disorderly fashion.

When I turned the corner from Rue Perrault, I instantly saw August's automobile, which was parked at the curb outside our house. He had returned! Suddenly, I forgot all about boiling feet, picked up my pace considerably, and noted that I still had sufficient strength to run up the stairs.

"August! I didn't expect . . ."

But the salon was inhabited by a lady I had never seen before. Effortless elegance characterized the slim silhouette, and her afternoon ensemble—lilac silk with abalone buttons—had clearly been chosen to match the striking color of her eyes. Her shining white hair had been arranged as only a very skillful personal maid can do it, and though she was advanced in age, there was still a freshness to her complexion that did not exclusively originate in a powder puff. She rose briskly to her feet when I entered and looked me over in a way that was only slightly less impolite than the gaze of the croissant-crumbling Barbier had been.

"I am afraid my grandson is not coming until later," she said. "I wanted to speak to you alone."

I stopped abruptly with the sensation of having run into a wall.

August's grandmother. The Empress of Heeringen. The woman who had raised him and overseen his education. The woman whose estate he was expected to inherit.

Of course, I knew that I would have to meet her one day. But couldn't it have been on a day when I had not spent several hours searching through dusty document boxes, followed by a wild-goose chase that had taken me from one unsavory back alley to another?

"Madame . . . ," I managed. I was not even sure how to address her. Her name was Constance Heering-Dreyfuss, and she did not, as far as I knew, possess any noble title, just vast resources of wealth. But surely owning an estate like Heeringen made her some sort of lady of the manor? Or a dowager. She certainly looked like a dowager to me. "Welcome. May I offer you . . ." What on earth did we have that I *could* offer? ". . . a glass of sherry, or perhaps a cup of tea?"

"Thank you. Your sweet little maid has already offered, but I am not here to be served. And you may relax, I will soon be leaving."

"Did you drive here yourself?"

She gave me a small tight smile.

"No. But thank you for not assuming that an old woman like myself would be incapable of learning something new. I sent the chauffeur down to the kitchen along with your little maid, so that the two of us may speak undisturbed. So. Do sit down."

We did not *have* a kitchen. Just the laboratory, where I assumed that Elise was even now boiling water on the Bunsen burner so that she could give said chauffeur tea or coffee.

"You and August are to be married, I understand. And he tells

243

me that you still wish to go through with the wedding, perhaps even sooner than you originally intended."

"Yes," I said. Could I perhaps serve myself a glass of sherry? My throat was terribly dry. But that would not do since she did not want any.

"He says you are an extremely intelligent and well-educated young woman."

"Thank you." It was only now that I registered that she was speaking French without a trace of an accent. Better than August, really.

"I am therefore convinced that you will understand what I am about to say," she continued. "*Everything* that I say."

"I hope so, madame."

"I know my grandson, mademoiselle. I have long hoped that he would find a suitable fiancée, but I have also always known that he was—and is—a complicated man. I am glad that you have an understanding of these . . . complications."

There was surely little doubt that Erich Falchenberg was one of the "complications" to which she was referring. I merely nodded.

"You must know as well that he, deprived of the professor's salary that he will now no longer receive, has only limited means."

"That is not why I want to—"

"Nonsense. Let us be practical. It may well be that you can honestly claim to love August dearly, but that is neither here nor there and will not provide you with sufficient income. However, there is no cause for alarm. I will support this marriage, and I have no intention of letting my own flesh and blood suffer in exile as long as I have the means to support you. In return, I have only one demand, but that one demand is not negotiable."

I felt caught by that lilac gaze in much the same way mice are said to react to certain snakes.

"What do you want from me, madame?" I asked, almost as an involuntary reflex.

She sniffed delicately.

"It is very simple. I want heirs."

"Heirs?"

"Yes. As quickly as may be, but I suppose we must give nature the time she requires. Let us say within two years. Then I shall be satisfied."

"But . . ."

"That should not be too difficult, especially not when you really do love my grandson?"

I was on my feet, boiling with indignation. Had the entire world entered into a conspiracy to transform me into a glorified broodmare?

"You are right," I said. "I love August. For better or worse. And we will manage. But we alone, he and I, will decide whether we are going to have children!"

She stiffened, but only a fraction. The lilac eyes narrowed infinitesimally.

"Come now, child. If you wish, I shall be happy to raise the child at Heeringen. Good nursemaids, the best teachers. A year of your life, that is all I ask for—nine months in the womb, three months nursing at your breast for the sake of the child's health. Surely you can indulge an old woman in that small respect?"

"I have no wish to discuss—"

"Very well. I shall hire a wet nurse. The only thing you need to do is bring the child into the world."

"That is not—"

"Is it the act itself that bothers you?"

"No! I—"

"Aha!" Her face lit up, and she too rose from her chair. She observed my face intensely, and to my great humiliation, I could feel that damnable blush spreading in my cheeks. "I can see you have already . . . with August? Yes, indeed. Well, then, so much the better!" Her eyes were not merely alight, they shone in triumph.

Apparently she possessed the ability to look right through me, at least in this respect. "Then I need hardly interfere. Au revoir, mademoiselle. A pleasure to meet you."

With the air of a field marshal returning in triumph, she prepared to leave. She did not attempt to shake my hand—she probably knew I would not let her. Instead she opened the door and called down the stairs with a stentorian voice that seemed considerably less elegant and femininely refined than the rest of her.

"Karl! We are leaving!"

There were noises from below, and a young man wearing a uniform consisting of a jacket, riding boots, and cap came clattering up the stairs to offer her his arm.

She turned in the doorway while I was still standing there as if nailed to the floor, filled with equal parts shame and indignation.

"Within two years, mademoiselle!" she said. "Get to it!"

When August arrived—quite late, it was almost ten o'clock—I was sitting in my nightgown and robe, with my feet in a basin of water and my wet hair spread across my shoulders. I had not expected to see him; at this late hour he would normally have gone directly to his lodgings with Madame Guille.

"I am sorry to come so late," he said, and threw a frankly lingering gaze at my extremely informal state of dress. I did not feel particularly ready to be so viewed. Because of the footbath I could not even get up and come to meet him—or flee up the stairs to dress myself more appropriately.

"I had to go to Strasbourg for the train, Grandmama had taken the automobile . . ."

"I know," I said heavily.

"You know . . . ?" He looked at me again, this time more at my face than at my body. Then he cursed. "She came here."

"Yes."

"With her mad talk of heirs and money."

"Precisely."

He smacked his hand down on the back of one of the arm-chairs.

"I told her not to." His voice was raw with anger. "Madeleine, I am so sorry. She is an old woman who is used to getting her own way, and she . . . she can be alarmingly practical."

"I noticed. She even offered to hire a wet nurse so that all I would need to do was lend a womb for nine months."

"Madeleine! She didn't say that." He paused. "Yes, of course she did . . ." He took my right hand in both of his. "It was in much the same way that she ended up being responsible for raising me. But I can see you survived the battle."

"I am not so sure about that," I said darkly. "It feels as if she won the first skirmish."

"How so?" His eyes fell on my other hand, the left, which had slipped down without my conscious notice and had placed itself against my abdomen just below the navel. Exactly where Porro would have begun his incision, I thought, and snatched it away. "Do you think that you are already—?"

"No," I said firmly and hoped that it was true. "But I will be if we . . . continue."

"There are methods . . ."

"None certain."

"Perhaps not. But would it be so terrible if . . . ? Grandmama has offered to raise it. You would be able to continue your studies, your work . . ."

I pulled my right hand from his grasp.

"That woman," I said with a rage that surprised us both, "that woman is *not* going to raise my child!"

He looked at me searchingly.

"She raised me," he said.

I think August was relieved that Papa was still at the hospital. My father had not exactly reached for his riding crop—not that he owned one—and chased my future husband out the door, but the natural friendship and mutual enthusiasm that had characterized their relationship from the very beginning had stiffened into long pauses, averted gazes, and backs held a bit too straight.

Elise brought out a bit of bread and cheese, and I watched him while he ate. His exhaustion was visible in every move, and I doubted that he had had much sleep in the past few days.

"How are you?" I asked at last.

He stretched and brushed a few crumbs from his chin.

"Not too bad," he said ironically. "*Pas trop mal.*" We almost always spoke French when we were together, though my German was probably almost as good as his French. "It has been a couple of . . . challenging days."

"Is there anything new from Heidelberg?"

"What news would there be? That the police have withdrawn the case, that the university has changed its mind, and that I am not, after all, unemployed and considered a criminal in my own country?" He spoke a little too fast and stumbled over some of the syllables, and for once I felt as if he was condescending to me—as if I was young and silly and naïve to even ask. Then he caught himself. "No, I'm sorry. None of this is your fault. But there is nothing remotely encouraging to say about the situation in Heidelberg. It will only get worse from now on—more friends distancing themselves, more accusations, more gossip."

"More accusations? Do you mean in addition to Falchenberg?"

He sighed so deeply that it was more of a moan. "Are you sure you want to know?"

"The truth, August!"

"Yes. That was a part of our agreement. So. Yes, there have been others. Not many, but it has happened before. I am thirty-four years old, Madeleine, and no monk."

"Women or men?"

"Both. Have pity, Madeleine. I solemnly promise to tell you everything you want to know, but . . . not tonight."

Something moved in his face, and I think he felt so hounded and exhausted that there were tears in his eyes. I could not be certain because he looked away.

There was an intimacy to sitting here that was not sensuous: his late supper, my state of dress or lack thereof—I had replaced the robe with one of my loose morning gowns and pinned up my wet hair but was still not what anyone would call presentable. It was like a taste of the casual daily companionship that would be part of being husband and wife, I thought.

"I want to hear about it one day," I said. "But you are right, it need not be now." After a brief hesitation, I reached across the table and placed my hand on his. I had not been raised with much physical intimacy, especially not after my mother died, and perhaps he had not either, because he jerked when our hands met. He did not pull away, but it felt a little stiff nonetheless. After a few moments, I withdrew my hand myself.

He looked up. "Thank you," he said. "You have no idea what an infinite relief it is to sit here, even though I lack the strength to discuss it."

"Do you want to hear what happened while you were away?" I asked.

"Beyond my grandmother's incomparable campaign? Yes. Please."

I told him about Althauser and the Pro Patria lecture. I even somehow managed to describe my embarrassing selection as the "foremother of the nation's future elite." I tried to present as concisely as possible what I had found in the commission's

249

archives and what Estelle Audran had said. He listened with interest.

"Do you think they have developed a new way of treating syphilis?" he asked.

"No," I said simply. "Althauser is not even a doctor of medicine. He is not particularly interested in curing diseases."

"Then what is your thesis?"

I shook my head in frustration. "I don't know if this is completely mad. But . . . I am fairly confident that Althauser, with the support of Pro Patria, is trying to develop techniques that can increase the birthrate."

"He did say that himself," August pointed out. "These new incubators—was that not what they were to be used for? To ensure that more children survive?"

"Yes, but that is still only a small number. I think they are attacking the problem in more drastic ways, or at least that they are preparing to do so."

"How so?"

"I think Althauser is experimenting with human insemination. Syphilis treatments do not make you pregnant."

He was six years old when he realized that his mother was not his mother.

They had recently moved into the house on Boulevard Saint-Augustine. His father had his practice on the ground floor in the early years, and Adrian was not allowed there. He had his own room in the nursery on the third floor, with Grandmama and Emmeline, who took care of him. He usually came down to the salons on the second floor for only a few hours in the afternoon if Mama was well enough and did not have visitors, and for a half hour in the evening before bedtime.

He loved Mama and Papa, of course, but he worshipped Emmeline. She was the one who dressed him in the morning, gave him his breakfast, accompanied him to his lessons at Maître Robert—he was not yet "mature" enough to go to the Benedictine brothers, said Mama—played with him in the park, bathed him before dinner; she was the one who said his evening prayers with him and put him to bed. Mama's health was delicate, and so was his, he was told. He was not quite sure what it meant, except that he was not allowed to play with the other boys in the park because they were "too wild," and that it also, in some way, meant that Maître Robert was a more suitable teacher than the brothers. That, and the monthly examinations with Papa.

They always took place in the evening, in the surgery, once all the patients had gone home. Papa's patients were mostly ladies. And that was a bit odd, really, since Papa's specialty was "pulmonary and respiratory complaints," and Adrian knew that was about breathing, and didn't men do that too? Rarely in Papa's surgery, it would seem.

First, Emmeline gave him his bath. That was his favorite thing in the world, because when she was bathing him, she took off her black blouse before tying her apron back on over her chemise so that you could see her soft white arms and the top of her round breasts. They were so fine, her breasts. Much better than Mama's. Or he imagined so. He had never seen Mama's. Perhaps she did not have any. In any case, it was Emmeline who had nursed him when he was a baby, she had told him that herself. "You lay right here," she said, taking him into her arms and rocking him playfully, "when you were a tiny little *bébé*." She always made sure the water was exactly the right temperature—steaming hot but not scalding. Sometimes, when she was in an especially good mood, they splashed each other, and she ended up getting almost as wet as he did. He loved her scent, the heat of the water, the sensation of being safe and clean and loved, because he was completely sure that Emmeline loved him. She said it herself, at least eight times a day. But when he was going down to Papa, she was serious, and then there was no splashing. He was dressed in his nightshirt, but no underwear or stockings. When he was younger, Emmeline had carried him downstairs; now he was old enough to put on his green felt slippers and go downstairs on his own.

Papa would be waiting below. Two lamps were lit, the one by the desk and the one above the examination couch.

"Good evening, my boy," Papa always said. "Let us see how you are doing."

Then he had to take off his shirt and lie down on the clean, soap-scented sheet on the couch. With his thumb and index finger, Papa opened wide first Adrian's left eye and then the right. He looked in his ears. Adrian had to open his mouth so that Papa could depress his tongue and look into his throat. Papa felt his neck and tapped his chest, squeezed his stomach, lifted up his little pee-pee and examined it, listened to his lungs both in front and in the back, and when it was all over, Adrian was given a caramel.

Adrian liked the examinations. There was something solemn and important about them, and they proved that Papa too cared for him and was concerned about his well-being. And afterward they would go upstairs to Mama, who was waiting in the salon.

"Well?" she said, and looked at Papa with an anxious gaze.

"He is a big, fine, healthy boy," Papa would say, and then Mama was happy.

But then one day. One evening. A few weeks before he turned seven. Emmeline had said he should wait, but he was a big boy now, he did not have to wait for her to give him permission. He could do it himself. So he crept down the servants' stairs to the surgery. The door was ajar, and Papa was in there, but he was not alone. The angry voices reached Adrian as he was making his way down the last steps and made him stop at the door.

"Here," Papa snarled in a tone of voice Adrian had never heard him use before, "you may have some mercury tablets. But this is the last time, is that clear? You'll have to go to the pharmacy like other people. I cannot help you anymore."

Papa stood behind his desk, and on the other side of it sat a woman Adrian did not know. She was wearing a very fancy shiny red dress, with a black cape on top, and her dark hair was piled under a black hat with a veil and black ostrich feathers. Her clothes were much fancier than Mama's and the ladies who visited her, thought Adrian. And you could see her breasts, or quite a lot of them, anyway.

"You don't care," said the lady. "I'm rotting up, and you don't care."

"What do you want me to do? If you want more money, then—"

"Money! You think everything can be bought. Do you know what you are? You're a bigger whore than I am!"

"Suzette! That's enough!"

There was something odd about the way the lady was speaking, Adrian noted. The words were thick and strange, as if she was drooling and bubbling like the snotty-nosed little *bébés* in perambulators that Emmeline insisted on admiring in the park.

At this point, Adrian was still more curious than afraid, so he took a step forward in order to see better.

Papa had his back turned, but the lady noticed him at once. She rose and came over to him.

"There we have him," she said. "What a fine boy he is!"

Adrian smiled uncertainly.

His father turned abruptly. "Adrian. Go upstairs. Now!"

But the lady had already reached him. She grabbed him around the waist with her gloved hands—the scarlet gloves were really quite dirty, Adrian noticed—and pulled him up into her arms. He caught a glimpse of her breasts quite close up—they were not nearly as nice as Emmeline's, but strangely wrinkled and covered with brown spots under the layer of powder—and then she hugged him so tightly to her that he could not see anything except her hair and one ear.

The stench hit him like a fist. Nasty. Rotten. Sickly sweet. It was made up of several things, of sweat and perfume and something that smelled a little like a mixture of onion and pee but wasn't either. But the stench of rotten meat was the worst and most overpowering. He had once found a dead blackbird in the park and picked it up, and it was not until afterward that he discovered that it was full of maggots and smelled really nasty. Emmeline had scolded him and said he was never to touch dead animals, and when they got home, she washed his hands with an ugly green soap that stung and was not nearly as pleasant as the one she usually used. The lady smelled just like the blackbird, only worse.

"Put him down!" yelled Papa. "Suzette, in God's name. Put him down!"

"Why?" The lady was almost as loud. "Isn't he my flesh and blood? I should never have let you take him. Every single day I have regretted it." And then the lady began to cry, with hoarse, thick snuffles, while Adrian squirmed to get free and wondered what it meant, that part about flesh and blood.

There was a crack like a branch breaking. Adrian fell because the lady fell. Papa had hit her with his cane. He was still waving it.

"Get out of here," he hissed. "If I ever see you here again, I'll sic the police on you. You are to have nothing to do with us anymore, don't you understand that?"

Adrian rolled to the side a bit to get away from the lady. His mouth hurt, and when he spat there were tiny droplets of blood in his saliva. Later, he discovered that his first baby tooth had been knocked out.

The lady sat up. The blow had dislodged her hat and veil, and for the first time, he could see her face. She had no nose. Her mouth was no mouth but just a hole, and the rest of her skin was a bubbling cratered wasteland of oozing black, pink, and yellow sores. One eye was completely closed by a boil, the other glinted at him, dark and wet and almost more frightening because it could see.

She was no lady. She was a monster.

And the monster opened its black maw and said, "How can you say that? I'm his mother!"

The next day, Emmeline packed her things. She cried and cried and said she would come and visit him very often, but she never did. The last he saw of her was the back of her jacket and bonnet on the seat next to the coachman. She turned around only once, and though he waved, he did not think she saw him, because she did not wave back.

It was hard to say his evening prayers without Emmeline. All he could think to ask the Lord was to please give him Emmeline back, but apparently the Lord wouldn't, not even though Adrian promised to be good for the rest of his life.

The following weeks he became aware of several things. Emmeline had been fired because of him—because he had gone down the stairs by himself even though she had said to wait. He also discovered that the monster had told the truth. His new nurse told him so. Her name was Nanette, and she was nothing like Emmeline. In all the places where Emmeline had been soft, she was hard. She had hard hands and thick nails and eyes that saw everything. She pushed and probed and dug out every secret, big or small. It did not take long for everyone in the house to be more or less afraid of her—even his father. She said she collected truths. And one of the truths Nanette quickly had seized on was this: The monster lady with the black maw was Adrian's mother. Adrian's father was Adrian's father, even if he was married to Mama and not to the monster lady. The monster lady was sick.

And perhaps Adrian was as well, and that was why Papa examined him so often. The monster lady had infected him while he lived inside her belly.

No one outside the house must know any of this. Adrian wasn't actually supposed to know either.

He had lost his first baby tooth, and he no longer believed that the Lord was merciful and just, or that He was the God of Light and Truth. Nanette taught him something new about truths. They were usually horrible and dark, but they were valuable, and they were everywhere. If you listened at the doors, if you hid under a table, if you found a letter or heard a rumor . . . She rewarded him every time he brought her something she did not already know. He still missed Emmeline, but in time he got used to doing without her. And once he himself had found an amazing little black pearl of truth about Nanette, she more or less let him do as he wanted. He was no longer anyone's little boy.

Nothing, thought Adrian, was so black that one could not turn it to one's purpose. It was better to know the awful truth and walk through the world with wide-open, seeing eyes than to live blind and deaf, like a dolt and a fool.

October 2, 1894

Althauser lived in a fashionable new apartment building on Rue Faubourg within comfortable walking distance of the university. His housekeeper let us in and asked us to wait in what she called the study. Others might have used the room as a salon, but "others" would probably not have been able to fill quite so many bookshelves.

Inspector Marot had noted the immaculate exterior, the black wrought-iron fence, the shiny brass door knocker, the elegant hallway. Now he looked around at the wealth of primarily professional and academic works arranged carefully and systematically on the mahogany shelves around us.

"Madeleine, are you sure?" he asked, and patted down one of his spit curls with an unconscious gesture I knew to be a nervous tic.

"We're not here to arrest him," I said. "Just to ask him a few polite questions."

At that moment, the door opened, and Althauser entered the room. He seemed entirely himself as I knew him from the university—correctly and carefully dressed without being conspicuously elegant, his face arranged in a dispassionate expression devoid of any trace of unease or curiosity. I could not even claim that the bulldog gaze rested on me with greater acidity than usual.

"Inspector. Mademoiselle Karno. To what do I owe the honor?"

"Thank you for seeing us," said Marot. "We are hopeful that you will be able to help us clarify certain aspects of a case we are currently investigating."

"We, Mr. Inspector? Should I interpret this to mean that

Mademoiselle Karno is now working for the police forces of Varbourg? The young lady demonstrates an alarming versatility."

"Mademoiselle Karno is here in a ... consultant capacity," said Marot. He himself had insisted that I should come. If I really wished to have a respected university lecturer questioned about "such things"—by this he meant the inseminations—then I had to be there to present the details. *He* certainly wasn't going to.

"I see. Well, with such excellent help"—a definite rise in acidity levels at last—"how is it you think I may be of service?"

Inspector Marot's left hand crept up to slick down an already perfectly positioned curl. But he stuck to his guns.

"On the thirteenth of January this year, a young woman by the name of Rosalba Lombardi was arrested and taken into custodial quarantine."

I was observing Althauser's expression minutely when Rosalba's name was mentioned. He did not bat an eyelid.

"That is as it may be. It is hardly my concern."

"You signed both the Public Health and Decency report that was the basis of the custodial sentence and the release papers three months later. How did that come about, monsieur? Is that not normally done by one of the commission's own doctors?"

Althauser did not alter his expression by a hair.

"I would imagine so. You probably know that better than I. The commission has generously permitted me to use these routine health examinations as a part of my research. If you say that this Mademoiselle Lombardi was one of the women examined, no doubt you are right."

"So you admit that Mademoiselle Lombardi was a part of this ... research project?" Marot pressed his advantage.

"I believe I have just said as much."

"What was the object of this experiment?"

"To develop a better and more effective way of treating syphilis."

"Can you describe the experimental treatment?"

"If it really interests you. I assume you know that syphilis in its first stage presents itself as nonirritant eczema lesions in the genital region?"

Marot grunted something that was construable as a yes.

"In women, such lesions often occur in the actual vagina and thus go undetected. Since they are neither painful nor itchy, the patient is completely unaware that she has them, but their existence is a source of infection for everyone who has intimate contact with her. The commission insists on regular examinations in order to ensure that prostitutes do not spread the disease, but at the moment we have no truly effective treatment. Mercury has been tried for several hundred years, with very limited results and several unpleasant side effects. However, I have developed a preparation that I hope will change that situation."

"And how . . . do you make use of this preparation?"

"It is applied to the infected areas. In women, this is accomplished by means of a vaginal spray that I have also developed."

"What are the . . . er, ingredients of this new wonder drug?"

"Mr. Inspector, that hardly has any bearing on your investigation. Let it be my little secret for the time being. The preparation has not yet been patented."

Marot sent a pleading gaze in my direction. I took a deep breath and placed Rosalba's file on the table. Althauser visibly started—the first reaction he had shown until now.

"As far as I can see," I said, "the result you were waiting for when you wrote this was not a cure for syphilis—a disease that we know from the autopsy that Rosalba Lombardi did not even have—but a quite different condition, noted here as *gravida*. The fluid you so carefully introduced into her vagina every other day for an entire month was not a preparation against syphilis, patented or otherwise, but something much more ordinary: male semen. Do you deny that?"

He raised a cushioning hand to his cheek, as if he had suddenly developed a toothache. Then he shook his head.

"You might have become a useful research assistant, mademoiselle, if you only had managed to liberate yourself from certain female weaknesses. You are right. It was not syphilis treatment we were experimenting with. But you also know the ultimate goal of our efforts—to save the nation from a threatening crisis. Inspector, this is an effort that is supported directly by the French state and by several prominent men from Varonne's more visionary elite. But the project is extremely confidential, and I myself have been sworn to secrecy. I hope I can rely on your discretion?"

"Of course," Marot answered automatically.

I cursed inwardly.

"Rosalba Lombardi is dead," I said. "As is her friend, Fleur Petit. If you are behind these killings, no vow of silence can save you, national crisis or not!"

Marot placed a warning hand on my arm, but it was too late. The words hung in the air. I had said them even though I had promised I would not.

"Mademoiselle. What is it you imagine I have done?"

There was no way back now. With a sensation of throwing myself into free fall, I attempted to present my dawning suspicions as if they were a fully consistent explanation for the two deaths.

"You attempted to remove Rosalba's fetus and uterus with the aid of Porro's procedure. You failed, and Rosalba bled to death. Thereafter you attempted to camouflage the procedure by making it look like the murder of Eugénie Colombe, then prominent in the headlines of our newspapers. And when Fleur discovered that you were behind it, you killed her and tried to mislead the police by using the same method a second time."

"I see," he said. "So I am supposed to be a simple murderer now? Is that what you believe?"

"Rosalba's death was not a murder, but Fleur's was!"

"Well, then you had better arrest me," he said calmly to Marot.

Marot cleared his throat. "Do you confess . . . ?"

"Of course not. But Mademoiselle Karno is not concerned with proof, testimonies, or confessions. She has already found the answer she wants, and nothing can shift her from her conviction. However, before we move on to summary justice and arrests, might I perhaps be permitted to ask when this murder of . . . what did you say her name was? Fleur Petit? . . . when this murder took place?"

Marot consulted his notes. "According to the autopsy, she died Friday evening, between six and ten. Where were you then, monsieur?"

An almost jovial smile lit up Althauser's heavy bulldog features. "Why, Mademoiselle Karno herself can answer that. She was there."

It was not until he said it that I realized what should have been obvious to me from the beginning. Althauser could not have killed Fleur. At the time of her murder, he had been in the rostrum of the Brotherhood of Freedom's Grand Hall, telling several hundred people about the threat against the future of France.

He was entirely correct. I had been there myself.

"It is probably best if I return this to its proper place," Althauser said, and took Rosalba's file from my numb hands. "I have a suspicion that Mademoiselle Karno did not receive the commission's permission to take it."

How could it happen? How on earth could I have made such an obvious mistake? I might have discovered my error, or not made it at all, had I been the one to perform the calculations and state the time of death. But thanks to my demonstration of feminine sensitivity down by the riverbank, my father had conducted the autopsy alone and had sent me home with Marie instead. Someone else, probably one of the morgue assistants, had been obliged to try to make sense of my father's notes for the report.

Marot escorted me out into the waiting hansom cab in silence and told the driver to take me home to Carmelite Street. I was clearly in the doghouse, and with good reason.

The house was empty. Elise must be out running errands or perhaps at home with her mother. I thought about visiting August's lodgings, but right now I would have found it difficult to look him in the eye. He considered me an intelligent person. I did not wish to lose that respect.

I went up to my room and sat in front of the mirror to loosen a couple of hairpins that were hurting my scalp. I had circles under my eyes, I observed. And felt sick.

Nausea. Still no menses. Gravida.

No. It was exhaustion. My monthly periods were often irregular. This meant nothing.

I lay down on the bed, still fully corseted, with the intention of resting for a moment. Instead, I fell into a deep sleep and did not wake until several hours later.

Someone was knocking on our front door. And the house was still silent—there was no Elise to open it.

I got up, considerably refreshed but still a bit fuzzy and with the disoriented sensation that often bothers me if I sleep during the daytime. On the steps stood a boy with slicked-back hair, unusually pale, and dressed in a suit that, in a slightly larger size, could have belonged to an undertaker or a bank clerk. It took me a moment to recognize him. It was Bruno, Aristide Gilbert's little laboratory assistant.

"Mademoiselle?" he said. "I have a letter for you."

He handed it to me. The hand that held it was shaking.

"Are you ill?" I asked. "Is something wrong?"

He shook his head.

"Read it," he said.

It seemed to me that the seal was a bit on the loose side. One might think the envelope had been opened and closed again—to judge from the way the paper was buckling from copious application of fresh saliva.

Dear Mademoiselle Karno,

You once showed me exceptional lenience. As I turn to you now, it is not in the hope of forgiveness, for such does not exist for someone like me, but with the plea that you will do what is in your power to see justice fully done. The poor little girl, I see her before me night and day. I thought the water would be kinder than the other thing, I thought she would be fulfilled as my poor Alice was, but it seems not all women are like that. I had no idea. I had no idea she would fight like that. And I am a monster, a coward, a sinner so great that not even God can forgive

The letter stopped abruptly midsentence. It was not signed, and I did not recognize the handwriting, but because Bruno had brought it, I must assume that Gilbert had written it.

I stared at the words. *The poor little girl . . . I thought the water would be kinder . . . I had no idea she would fight like that.*

I did not know who "poor Alice" was, but "the poor little girl" . . . could it be Fleur?

"Won't you come?" said Bruno, who looked as if he wanted to grab my skirts and drag me off there and then. "Please won't you, mademoiselle?"

At first glance, there was no one in the atelier. It occurred to me—belatedly—that if the letter meant what I thought it did, I should have brought Marot along, or at least have fetched the policeman who directed traffic on nearby Place Picault. There was a heavy smell of absinthe and vomit, but no visible signs of either bottle or regurgitated alcohol. The stuffed dog was staring into the distance with its squinting glass-bead eyes, and the potted plants looked so mummified that they were probably beyond salvation.

"Monsieur Gilbert?" I called out, without much hope.

"The darkroom," whispered Bruno. "He is . . . maybe he is in the darkroom."

The door was ajar, so if he was there, he should have been able to hear us. On the other hand, there was such despair in the brief letter that it made me assume the worst.

I pushed open the door. The room was surprisingly large but, of course, it had no window. I could not see very much, but there was a bulb hanging from the ceiling, the kind that is usually turned on by pulling a chain. I located the chain and pulled. The bulb did give off light—not white or yellow, however, but red, which gave everything an unreal glow, as if part of some distorted nightmare.

Along the back wall was a zinc-lined wooden tub. I was not sufficiently familiar with photographic processes to know whether it belonged to the darkroom's inventory, or whether it was there just because the room was an old bathroom, but I suspected the latter. It was, in any case, large enough to hold a human body, and I would have thought such volume was excessive if all one wanted to do was expose photographic plates the size of a book or a postcard.

The bathtub was full. A pair of fully dressed male legs were dangling over the rim. When I took a few steps farther into the room, it was no longer any great surprise that the rest of Aristide Gilbert was lying on his back on the bottom, staring up at me with eyes as huge, blank, and dead as those of a cod on a fishmonger's slab.

On the 27th April, 1890, two ova were obtained from an Angora doe rabbit which had been fertilised by an Angora buck thirty-two hours previously; the ova were undergoing segmentation, being divided into four segments.

These ova were immediately transferred into the upper end of the fallopian tube of a Belgian hare doe rabbit which had been fertilised three hours before by a buck of the same breed as herself.

It may be well to mention here, I bought this Belgian hare doe some three months before; the man from whom I bought her bred her, and guaranteed her to be a virgin doe of about seven months old. During the time I had her, until the 27th of April, she had never been covered by a buck of any breed, kept always isolated from the various bucks in my rabbitry.

In due course this Belgian hare doe gave birth to six young—four of these resembled herself and her mate, while two of them were undoubted Angoras. The Angora young were characterised by the possession of the long silky hair peculiar to the breed, and were true albinoes, like their Angora parents. Both presumed Angora offspring were males.

—WALTER HEAPE ON HIS FIRST SUCCESSFUL EGG
TRANSPLANT, 1890

October 3, 1894

They lay side by side, the murderer and his victim. The morgue made no distinctions. In death there was no barrier between them, unless one counts the sheets with which the naked bodies were covered. There were married couples who never came closer to each other than these two.

I could not make it fit, and yet it fit as a key fits its keyhole. Under her shredded, broken nails were the remains of his skin. On his arms and neck were scratches she had made in her mortal struggle. I had to believe it *was* Aristide Gilbert that Fleur had seen with her wide-open eyes.

But why?

I had known Aristide Gilbert for years. He was a quiet, melancholy man, and if I had been called to comment on his ability to murder another human being, I would have said that he could not hurt a fly. Now he was lying here, and Police Inspector Marot had already completed a report that said he had killed and disfigured at least three women. The proof included a scalpel still marked with traces of blood, as well as two thick leather-bound portfolios found in the search of his studio. Here he had hidden, so it seemed, every single photograph he had taken of a dead woman during the past five years. I had seen those portfolios, and it was like paging through a catalog of the dead of Varbourg, or at least those dead who were female. I knew a number of them because I had taken part in their autopsies.

Only a small portion of them were police photographs. As Gilbert had remarked himself, there were not enough crimes committed in Varbourg to supply his needs. Instead he had made use of his access to the morgue and the Commissioner's archive, it turned out, and had sought out the survivors with a handsome offer. For a very modest price he would take one last picture of their deceased relative. I had read some of the witness reports as well.

"He was very polite and kind," said a mother whose daughter had died in an accident at the textile factory. "He asked us what she was like, what sort of things she liked . . . and the picture . . . the picture turned out to be so beautiful. You can't even tell that she is dead."

It was almost true. Perhaps Aristide Gilbert had never been very good at portraying the living, but it was only because they did not interest him. He had reserved all his compassion, insight, and imagination for his preservation of the dead. He had dressed them in the clothes they liked best; they were surrounded by people and things they had cared about; for their sake he worked with light and shadow until the tender portrait took on the life the subject no longer possessed.

There were more than a hundred of them. Even for someone like me who was used to death in all its forms, it was strange to see so many lifeless faces all at once. The oddest pictures, however, were the first three. They were close-ups. A young woman lying with closed eyes, slightly parted lips, and her head at an angle. Normally with the dead that would mean that the features collapsed, that flesh and skin fell away from the bones because there was no longer any elasticity in tissue and muscle. Some undertakers place small amounts of wax in the nostrils and mouth to remedy this phenomenon and make the deceased look more like their living countenance, and perhaps Gilbert had done the same thing, but in addition this woman was half immersed in dark, shimmering water, which returned to her some of the buoyancy she had had in life. Her blond hair was loose and billowed around her head so that she looked like a sleeping mermaid. It was poetic and bizarre, living and dead at the same time, and in all ways a portrait I would have a hard time forgetting.

The picture of Rosalba was equally unforgettable. It was not one of the raw, unvarnished police photographs—Gilbert had not saved any of those, at least not in these portfolios. She too was lying down, with her head turned slightly to the left, in much the same position as the mermaid. Her hair was arranged decoratively around her head, and beneath her one could make out the gleaming thick folds of some silky fabric that, with their wavelike contours, created a further similarity with the mermaid pictures.

Yes, I realized. Of course he had used wax, like the undertakers. I had found traces of it in Rosalba's mouth and had wondered about its source. Not cheese rinds, as I had once speculated. It was simply what remained of Gilbert's attempt to make her look alive.

This picture was proof; I had to acknowledge that. There was no possible way he could have taken it unless he had been present between the moment of death and the moment of discovery. He had not had access to the corpse afterward.

There were no pictures of Fleur. Not even the pictures I had seen him take that morning on the riverbank.

Aristide Gilbert had drowned as well—of that there was little doubt. We found foam in his mouth and water in his lungs. When he went underwater in the bathtub, he had still been able to breathe. In his stomach sloshed most of the bottle of absinthe I had found on the floor of the darkroom. This, with the letter, made it easy to imagine he had climbed into the tub and drunk himself unconscious, well aware that there was a high risk, perhaps almost a certainty in this helpless condition, that he would drown.

"I've seen it before," said the Commissioner. "In a judicial and religious sense it isn't suicide but rather death by misadventure, which at least provides the bereaved relatives with a more palatable conclusion to the case, whether it is an insurance settlement or simply a Catholic burial that is at stake."

Aristide Gilbert seemed to me to be a man with a startling lack of loved ones.

"Did he have a life insurance policy?" I asked.

"I have no idea," said the Commissioner. "It was meant as an example."

"But why . . . with all his clothes on?"

"To maintain a bit of dignity in death? Many suicides dress themselves in their best, after all."

This was true; I had seen more examples than I cared to think about.

The proof was there. The key fit the lock. I just did not understand why.

"Maddie?" said my father. "Let us leave. There is nothing more we can do."

"You go ahead," I said. "I'll just clean up."

The Commissioner and my father exchanged a brief look.

"Jean-Baptiste can do that," said the Commissioner.

"I would prefer to do it myself. Then I know where everything is. I might as well enter the notes in the records at once."

"Is there such a rush?"

"Papa. I would like to be alone a little."

He raised his hand in a halfhearted farewell gesture.

"You are a grown woman now. Engaged, even. You can come and go as you wish."

"Thank you," I said, though it struck me that it was neither my work here nor my acceptance at the university that had made him consider me a "grown woman." It was my upcoming marriage.

They left and let me be alone without further objections. In the doorway, the Commissioner turned one last time.

"Dear Madeleine," he said quietly. "Everyone makes mistakes."

I lit candles for Fleur just as I had for Rosalba. I recalled how she had thanked me for that. Then I sat next to the bier in the glow of the candles and read the autopsy report that I had not had any part in. For each point, I examined as far as was possible whether the reality matched the words. I looked at all the tests and at the organs that had been removed. I even cut the stitches with which the abdominal incisions had been closed, so that I could make sure that nothing had been overlooked. Some might think this an insult to her memory. For me, it was the opposite—a memorial service, an almost holy duty, and one last attempt to keep the promise I had made to her.

In this way, I collected a list of points that seemed to me anomalies not sufficiently explained. It is often like that—we do not always know why the deceased has a bruise on her hip or has been in the proximity of something that left a tar-like stain on his left palm. Life marks our bodies constantly, small accidental occurrences that become interesting only because death chose to stop the process on a particular day so that the bruise never healed, and the traces of tar on the palm were not worn off in time. Even in the case of a homicide, not all marks and traces are connected to the murder.

As far as Fleur's corpse was concerned, I noted the following:

She was considerably undernourished and dehydrated. Both the stomach and intestines were empty, and there were many indications that she had not had sufficient fluids. Her lips were cracked, and lividity spots were not as prominent as they would normally be—in a dehydrated body the blood does not pool quite the way it normally does in the lower tissues. The kidneys were yellowish, the bladder affected; nor did the liver have the weight and water content one would expect. She had clearly been drowned, and yet she had at the same time been dying of thirst. The irony was painful.

She had a large number of scratches and bruises both on

her hands and knees. The tissue along the edge of her hand and little finger was damaged to such an extent that it might best be described as crushed, the knuckles on both hands were skinned and in some cases fractured. Back on the riverbank where we found her, I had already noted that she had fought for her life, but some of these bruises had occurred earlier and had had time to begin to heal. The oldest she had received several days before her death, and probably not from hitting Aristide Gilbert. He had some scratches and the odd bruise, but no lesions that matched the power of desperation Fleur must have had to hammer her hand so hard against someone or something that it fractured. Further, at the time of her death, she must have been considerably weakened from the dehydration and no longer capable of inflicting such great damage on herself. In any case, I did not think the object of her blows had been anything as soft and yielding as a human body. One might certainly break a knuckle if one struck something hard like the jawbone or the skull with sufficient force, but the pulping along the edge of her hand had required something more solid—a wall, a door, a floor, something that did not yield at all and thus transferred the full power of the blow to the tissue instead.

The last thing I noted was significant amounts of dirt under Fleur's broken nails and in the half-healed scabs on her hands. On her knees too were dark patches where this same grime—a mixture of blood, earth, and coal dust—had become so ingrained that not even the river had been able to wash it away.

Fleur's undernourished condition was not in itself so surprising. On the day I had seen her for the last time, she had already seemed thinner and weaker than she ought to be, as if Rosalba's passing had robbed her of her interest in food. But it is extremely rare for someone thirsty and dehydrated to the point of death to *not drink*—if that option still exists.

A place began to appear before my inner eye. A place without windows, a place with walls and doors against which one might shatter one's hands without being heard, without being released. A place where the floor was earthen and the walls of stone, and both were black with coal dust and dirt. A cellar. Perhaps a coal cellar.

Several of the unanswered questions raised by Rosalba's death concerned the place where she had been found. Why leave her like that, in the coal merchant's backyard in Rue Colbert? How had her assailant been able to bring her there without being seen? I remembered the curious men, women, and children leaning over the window ledges in the yard like spectators from theater balconies, eager to take it all in. Even on an ordinary night it would be difficult to come and go unobserved in Rue Colbert, and this had not been an ordinary night. The president had been murdered, and the streets had been full of alert, angry, and frightened people. And for every person on the street there had to have been at least two sitting in the windows following what was going on.

Yet still no one had seen a thing. Marot's men had gone door-to-door, and while this was not a neighborhood where people fell over themselves to help the police, it was nevertheless remarkable that this heroic effort had not turned up a single witness.

But Rosalba's hands had been clean and whole. Even her feet had been unblemished. The contents of her stomach had been negligible, and she would had to have been fasting for about twelve hours preceding her death, but she had not been dehydrated. I could not at present connect her fate to Fleur's and that grimy and merciless prison I had built in my mind from the clues Fleur's silent and lifeless body had offered me.

The facts first. Then the conclusion.

Had I learned nothing from my ignominious mistake?

Still. Still I could not shake off the assumption that there *was* such a room, and that it was located in the immediate vicinity of the coal merchant's yard.

I gathered my notes on Fleur and added those my father had made during the autopsy of Aristide Gilbert. I had meant to make a fair copy of them and bring the records up-to-date, but I simply could not concentrate on them right now; I would have to do it later. I placed both in my bag to bring with me when I left.

I covered Fleur's tiny battered body with the shroud and tied a new piece of gauze around her jaw to keep it in place. I could not bring myself to blow out the candles.

There was nothing in that cold room that would let them start a fire. Let them burn out on their own, I thought, and quietly closed the door behind me.

It was evening when I left the morgue. The streets were busy, as many people were on their way home from work, while others were heading for restaurants or other places of amusement. It was the same in Rue Colbert. An ordinary weekday at the beginning of October, with the daylight fading softly into dusk while a very fine light rain was falling. Quite pleasant, really, since it made the dust settle without being sufficiently heavy to soak through my jacket or transform the dirt into mud. An elderly woman stood on a corner beneath a worn parasol, making crêpes in a huge pan balanced over glowing coals and selling them to those tempted by the sweet golden scent.

I had no idea how or where to start my search. How was I supposed to find anything that Marot had missed? But he did not know about Fleur's prison, I told myself. He had been looking for witnesses and the scene of a murder, not for a cellar where a young woman could be kept captive for several days without anyone noticing.

I was a stranger in the neighborhood and I had been noticed.

A straggling line of street urchins had collected in my wake, shrill voices pealing out in the gathering dusk.

"A copper, mam'selle. Give a copper to a poor starving boy."

"Come on, lady. Be nice!"

At first, I ignored them, especially the ones who turned their reedy voices to homemade chants, presented in a patois so thick that the words were barely distinguishable. Probably just as well, from what I could make out.

"One-two-three, howd'ya like my ass to see, four-five-six, it can do some cunning tricks, lady watchya clever jack, and pop a centime in the crack . . ."

This was followed by wild giggling, and they liked their song so much that they repeated it a few more times.

I stopped. "Do you live here?" I asked.

"'Course. Where else?"

"I am looking for a cellar . . . a specific one. It is probably a coal cellar."

They looked at me with a collective grin that managed to cast severe doubts on my sanity.

"All the houses have a coal cellar, lady," said a big-boned, stocky boy of seven or eight, whose hair had recently been cut so close to his scalp that you could see the pale skin through the dark stubble.

"This one is no longer used for coal," I said. "And it is closed off. Locked. And the walls must be pretty thick. Perhaps the usual entrance has even been walled over."

"How d'ya get hold of the coal, then?" asked one of the smaller boys.

"Dumb nut. She said there wasn't no coal in it any longer," pointed out the bony one, who seemed to be the spokesman.

I lowered my voice and made it suitably dramatic. "That's right. Because it's a secret cellar. If you find it, there's a demi-franc for a finder's fee—and hot crêpes for everyone."

That had about the same energizing effect as Galvani's instruments on the quadriceps femoris of a frog. They jumped up and raced in all directions, whooping and cackling, and the bony one yelled back over his shoulder: "Wait here, lady. You might as well order them pancakes right away!"

Having endured a mild nausea all morning, I was now suddenly starving. I bought one of the tempting crêpes for myself and consumed it with an eagerness I usually did not feel for fried batter.

Nausea. Menses nil. Sudden cravings?

I did not care at all for the messages my body was sending me. I stared at the last sticky remains and felt most of all like throwing them away, but the hunger was merciless. I wolfed them down and licked the syrup from my fingers like a badly behaved child. After that, I had to get out my handkerchief to return my hands and lower face to a reasonably respectable condition.

One of the street urchins came racing back.

"We've found it," he whispered conspiratorially. "Come and look, lady!"

My heart jumped, and I followed him farther down the street, in through not just one but two back courtyards.

"There!" he said, and pointed.

At first, I could not see what he meant at all. Some minor construction was in progress—a shed in the middle of the courtyard had been torn down and was, judging by the mason strings and foundation excavation, to be replaced by a larger one. But I could not see any cellar.

"Where?" I had to ask.

"Over in the corner!" he said triumphantly. "You said it was secret and maybe walled in . . ."

Now I could see what he meant. There *was* a cellar, or there had been. At present it was full of rubble from the demolished

shed, and when the floor of the new one went in, it would disappear entirely.

I felt a momentary chill down my spine. The thought that there was a hollow down there, and that it might be big enough to hide a person . . . It would be like being buried alive.

But Fleur had not been buried, I reminded myself. The prison she had found herself in *had* an exit—at least for her jailers.

"Are there other entrances to that cellar?" I asked.

"Nah, don't think so. Wouldn't be a secret, then, would it?"

"I'm sorry," I said, "but that is not the right one. The right one has a door—but it probably isn't easy to find."

He looked crestfallen.

"Listen, lady," he said. "Now don't try saying it's not the right one even if it *is*—just to get out of paying. Right?"

"No," I said, and traced a finger across my neck in a throat-cutting gesture I had not used since I was about seven and still played with Paul Tessier. "Cross my heart and hope to die." I clicked my tongue to emphasize the seriousness of the promise.

"Good," he said. "'Cause we don't like cheats around here!"

The next two cellars they showed me did in fact have doors, but they were basically ordinary coal cellars to which all of the inhabitants of the house had access. The darkness had deepened and the evening had grown colder, and the flock had thinned because some of them had been called home to supper. It was time to call off the hunt, at least for today.

"Listen," I said. "I can't give you the half franc. It will still be waiting for you if you find the right place and come to Carmelite Street with a message. But you have worked hard, and you have earned at least a part of the reward."

I bought ten large crêpes well filled with thick black treacle—it was cheaper than honey—and parceled them out among the boys. It worked out to about half a pancake per boy. The crêpe seller was quite pleased but still asked us to retreat a little up the street while we ate so as not to scare off the more respectable customers.

Ten crêpes—eleven with the one I myself had devoured earlier—made a significant hole in my petty cash, especially since it had not yet quite regained the two francs I had given to the rebellious Pauline. If I were to continue scattering various forms of bribes in this way, I would have to start looking for a paying job. As it was, I had to cover my expenses from the already distinctly unimpressive household budget in Carmelite Street. Perhaps it had been a little hasty of me to reject Constance Heering-Dreyfuss's generous offer outright, I thought with an ironic smile. Then I remembered the morning's sickness.

Nausea. Menses nil.

The thought of the dowager's bargain was suddenly no longer the least bit amusing.

On the way back to the streetcar stop, I threw a last glance into the coal merchant's yard. There were lights in most of the apartments, and the smell of frying onions came wafting down from several open windows. A woman emerged from one of the back doors with a slop pail that she emptied into one of the big galvanized barrels waiting for the honey wagon. She sent me a curious look, and I greeted her politely.

"Good evening, madame."

She did not answer, but instead stared at me for so long that I myself took another look at her.

I had seen her before, I realized. She was Adrian Althauser's housekeeper. She banged the lid of the container down with a clang and hastened back toward the open door to the stairwell.

"Wait," I said. "Please! I just want to talk to you!"

It was clearly not mutual, but I set aside my dignity and sprinted as fast as I could. I managed to get my foot in the door just before she tried to slam it.

"Please stay," I said. "I only want to ask you a couple of questions."

"I'm busy," she said. "My husband's waiting."

"It probably will not hurt him to wait a few more minutes," I said.

She sent me a frightened look and let go of the door. She rushed up the stairs, and if I wanted to continue the conversation, I would clearly have to run after her. She disappeared through a door on the first floor, but I managed—barely—to repeat my doorstop performance.

"Madame," I said, "be sensible."

"Go away."

"If you don't want to speak with me, I'll have to send the police instead," I tried.

"Clothilde?" a voice sounded from inside the apartment. "Who is it?"

The fight leaked out of her.

"A lady," she said. "She's just leaving."

"Why? Ask her inside, Clothilde. We have so few visitors."

"So this is where you live," I said. I think I had imagined that she had a room at Althauser's.

"Yes," she said. "That's no crime, is it?"

"Of course not."

But it *was* a striking coincidence, I thought. Yet another thread that somehow tied Althauser to Rosalba Lombardi's death. If I could only figure out how . . .

The apartment was not large, but it was neat and cozy. Kitchen, bedroom, and a small living room, from what I could see. There were light muslin curtains and potted plants in the windows, and in a comfortable-looking armchair upholstered in mossy green bouclé sat the master of the house, a small, lively looking man with muttonchop sideburns and a pomaded center parting that gave Inspector Marot a run for his money. Apart from that, the most striking thing about him was the empty trouser legs that had been folded up and stitched closed so that it was instantly obvious that both his legs had been amputated just under the knees.

"Do please excuse me for not getting up," he said with a dead-pan humor. "Henri Arnaud, at your service."

He was open and extroverted as she was closemouthed and tense. He asked my name and errand, invited me to sit down, asked Clothilde Arnaud to bring us coffee and "refreshments." So I knew the professor from the university? Well, he must say that was most impressive for a young lady. For sure, he himself had neither the brains nor the nerves for that kind of work. Clothilde certainly had a lot to report when she came home. Dismembered animals and dead bits and pieces in glass jars, as though they were preserved pears! No, that was not for him. But he was a gentle-man, the professor, in spite of the peculiar things he studied. He paid Clothilde well and on time. And that was just as well, because after his own little accident—here he waved a casual hand at his stumps—he had had to move his workshop up here, so no one came in off the street anymore, and only a few of his old customers stayed loyal.

"What is your trade, then?" I asked, while I sipped carefully at the coffee. It had clearly been standing on the stove for a while and was about the consistency of chimney soot.

"I am a saddler," he said. "Well, it's tough to handle the larger commissions, but I can still repair bags and harnesses and that kind of thing. And resole a pair of boots, if necessary."

I spoke with him for another ten minutes or so while I tried to down the burned coffee, but really I was by that point almost as eager to get out the door as Madame Arnaud was to get rid of me. Something had occurred to me, and I could barely wait to see whether I was right.

I got up at last, thanked them for the coffee and the "nice

chat"—Madame Arnaud's eyes narrowed in her anxious pale face—and said good-bye. She herded me out onto the front steps this time, and I made no objections.

Outside, in the increasing downpour in Rue Colbert, it took me another fifteen minutes to find it. The windows that had opened on to the street had not just been shuttered or boarded over; they had been bricked up. So had the door. But on the wall, above the recess where the door had been, a faded sign could still be made out: H. ARNAUD, SADDLER.

I stared at the walled-up entrance while the rain pounded ever more forcefully against the sidewalk and quickly soaked through my thin linen jacket, now more charcoal than ecru. There had to be an entrance somewhere, all I had to do was find it. There was something in there, and I had to find out what it was. Among other things, I was fairly certain there was a cellar . . .

There was the sound of hoofbeats behind me, and a hansom cab stopped a few meters away. The passenger opened the door and leaned out.

"Mademoiselle Karno! May I take you home?"

I stared. It was Christophe, complete with bow tie and an entirely inappropriate boater.

"Are you following me?" I asked heatedly.

"On occasion," he admitted cheerfully. "When I have nothing better to do—and when the weather is less unpleasant. You frequent such *interesting* places, mademoiselle."

"Is that even legal?" I asked.

"Oh, absolutely. As long as I'm not bothering you."

"But you are!"

"By offering to save you from this inclement weather? That is hardly a grave offense. Oh, do hop in, you are absolutely soaked. I promise to behave like the gentleman I really am!"

I was almost tempted, but I gathered the remains of my sodden dignity around me.

"No, thank you," I said. "There is an excellent streetcar awaiting just round the corner."

"As you will, but may I at least present you with today's paper? I am sure you will find it interesting."

The hansom cab clattered on. I unfolded the newspaper and the headline jumped out at me.

"DEATH'S PHOTOGRAPHER," it said, across most of the front page. I could not help reading it, in spite of the big wet drops that spotted the paper and made the print blur.

Christophe was in top form. As far as I could tell, he and Aristide Gilbert were responsible for almost seven of this edition's pages. In the front-page article, he described how Gilbert had hidden "dozens" of photographs of dead young women and somehow made it sound as if Gilbert single-handedly murdered all of them. There was even a drawing that depicted "the scene in the darkroom where Mademoiselle Death finds the murderer's self-slaughtered body."

So far, there was nothing in it that I did not already know, give or take a wildly exaggerated hypothesis or two. But in "the following article on page 5: The drowned wife," the apparently quite effective Christophe had dug up information about Gilbert's past that I did not think even Marot knew of yet.

THE DROWNED WIFE

Alice Anderson was just seventeen years old when she first came to the resort town of Hyères to improve her health. Here she met Aristide Gilbert, who was working as a bathing assistant at a facility run by English Doctors Griffin and Madden. She fell head over heels for the young Frenchman, and some months later they were married, in spite of the doubts felt by Miss Anderson's parents. We now know just how right they were to doubt. When the beautiful young Englishwoman drowned in 1890, at the age of twenty, Mr. and Mrs. Anderson expressed their fear that this was not just a tragic accident, as her husband claimed. Gilbert, however, escaped prosecution because a relative, Madame C. Aguillard, swore under oath that he had been visiting her at her home (she was elderly and bedridden) on the day that Alice Gilbert drowned during a bathing excursion. *Varonne Soir* has now sensationally come into possession of a letter from photographer Gilbert to Madame Aguillard, now deceased, which reveals that this alibi was false! The letter is printed in its entirety on page 12.

What kind of man was Death's Photographer? How many killings did he have on his black conscience before he took his own life? Read more on page 12!

Naturally, I immediately turned to page twelve. The newspaper had arranged for "the six-page-long letter of confession" to be photographed, so you could see the wavering, emotional handwriting and the many deletions. I would have to compare them side by side to be sure, but I thought I recognized the handwriting from the letter Aristide Gilbert had written to me.

Dear Aunt Celeste,

Two people can hardly be more destined for each other, and yet be more remote than we are. No. Than we were.

My Alice is no longer. The darkness took her, and there was nothing I could do.

She was ill last winter, a cough that would not quite loosen its grip, perhaps that was why. In any case, it began again. She had headaches and could not sleep, she took no pleasure in anything, did not feel comfortable indoors or out, had only the slightest appetite for food and drink, and turned away from me in bed. I apologize, dear Aunt, but you were married for more than twenty years, after all, you know how it is between a man and a woman. Or how it should be.

When she came to Hyères for the first time, it was for the sake of her health; that was how we met. Every day during the two months she was with Dr. Madden and Dr. Griffin, she bathed, and I was her dipper every time. Where she had been terrified to have her head underwater in the beginning, she now tried to get me to hold her down a little longer—"Just a few seconds, dear Ari"—and then a little longer still. She called it her daily rebirth. "It is like wandering through the Valley of Death and coming out on the other side," she said one day. "I am sure that the resurrected souls feel this way when they are freed from their fleshly prison." Dear Aunt, I know it is blasphemous, but I felt then as I think John the Baptist must have felt when he offered believers a new life. It was only later that I understood that what she experienced was not a resurrection but rather something that should happen between a man and a woman and not between a woman and the dark cold water.

When we became man and wife, it ceased for a while. She was satisfied. And heaven knows, I was too. Oh, my Alice.

But then she became ill. And she was sure that the only thing that could restore her good health was the baths. Dear Aunt, I was afraid. She would have gone by herself if I did not go with her. I thought that I could at least make sure that she returned. And she was so grateful. She clung to me before and after her body shuddered, and everything between us was fresh and new as if it was the first time.

I will remember that day as long as I live. The last one. Because neither she nor I have really lived since then.

It was at the beginning of November, and the water was warmer than the air. The season was over. The machines had been pulled up on land for the last time, shutters had been hammered across the windows in the boathouses and bathing cabins. The wind had been blowing hard for several days, but now it had died down, and the sea was completely still, heavy, and silklike to look at.

"Today we can do it," Alice said triumphantly. "You can't say that it is too windy today!"

"But it will soon be winter," I objected.

"All the more important, then, that I regain my health."

I could not resist her. There was a light in her face, and I did not want to be the one to extinguish it.

We were the only people in the world, it seemed to me. Our footprints in the white sand were the only ones, our voices the only sound one could hear except for the screams of the seagulls.

"My love. This has to be the last time this year."

"Yes, yes," she said, as if she would promise anything. "Hurry up. I have not slept well for several nights; how am I supposed to get well if I cannot sleep?"

"I thought you were doing better."

"Yes, a little, perhaps. But only thanks to the baths."

We changed in one of the abandoned cabins. She was still using the same blue-and-white costume as the very first time I saw her. Still just as slender, still just as young, it seemed to me, though I had had days and months and years together with her. For better or for worse, as it says.

The air was cool, and I could see the goose bumps on her arms.

"It's too cold," I said. "Let's go home."

"No," she said, though her teeth were chattering. "Ari, I beg you. It will only take a moment . . . and the water isn't cold, not yet. Not really."

The water was in fact a few degrees warmer; we could both feel that.

"See," she said. "What did I say! Do it now, Ari . . . one of the long ones."

"The long ones" had gradually become sixty seconds. The normals were thirty seconds, and the short ones ten. I still counted, just as Dr. Madden had taught us back when I started. He, however, had never asked me to hold a patient underwater for more than ten seconds at a time.

She willingly leaned back, supported by my right arm. With my other hand I pushed her under the water and held her there. I looked down at her, a shimmering, blurred image, while I slowly counted the seconds.

". . . fifty-seven, fifty-eight, fifty-nine . . ." She hung limp in my arms and did not begin to fight until I reached "sixty!" and began to raise her up again.

"No!" she scolded as soon as her face broke through the surface. "It's too soon! You're not doing it right! I said one of the long ones!"

"That was one of the long ones."

"No. No, it wasn't . . ."

"My love. Why would I lie?"

"You did not want to come down here. Now you want to go home quickly, and that is why you are cheating!"

"I am not cheating!"

"Then why isn't it working?" She began to cry. "You don't want me to be well. You don't want me to be happy."

I held her close and tried to comfort her. What kind of talk was this, I said, when she knew very well that I loved her and would do anything for her. I stroked her back, her wet back, and the narrow shoulder blades, which I could feel through the fabric. But it was not enough; I could not hold her tight enough or long enough. She always wanted something more than me. Something else.

"Do it again," she said. "And do it properly this time."

Lord have mercy. I did it.

I held her under the water while I counted to sixty. And then to seventy. I thought that now it had to be enough. This time it had to be enough so we could go back, so I could get her to come home. She lay heavy and relaxed in my grip and did not resist. Not when I brought her to the surface either, not this time.

I don't even know when she died. If she let the water slip into her throat at once, or whether long seconds passed before it happened. When I worked for Dr. Madden and Dr. Griffin, there were rumors about a patient who had suffered a seizure at the very first dipping, somewhere in another health resort along the coast, but I don't know if this was true, and I don't know if this is what happened to my Alice. Would I not have been able to feel it? Would there not have been spasms, cramps? I held her in my arms, and I still could not feel it. I just know that when I raised her from the waters she was gone, and nothing I tried to do could bring her back to life.

You will probably think that what I did next is unforgivable. I think it is. But fear gripped me because I knew what her parents would say when they heard. They would say: He murdered our little daughter. He killed her. He was only after her money, and now he has killed our darling girl. That was what I thought they would say, and I was right, that is precisely what they are saying now.

291

How could I prove that they were wrong? Who would believe what I have just told you? That a young woman may fall so passionately in love with the darkness under the water that she worships it as Alice did? Who would believe that?

So I left her.

I left here there at the water's edge, like something the storm had washed up, but there was no storm, only the still, dark waters that had taken her from me. I was trembling and weeping while I did it, but that does not lessen my guilt. I fetched my dry clothes from the cabin and changed. And then I pulled the wet ones after me and erased my tracks in the sand, every print, until only hers were left. The wind had risen again, and grains of sand tumbled over each other, one by one, and fell into the indentations so that the edges were blurred and the lie stood out more clearly: that only one person had walked here, that only one person had met the sea and found her death here.

I am telling you this now because you are perhaps the only human being in the world who will believe me. You who have known me since I was a small child wriggling on my belly. You who have comforted me and kissed my scraped knees better, you who helped me learn my catechism, who said to Papa that he should leave me in peace, I was as I was, and I was a good boy even so. You who listened to me when I poured out my heart because I had fallen madly and hopelessly in love with a young English lady from Birmingham. You who cried at our wedding and blessed us both when no one else would.

If you who know me and know the whole truth now cannot forgive me, then no earthly forgiveness is possible. And then I might as well let them lead me to the guillotine or let the sea take me as well.

I hope this finds you in better health than when I saw

you last. I do not know if we will ever meet again in this life, but if that is not to be, then take this as assurance that I love you now and always will.

> *Yours in devotion—in this life and the next—*
> *Aristide*

I folded up the newspaper. It was so damp now that it tore. I shall have to buy a new one, I thought with the part of my brain that was still continuing to deal with the mundane.

He must have received the forgiveness he sought—otherwise his aunt Celeste would not have perjured herself for him and given him a false alibi. Finally I understood, in part, at least, what Gilbert had meant by those cryptic words: *I thought the water would be kinder than the other thing, I thought she would be fulfilled as my poor Alice was.*

He really had killed Fleur. I think it was only now that I entirely believed it in spite of the clear connection between her nails and his scratches. He had actually done it. This former bathing assistant had held Fleur's small and weakened body underwater until she drowned. I just did not understand why.

I suddenly remembered how affected he had been when he had had to photograph her body. He had been sick, had vomited. He had perhaps not counted on having to confront in the light of day what he had done in the evening darkness.

Then a fairly obvious question hit me. How on earth had the newspaper got hold of this letter?

I might as well have accepted Christophe's offer of a ride home. I would have been less wet now, and it would have saved me the trouble I now had to take: to seek him out.

When *Varonne Soir* turned on its electric sign for the first time at the beginning of December 1891, it had been an event that attracted several thousand people. For a while, there had been a small daily crowd waiting for the switch-on—at five in the winter months and seven in the summer—staring up at this wondrous and entirely free entertainment. Now people had become more blasé. There were other incandescent signs, and when someone did stand staring these days, citizens of Varbourg smiled indulgently and mentally categorized the gaping spectators as "from the country."

In the darkness and the rain this evening, no one had stopped. Nor did I, though the sign was worth a peek or two. Perched on the roof, it stretched across almost the entire length of the building and was so cleverly designed that, as the incandescent bulbs automatically went on and off, it looked as if a golden trail of fire ran across the sky and lit the torch of enlightenment that was the paper's trademark. It flamed cheerfully for a few moments, and then the whole performance repeated itself. The reflected glow from the yellow, orange, and red bulbs painted colored streaks in the puddles and across the dark, wet cobblestones.

At this time of day—or evening, rather—the newspaper's pompous headquarters were humming with activity. In spite of its name, *Varonne Soir* came out in two editions, an early one that was on the streets by one in the afternoon, and a late edition timed, at eight o'clock in the evening, to catch both those heading home after work and the crowds going out for a meal or an evening's entertainment. The newspaper Christophe had given me was so fresh off the press that the paperboys were still clustered around the gates to the loading bays, waiting to have their bags filled. As soon as this was accomplished, they would race off, and you could hear their shouts through the rain: "Death's photographer! Read about the women he murdered!"

For the journalists and the editors, that edition was already history. They were beginning to convene again to plan tomorrow's early edition, and this was why I was hoping to meet Christophe here.

The young man at the reception desk did indeed helpfully suggest that I should be able to catch "Monsieur Christophe" before the editorial meeting at eight thirty. He willingly gave me directions to "go up the steps to the third floor and then to the left" and otherwise just turned me loose. I think I can therefore say that I succeeded in surprising my public nemesis entirely.

He was sitting at his desk in a corner of a large room holding fifteen or sixteen similar desks, most of them in a row by the windows so as to make the best use of the daylight. Right now, there was of course no daylight to be had, and at the occupied tables—all of them, more or less—reporters were reading, writing, or making notes, each in his own little bubble-like sphere of light cast by the green-shaded brass lamps that seemed to be standard inventory here.

Here, in his professional surroundings, he looked more serious and less of a dandy. True, the boater hung on a hook behind him, and he wore no jacket, only a gray silk waistcoat and shirtsleeves, while he was hammering away at an apparatus that must be one of the new Remington typewriters that seemed to have taken over most of Varbourg's offices in the past decade. It was very loud, and I could not help thinking that a clear and elegant handwriting would not only have been more aesthetically pleasing but also easier on the ears.

He did not look up until I had nearly reached his desk. When he recognized me, he hastily pushed back his chair and got up.

"Mademoiselle," he said. "This is . . . unexpected."

"Good evening," I said politely. "Are you busy?"

"Ahh . . . never too busy to speak with you," he answered gallantly. "But I was left with the impression that *you* preferred not to speak with *me*."

"Perhaps you are familiar with John Stuart Mill's thoughts on utilitarianism?" I said. "At the moment, it so happens that it will contribute to the common good here in Varbourg if you and

I help each other. I am therefore prepared to consider you if not a friend, then at least as a potential ally."

"If you say so."

"You have something I would like to see. I too have information and evidence that will be of interest to you. Is there somewhere we can talk without being disturbed?"

The letter from Aristide Gilbert to Celeste Aguillard was in its original form almost six pages long. I wanted to see it, not because of the contents, which I was already familiar with, but to compare the handwriting to that of the unfinished letter that Bruno had brought me.

Achieving this took some hard bargaining.

"You speak of utilitarianism, mademoiselle, but what do you have that could be useful to me?" he began.

I had given it considerable thought on the way here.

"Are you aware," I said, "that the public decency laws are being misused in order to conduct experiments on this city's so-called public girls?"

"What kind of experiments?" he asked.

I explained. He frowned.

"You mean that . . . that this Althauser . . . impregnates these women?"

"Yes."

"With this—what was it you called it?"

"Insemination. It comes from semen, the Latin word for—"

"Thank you, I can follow you that far," he said quickly. "Can you prove it?"

I no longer had Rosalba's file—Althauser had secured it for himself. But I still had some names and addresses I could look up, and perhaps Estelle Audran would be willing to tell her story with a bit of persuasion and payment.

"I might be able to convince one or more of the women to talk to you," I said.

"Prostitutes? Mademoiselle, this is a respectable newspaper."

"So in other words, the newspaper will write about them when they are murdered in a sufficiently spectacular way, but not let them speak while they are still alive?"

"Mademoiselle Karno, please pardon my language, but that a whore gives birth to a bastard is not really news."

"The *way* it is happening is news."

"Yes, you're certainly right about that. But I can't imagine that my editor will give me permission to describe that. We are Varonne's second-largest newspaper, mademoiselle. We really cannot use words like . . . uh, *semen*."

"Then don't. Just write that the women were subjected to 'medical experiments' or something like that. Without their knowledge. And that Althauser and Pro Patria are behind it. Imply that these experiments cause the women to become pregnant and let the reader's imagination do the rest."

"What you want us to insinuate is decidedly indecent!"

Not more so than what actually happened, I thought, but kept that thought to myself.

"It may perhaps be perceived that way by some, but for the pure of heart everything is pure," I said piously.

He looked thoughtful.

"It could perhaps . . . hmmm. I have to speak with the editor. But . . . perhaps . . . not uninteresting. But also not enough, mademoiselle. What else do you have?"

"I imagine that you might like to see Aristide Gilbert's suicide note," I said, knowing full well that I had probably just given him the headline for tomorrow's newspaper.

His somewhat languid expression came sharply alive.

"Yes, that . . . I would," he said. "Very well. Let us exchange letters and favors, for the common good."

Thus, the two letters ended up side by side on a conference table in the empty premises of the editor of the Sunday special.

"If I may?"

"Just don't crumble it," he said. "We will most likely have to turn it over to the police as soon as they have read today's paper."

This caused me a pang of guilty conscience because I still had the notes on the autopsy in my bag, but it was only a momentary twinge. The autopsy notes were the reason why I had the letter with me in the first place—it was to be included in the file. Both would reach the Commissioner's desk soon enough so that they could be stamped and certified and added to the files of a case that everyone but I clearly considered closed.

Here, in the electric light, it was obvious that the handwriting in the two letters was the same.

"How did you get your hands on this?" I asked Christophe.

"It was sent to us," he mumbled while his eyes flew over the desperate lines in the good-bye note. "Anonymously."

"How did you know it was real, then?"

"We called Hyères on the telephone and had a number of details confirmed that an outsider could hardly have known about. That bit about the erased footprints, for example. There was a note in the police report that said that because of the blowing sand one could not exclude the possibility that there had been more than one person on the beach. This was not made public because Celeste Aguillard's testimony made the case fall apart."

"Who do you think sent it?"

"Himself, probably. He was looking for penance and forgiveness, wasn't he? But this ends a bit abruptly, doesn't it?" Christophe pointed at the letter's last sentence: *I am a monster, a coward, a sinner so great that not even God can forgive*

A sudden anger rose up in me. All that babbling about forgiveness. It might be that Alice's death was an accident of sorts, but Fleur's was not. She had fought. With open eyes and all her strength, while the water forced its way into her throat and lungs. If he had wanted to die with a clean conscience, he should not have done that. I refused to feel sorry for him now.

"What should he have added?" I said. "'I'm really, really sorry, I'll never do it again'?"

"You're a hard woman."

"She was half his size. It must have been like drowning a child."

"What I am wondering is . . . There is not even a full stop at the end. Nor has he signed the letter. Suicides usually do. And take a look at the edge of the paper."

I could see what he meant. Compared to the other three sides, the bottom of the sheet was neither as crisply cut nor quite as straight.

"You mean . . . something is missing?"

"Yes."

"But how . . ." I hesitated. "Who would . . ."

"He asks you to 'do what is in your power to see justice fully done.' If he and he alone committed this crime and is now punished by his own hand—what justice is left to pursue?"

It was obvious now that he had pointed it out.

"He was not acting alone," I said slowly. "That is what he means. What he wants me to do. He wants his accomplice stopped and punished." I sat up straight and tried to line up my thoughts in a logical fashion.

"This letter," I continued. "No, not the note, the one addressed to 'Aunt Celeste' . . . What if it was not Gilbert who sent it . . . When did you receive it?"

"In the morning mail."

"And when does that arrive?"

"Around ten. We only just missed getting it into the afternoon edition."

"Do you still have the envelope?"

"Yes." He took it out of the same folder in which he had kept the letter.

It was an entirely ordinary envelope, except for the lack of a return address. But what interested me was the postmark. It indicated that the letter had passed through Varbourg Ouest, the post office in charge of delivery to and from the city's western parts. In other words, a local letter, posted yesterday.

I did some mental calculations. In Varbourg, the mail was delivered twice a day, in the morning and late in the afternoon between five and six. To make the late delivery, a local letter needed to be handed in for sorting by three at the latest. So we had to assume that the letter had arrived at the post office sometime after three, or it would have been delivered the same day.

"He cannot have sent it himself," I said.

"How do you reach that conclusion?"

I explained. "At three in the afternoon, Aristide Gilbert was lying in his bathtub. He may not have been quite dead yet, but he was definitely so inebriated that it would not have been humanly possible for him to go and post a letter."

"If you say so. All right, so he was not the one who sent it. Why are you looking as if someone just handed you the keys to a confectionary?"

"Let us agree on two things," I said. "First: Anyone who had this letter in his possession while Gilbert lived had a terrible power over him."

Christophe considered this, but only briefly.

"Of course," he said. "This person could send him more or less directly to the guillotine simply by showing the letter to the police."

"Second: I assume we agree that it was not a coincidence that this letter was sent on the same day Gilbert died?"

"That is obvious. The two things are connected. The letter was sent *because* he died."

"Thus the sender must have known about the death before the morning papers were on the street."

"You mean . . . No. I don't know what you mean. Explain."

"I think that both of these letters are . . . what should I call it? Props in a *staged* event. A guilt-ridden murderer writes a suicide note and takes his own life. The suspicions against him are quickly confirmed by another incriminating letter, revealing that he has previously been guilty of killing. Together they create a prettily embroidered silhouette with all the loose ends neatly tied up. Only . . . the details do not fit. The apparent suicide note has been cropped and a part of it is missing. The letter addressed to Celeste Aguillard is sent by someone who knows a little too much a little too soon. Someone who might even have staged the suicide itself . . ."

"Is that possible?"

"I would think so," I said. "He—I am fairly convinced it is a man—he seeks out Gilbert yesterday. Gilbert is possibly already inebriated, possibly already suicidal . . . He was an absinthe addict, and I am willing to believe that the killing of Fleur Petit really did torment him intensely. He must have already written the letter that becomes his suicide note in the abbreviated version. Manhandling his incapacitated body into the bathtub would no doubt have been odious, but far from impossible. After that, it is only a matter of time before he drowns. If you want certainty, pushing his head underwater for a little while will do the trick. Or even better . . ." I suddenly remembered how Gilbert's legs had stuck out of the tub. "Even better: Simply grasp his legs and pull so that his entire upper body is submerged. Even someone fully alert would find it difficult to save himself from that position. For a man already paralyzed by alcohol, death would have been inevitable."

Christophe observed me for a while.

"You have a frightening imagination, mademoiselle."

"No," I said grimly. "I have frightening *knowledge*."

"And this man . . . this accomplice . . . do you also know who he is?"

First the facts. Then the conclusion. Not the other way around. There was quite a lot I still did not know, and even more that I would have a hard time proving.

"Perhaps," I said carefully.

Madame Arnaud was once again standing in the door to the study, though he thought he had sent her home several hours ago. She was wearing her coat, he noticed, and stood clutching her soft black velvet hat in white-knuckled hands.

"She has been to Rue Colbert," she said.

"Who?" He sighed.

"Her. The one you teach."

"Mademoiselle Karno? She is no longer my student."

"That may be," said his housekeeper, "but she is still poking around. She spoke to Henri, and later I saw her standing outside the shop."

He stiffened in his chair but controlled any other outward reaction.

"Are you sure?" he asked. "I mean are you sure that she didn't just coincidentally stop there?"

"Yes," she said, agitated. "It was not a coincidence. I saw how she looked when Henri started prattling on about the shop. M'sieur, what if they find her? They will not know . . . They will not understand. M'sieur, you have to do something."

"Madame, control yourself. You know that I do not care for these emotional outbursts."

"Yes, I am sorry, m'sieur, but . . ."

"I will take care of it."

"Thank you, m'sieur."

He really would need to find a replacement for her—however

difficult that might be. She had become much too emotionally affected, it was not bearable. He thought for a moment. Then he wrote a brief note on a piece of his own stationery and another on a blank piece of paper that carried neither his nor the university's address.

"This," he said, and gave her the first, "you may send to the lodgings of the German. Find some reliable errand boy. You, yourself, must go to Carmelite Street. If you find Dr. Karno at home, make sure he receives this message. And then go home to your husband, where you belong."

"But you will make sure that no one discovers her?"

"Yes, I said so. Now go, madame!"

When she was finally gone, he slid the point of his letter opener down behind the desk's bottom molding until he found the right place. A quick turn, a click, and the molding could be pulled out to reveal the secret compartment. The photographs were stored here, along with a few other things that he did not wish Madame Arnaud or anyone else to come across.

Had it been wrong of him to have them taken? Back then it had seemed the ideal solution. But he could not have known, of course, that the silly woman would die in the middle of the operation.

The problem with insemination was that it required semen. For the sake of the project, it could not be semen from, for example, the gendarmes working for the Commission for Public Health and Decency. While no doubt willing, they were of less than ideal stock.

The young Italian girl had not been like the majority of the prostitutes he had been forced to associate himself with. She had regular, unblemished features, her body was healthy and shapely without being overly ample, and most important, she had an instinctive grasp of cleanliness and hygiene. She did not seem to find it odd that he had no wish to touch her. Before the successful insemination, he had used her several times as an effective stimulus, but he knew that she would not want to oblige him again after the operation. The two photographs preserved, in the simplest manner, the scenario he needed for release, and once in possession of them, he would no longer be dependent on the presence of a living woman. It seemed to him an altogether elegant and hygienic solution. He did not trust the photographer, but that problem too he had solved to his satisfaction. Were one or several copies of the photographs to fall into the hands of strangers, no one would be able to tell who the gentleman observer was. He even found that it had excited him that he could see the entire naked woman while she was unable to see any part of him.

The latest development, however, made it advisable for him to get rid of them. They might not constitute definite proof, but there was no reason to hand the good inspector even this circumstantial piece of evidence. He could always have some similar pictures taken later—it made no real difference who the woman in the bath was.

He threw both photographs into the fireplace. Then he sat down to wait for the German.

"Madeleine. You're soaked!"

I met August in the stairwell. He was on his way out and far more sensibly dressed than I, in a long oilskin coat and a heavy tweed cap.

I sneezed. He took hold of both my elbows and pulled me close.

"Have Elise prepare a bath," he said. "Your father was called out to an accident, but there is food for you in the salon, and there is hot tea. By the time you are warm and dry and full, I'll be back. And then you can tell me what you have been up to."

He wanted to kiss me, but I resisted.

"Where are you going?" I asked.

"I have to meet someone."

"The truth!" I demanded, invoking the pact we had made with each other.

He sighed. "What I am doing is for us," he said. "So we can live in peace and perhaps not in the deepest penury."

"You're meeting with *him*!"

"With Erich. Yes. He asked if I would come, and I said yes."

My hands closed spasmodically around his upper arms.

"Why? How is that going to help?"

"I hope I can get him to withdraw his testimony. I don't understand why he did it—it hurts him as well."

"I don't want you to do it. I don't want you to go!"

He kissed my wet hair.

"Sweetheart. We must, as Grandmama usually puts it, be practical. You have nothing to fear, I promise you. It is, after all, you I want to marry, not him . . ." He smiled crookedly, clearly trying to inject a little humor into the last remark, but I could not quite see the funny side, and the reference to his grandmother in no way helped the hilarity.

"August . . ."

"Go on in and have your bath. You're shaking."

He was right. It was as if his concern for me had released a wave of weakness. My knees trembled. My hands trembled. He loosened my grip on the oilskin coat and kissed me again, this time on the mouth. Then he left, and I just stood there and let him.

The kerosene lamp in the laundry shed was not lit, and I could not see Elise anywhere.

"Elise?" I called.

There was no answer. I could hear a faint hiss from our improvised water heater, and the gas flames threw a faint blue glow over contours of the room, but the tub was empty. With a frustrated groan, I put down the pile of dry clothes I was planning to change into after my bath and made my way to the copper, edging past some crates full of broken specimen jars and chipped flasks—Papa never threw anything away, not even if it had long since lost all usefulness. The bucket with which we normally filled the tub was gone.

I was wet, cold, and tired. I had left my sodden jacket in the hallway, but the blouse underneath it had not fared much better, and my corset had chafed me under my arms, as it often did when it became damp. It would have been wonderful if a steaming tub had been ready and waiting, but apparently it wasn't going to be that easy. Where was that bucket? Where was Elise?

The laundry's old back door was open, I discovered. It led only to a long, narrow passage that could barely be described as a yard; we kept the garbage pails there, but apart from that its only function was to provide a shortcut into Rue Langoustine—a winding, gloomy little alley whose delicate nomenclature was shrouded in mystery; it was definitely not so named because its denizens ate lobster every day.

I could not think what Elise and the bath bucket might be doing out there but, on the other hand, I could come up with no other explanation as to where they might have disappeared to.

"Elise?" I called again, louder this time.

There was a clattering from outside, as if someone had bumped into one of the garbage pails, and then a thin, reedy sound that might almost have come from a rat. Almost—but not quite.

"Elise!"

It took me only a few paces to reach her. She was lying in a huddle against the closest garbage pail, only barely conscious. Next to her lay the missing bucket.

I was reaching to feel her forehead—

Before me rose a figure from its hiding place behind the pails. In the dark, I saw nothing but a shadow that was darker still, topped by a grotesque face, painted black on white, just gaping black eye sockets and a crudely drawn black smile. No phantom vision this time, but reality.

All my muscles froze. My throat constricted. For a few seconds, I stood completely still, paralyzed by shock. And in those seconds, I was seized from behind by someone whose strength made a mockery of my brief attempt at resistance. My head was jerked back, and I recognized the strong smell of ether the instant before the rag was forced against my nose and mouth.

I was being carried, slung over someone's shoulder, with my head dangling unsupported at every step. It was very uncomfortable. If I had been properly awake, I would have done something about it. But I could not seem to locate and connect the nerve endings and muscle fibers I normally used to direct my body.

Two men were arguing.

"You're mad," the one carrying me said, in rather poor French. "Do you really think that it will not be discovered? That you will not be found out? For nine months?"

"I don't need nine months," said the other one. "Just a few weeks until the cell division is well under way."

"What do you mean?"

"If it can be done with an Angora rabbit, it can no doubt be done with a woman. The differences are not that great."

"You're mad!"

Then my head knocked against something, and the voices disappeared.

I was thirsty. My throat was raw and painful. But I could not lift my arms or open my eyes.

A child was swimming through the darkness. No, it was not a child; it was a fetus. No, it was not a fetus. It was a child so small that it should not yet have been born. It floated in the dark, severed and free, and something in me ached to see it like this.

"Children that small should not be alone," I whispered.

But I could not hear my own words, and no one answered.

Thirst. Darkness. Cold. A nagging anxiety that would not leave me. Where was the child?

October 4, 1894

"Where is the child?"

This time I could hear myself, but at the same time I wondered at the words coming out of my mouth. What child?

I opened my eyes. It made no difference. The darkness was absolute and I could see absolutely nothing. I felt so nauseated that it was difficult to breathe. For a while, that was all I could manage—to inhale and exhale, without throwing up. Then I threw up. Then I inhaled and exhaled some more until the nausea receded enough for me to have two coherent thoughts.

The cold made me uncertain whether I was inside or outside. But outdoors, darkness is rarely so complete. What I was lying on must therefore be not bare earth but some sort of floor, damp and gritty though it was, smelling strongly of dirt, urine, and wet coke.

It was when this information made its way from my nostrils to my consciousness that I began to understand where I was.

In a room without windows, a room with walls and doors against which one could shatter one's hands without being heard, without being released. A room where the floor was dirt and the walls were stone, and both were black from coal, dust, and filth. Fleur's prison.

I did not call for help. I knew it would do no good—it had done nothing for Fleur. But I tried to stand up so that I might at least learn the dimensions of the room. I was dizzy and weak at the knees but managed to get to my feet, observing that I could at least stand upright without hitting my head on the ceiling. Carefully, I stretched my arms out in front of me, then to both sides and at last up above my head. I did not meet resistance anywhere.

I cautiously took a step forward. Then another.

With the third, I stumbled and fell down on my knees on top of something living. A thick German curse made me scuttle back so that I ended up squatting a few meters away.

"Herr Falchenberg?" I whispered.

He did not answer, but I was nevertheless convinced that it was him.

Abruptly, I recalled the angry discussion I had overheard during one of my brief befuddled moments of semiconsciousness. *If it can be done with an Angora rabbit, it can no doubt be done with a woman. The differences are not that great . . .*

"What . . . happened?" I asked, and sincerely hoped that he would answer.

A not very articulate moan was all the reply I received. I thought I could distinguish the words *zum Teufel*, but I was not sure.

If someone . . . no, if Althauser, let us give the devil his proper name, if Adrian Althauser had inserted a glass tube into my vagina, would I be able to feel it now? Probably not. It was not in that sense a violent intrusion. It was only the effects that . . .

I did not wish to complete the thought.

Only a few of the unsuspecting women he had experimented with had become pregnant, I tried to assure myself. In the successful cases, he had performed the procedure repeatedly, often for more than a month.

I did not feel particularly reassured. If that was his intention, what was to prevent him from doing it to *me* repeatedly? Fleur had not found any way out of this prison. Would I be able to?

"Herr Falchenberg?" I called once more.

"What?" he mumbled, still in German. "Go away."

"There is nothing I would rather do," I said. "But unfortunately I don't think it is possible."

I could hear him moving in the darkness—a quiet rustle of clothes against clothes.

"Where are we?" he asked.

"I had hoped you would be able to tell me that."

"Damnation. Why is it so dark? And cold." His voice sounded slurred and uncertain, and I wondered if he was plain drunk. But no—I would have been able to smell it.

"Are you injured?" I asked.

"I don't know. I . . . my head. Something has happened to my head."

"Are you in pain?"

"Yes, damn it. I just said so."

I ought to do something. Examine him. Find out whether there were external injuries, internal damage. If he was bleeding . . . But I was not sure I could bear to touch him. And what good would it do anyway? I did not have a medical bag with me; I could not even see. Beyond placing a compress if he was in danger of bleeding to death, I did not see how I would be able to help him.

"Are you bleeding?" I asked, just to be certain.

"I think I was," he said. "There is something sticky . . ." And then his voice suddenly came clear as day and sharply indignant: "He hit me. He hit me with that damn cane!"

"Althauser?"

"Who else?"

"Why would he do that? I thought you were . . . conspirators." Because it was Falchenberg who had carried me through the dark while he argued with Althauser, and I was fairly sure he was the one who had grabbed me in the passage behind the laundry shed and held the ether rag over my face.

He was silent for a while, then he said, "You don't know what he is like."

I felt a strong urge to say that I knew perfectly well, but I controlled myself.

"What are you referring to?" I asked instead.

"He has this knack . . . He quietly turns you inside out and

313

studies what he finds. He picks at your intestines. He observes you when you are not looking at him, and when you turn around, he looks away. He notes what works and what doesn't. And once he knows what the bleeding, pulsating heart of an Erich looks like, and what makes it beat . . . then he rips it out. Once he holds it in his hand, you are at his mercy. You must do what he commands."

I could not protest. Althauser had done what he could to dissect the heart of a Madeleine as well. He had quickly discovered what my most precious dreams were, which parts of me reacted if he compressed a nerve ending *here* or pulled a tendon *there*. If the clumsy Vice Marshall Delafontaine had not revealed the great plan a little too soon, might my clever tutor ultimately have discovered which part of the living flesh he must probe with his scalpel to make me accede to his will in this too?

You and Malleau are without a doubt the most promising intellects in the class. I cringed when I thought how eager I had been to lap up his praise, the things I had done to myself and to innocent living creatures to humor him.

"Surely you are possessed of free will," I said in spite of my own thoughts. "You could refuse."

"Could I? When he possesses my innermost secrets? When he knows my deepest love—and uses it against me?"

I recalled how he had lurked for hours in that doorway in Carmelite Street, hoping for August to pass by. How wretched he had looked. How guilt ridden he had seemed.

"Did he get you to testify against August?" I asked.

Again he was silent for a while.

"Yes," he finally said.

"But . . . did that not make your innermost secrets public?" I asked. "What could he do to you after that?"

He snorted. "You think I mean August. That he is the one I love."

Now I became confused. "And isn't he?"

"No. I am fond of him, and we . . . we enjoyed each other's company. He helped me to recover after . . . after the terrible thing that happened. He showed me that I could still find joy in life. I was grateful for that, and that is why it was such a . . . a *devilish* thing to have to do to him."

I did not at all care to hear him describe how he and August had enjoyed each other's company. But I could not help being curious.

"Why did you do it, then?"

"You know why. Because Althauser told me to."

"Yes, but . . . why did you think you had to obey him?"

"Why should I tell you that, Fräulein?" A bit of the old arrogance crept back into his voice.

"That is up to you, of course," I said. "But I may perhaps be allowed to point out that the chances of us getting out of here are quite slim."

"Why do you think that?"

I told him about Fleur. About how I had found the saddlery shop and its bricked-over windows and doors.

"And you think this is it?" he asked.

"I am convinced of it. And he has not put us here for the sake of our health."

"Oh, you have nothing to fear," he said. "At least not for the first few weeks."

"Nothing to fear?" My voice had grown shrill. "Beyond being . . . being opened up like an Angora rabbit?"

"Oh," he said. "You know."

"I heard. And unfortunately I know precisely what Walter Heape did to his rabbits."

"In a way, it is a compliment," said Falchenberg. "He would not go to such lengths to secure your hereditary traits if he did not consider your intelligence unique."

"Thank you, but I would prefer to do without such compliments. No doubt I am merely the first woman he has met who did not faint when she was asked to cut into a living squid. I am not at all sure that this is an admirable trait."

More silence. I could hear his breathing and the slight sounds he made when he changed his position. But when I listened for other signs of life—footsteps, voices, hoofbeats, anything at all that suggested that we were not alone in the world but were in the middle of a crowded, living city—I heard nothing.

I had the feeling Falchenberg was falling asleep. His breathing changed, became slower but also a bit uneven. I hoped it was not because he was dying. Damage from a blow to the head could come like a thief in the night, I knew. A seeping of blood beneath the skull, gradually pressing harder and harder on the brain's soft tissue. Body functions that quietly shut down, one by one . . .

"Are you awake?"

He did not answer. I crept across the floor until my fumbling hand met a sleeve.

"Falchenberg!"

"Leavemealone," he slurred.

"Wake up," I said "Talk to me." Why did we have no light? It was impossible for me to check the state of his pupils.

"Go'way."

"I mean it! Sit up! If you fall asleep, you might die without me noticing."

He finally moved.

"Well, that would be unfortunate," he said dryly. "Far better to die while you can enjoy every single cramp."

"That is not what I meant."

"I know. I apologize."

"Then say something. Keep talking, so I know that you are not losing consciousness."

"What should I say?"

"Whatever you want. Or if you can't think of anything, then . . . sing. Whistle. Anything at all."

He snorted. After a pause, his voice came out of the darkness, not without a certain irony: "*O Tannenbaum, O Tannenbaum, wie treu sind deine Blätter . . .*"

I could not help smiling. And at the same time the old melody loosened something in me so that the tears also began to flow, quietly and warmly, unaccompanied by sobs. I began to sing along: "*Du grünst nicht nur zur Sommerzeit, nein, auch im Winter wenn es schneit . . .*"

After the first verse, he stopped.

"Fräulein," he said.

"Yes?"

"I am sorry, but . . . you are no Jenny Lind."

"Are you implying that I am off-key?"

"Only on every other note," he said. "But do continue. You sing off-key in a most . . . *charming* manner!"

One loses all sense of time in a darkness as complete as the one in which we found ourselves. Especially if one dozes off. And we did doze, in spite of all our good intentions. The body has its own laws. That is why I discovered at some point that I was lying snuggled up against him because my sleeping self had sought out the only source of warmth that existed in this damp, cold room. Had anyone told me a month ago that I would be sleeping arm in arm with Erich Falchenberg, I would have considered their sanity and intelligence considerably at risk. But other rules were in effect here.

We spoke. We sang. We argued. And we told stories. We explored our prison as well as was possible—about two meters in one direction and three meters in the other, cold stone walls, earthen floor. We experimented to see if one could dig under a wall. One couldn't, not without tools. A shoe, bare hands,

Falchenberg's belt buckle—none of these made any significant impression on the compacted dirt.

"It's no use," said Falchenberg. "We'll die of hunger long before we get under the foundation."

"Or of thirst," I said dejectedly, thinking of Fleur's dehydrated organs.

"Perhaps I can at least make a hole that can be used as a form of latrine," he said. "I'm sorry, Fräulein, but . . . it will come to that as well."

After what seemed an endless time, a few narrow slivers of pale gray light appeared somewhere above us. It was morning.

I got up and stared upward. The ceiling was much farther up than I had expected—between three and three and a half meters, I estimated. The faint glow of light I could see was daylight penetrating the cracks in the floor of the room upstairs. This probably *was* a coal cellar—or at least, the surface beneath us was the floor of such a cellar. Someone had removed the partition between the cellar and the saddler's shop above it, so that it all became one high-ceilinged room. One could still make out the remains of the decaying beams that had supported the floorboards.

To call it daylight would be an exaggeration, but after the total darkness it was still an encouraging transformation. I examined Falchenberg's head and found a total of six bumps and cuts left by Althauser's cane—one on his forehead and one at his temple, and four scattered across the back of his head.

"You must have an unusually thick skull," I said. "In my opinion, it is a miracle that you are still alive."

"I don't think he is used to hitting people," said Falchenberg. "His customary methods are less direct."

The light was wonderful, but after a while I must have fallen asleep again. I was woken by creaks and rustling from above. Then there was a scraping noise, as if a piece of furniture was being pushed across the floorboards.

"Lie down," I whispered to Falchenberg. "If he comes, it's best that he think that he actually *did* kill you."

He did as I said.

But when a square of blinding daylight appeared above us, it was not Althauser's voice we heard.

"Mademoiselle?" It was Madame Arnaud, the saddler's wife and Althauser's anxious housekeeper. "Mademoiselle? Are you awake?"

"Yes."

"What about the young man?"

I looked at Falchenberg. He was giving an excellent imitation of a corpse.

"He's dead," I said in a hard voice. "Madame, you are working for a murderer. Go to the police. It is your one chance to avoid punishment."

"He said that I was not allowed to listen to you," she said. "He said I should not let you speak. If you say anything more, you will not get any water."

Water. At that moment I think I was prepared to do much more humiliating things than just keep my mouth shut, if it meant that I would be allowed to slake my thirst.

"I'm sorry," I said. "I promise to remain silent."

"I will lower the bottle down to you," she said. "Drink from it and then let it go so I can pull it up again."

She sounded as if she was reciting her catechism. I had no doubt she was repeating Althauser's instructions word-for-word.

The bottle came down at the end of a long piece of string, swaying and jiggling. I grabbed it and drank. I drank until it was almost empty, and then I filled my mouth as much as I could.

"Let it go," said Madame Arnaud.

I did as I was told and the blessed bottle disappeared up through the hatch. Then the hatch was slammed shut again, and we could hear the furniture—whatever it might be—being pushed into place again on top of it.

Falchenberg cursed very quietly and whispered, "The next time I don't want to be dead. The next time I want something to drink too."

I placed a hand on either side of his face. His stubble scratched my palms, and I saw his eyes expand in shock. He must have thought I was going to kiss him. Instead, I slowly delivered the water I had not swallowed into his open mouth, and when he realized what I had in mind, he received it as only a thirsting man could.

"Thank you," he mumbled afterward.

"I know it was not much," I said. "But at least it may relieve the dryness of the mucous membranes."

"You really *are* a most unusual woman," he said. "I don't know many people who would have thought of doing what you just did."

The knowledge that there was a hatch above us was an insistent, nagging hope.

"If you sat on my shoulders . . . ," Falchenberg suggested.

We tried. Erich Falchenberg was nearly two meters tall, and I had luckily inherited my body type more from my father than from my petite mother. I could reach the hatch, I just could not move it even a millimeter. Whatever it was that had been placed on top, it was much too heavy for me to move.

I looked calculatingly at Falchenberg's broad, athletic shoulders.

"Perhaps you should try."

"You could hardly carry me."

"We must at least make the attempt!"

Unfortunately, he was proved right. Even with the exertion of all my strength, I could not remain upright long enough. I staggered, and we both tumbled to the ground in a hard and awkward fall.

"Blast it," I cursed. What good was it that one of us was built like a medieval battering ram if we could not get the ram within striking distance of the castle gates?

We tried a few more times, without luck. Then Falchenberg had to sit down for a while.

"Are you dizzy?" I asked. "Does your head hurt?"

He smiled crookedly. "It's kind of you to ask, but . . . even if it does, what do you propose to do about it?"

He was right. There was nothing I could do. But it was second nature to keep an eye on his symptoms.

"Last night . . . when you asked August to meet you," I said, "was that just to get him out of the house?"

He nodded without meeting my eyes. "Althauser sent a false message to get your father out of the way; I was to write to August. He knows my handwriting, so he would not have been convinced if the letter had been written by someone else."

I observed him in the dim light. There were copious quantities of congealed blood in his hair and a bump the size of a hen's egg where Althauser had hit him on the forehead.

"I still don't understand why you think you have to do everything he says."

"No," he said simply, "you probably don't." That was all. No explanation, no apology.

"Do you have any idea why he hit you?"

"I should think because I disagreed with him. And because time is running out for me."

"What do you mean?"

"I'll soon be a tool he no longer needs. I can only be used against you and against August. He has you under control, and August . . . August he has pretty much managed to push into the gutter too."

"With your help."

"Yes, damn it! With my help. How often do you want me to confess?"

He expelled the words with such force that he silenced me. We sat next to each other for a while and brooded over our private thoughts. Finally, he broke the silence.

"His name is Jacob. He is two years younger than I. And when his father discovered what was going on between us, Jacob tried to kill himself. I have not been allowed to see him since, have not been able to write to him or speak with him. All I know is that a court case would kill him. August can survive it. So can I. But it would kill Jacob, it honestly would. That is why I need to protect him. Can you understand that?"

It was so . . . upside down. I had spent so many months fearing and hating this man because I believed he was a threat to my relationship with August. Now it seemed that that had never seriously been the case. Though he had harbored no tender feelings for me back then, he would hardly have traveled all the way from Heidelberg to Varbourg just to harass me.

"The bladder of pig's blood," I said. "Was that your idea?"

"Yes," he admitted. "Though it was actually lamb's blood. Just in a pig's bladder."

"But . . . why? Since I had not actually stolen the love of your life, why all that anger?"

"I don't know. And I really am sorry—it was a low and disgusting thing to do. I was so . . . frustrated. I was homesick. I was in despair over what happened with Jacob. I thought you were an insufferable little busybody. I probably needed you to be that, because then it was easier to do what I had to do for Jacob's sake. If you actually deserved it, I mean . . . but you didn't, and I'm sorry."

I smiled crookedly.

"You have actually apologized once already. Very articulately too."

"Yes. But that was only because Althauser forced me to so he could appear to be a hero in your eyes."

I thought about it for a while.

"You say you love this Jacob. Is there a great deal of difference? Between the love of two men and the love of a man and a woman, I mean?"

"I don't know, mademoiselle. I have only tried one kind. Perhaps you should ask August?"

"If I ever get the chance . . . ," I said despondently. But the thought of August somehow made my tired brain start working again.

"I have an idea," I said. "Perhaps it is foolish to aim for the hatch—that is exactly the spot that has been most fortified. What if there is a board we can wrench loose?"

"With your bare hands, Fräulein? You may be a remarkable woman, but . . ."

"With my bare hands," I said. "And the stays in my corset."

He began to laugh.

He helped me undo the hooks of my corset. If nothing else, I'd be able to breathe more freely now, and after the water-kiss we seemed to have few physical secrets from each other. We used the tongue of his belt buckle to undo the stitches. The stays were almost forty centimeters long and made of spring steel, and though they were meant to yield a little to follow the movements of the wearer, they turned into quite an effective slender crowbar when we combined several of them by tying a strip of fabric around them.

Once again, I climbed onto Falchenberg's shoulders, and we proceeded systematically. Every crack was examined. There were only a few places where the crack between the boards was wide enough that my improvised crowbar could be inserted. Every time I succeeded, I tugged energetically at it while Falchenberg offered me well-meaning technical advice.

"Don't yank. Use a steady pressure. Push it in farther before you try. Yes, that's better."

Finally one of the boards gave. The nails squeaked, and the wood began to splinter. I could feel Falchenberg's shoulders shaking with effort, but he stood solid as a rock despite my unco-ordinated rocking and tugging.

Then the board snapped with a crack like a pistol shot. I completely lost my balance and brought Falchenberg down with me. But when we sat up and looked toward the ceiling, there was a new hole—about twenty centimeters wide and sixty centimeters long.

"One more board," said Falchenberg. "Then a slender young lady like yourself should be able to wriggle through with no problem."

It took time, because while the first board had been somewhat rotten and worm-eaten, the boards next to it were more solid. But we succeeded at last. I hauled myself up as far as I was able and ended up using poor Falchenberg as a kind of ladder. I think I even stepped on his abused head, but he did not complain.

I found myself in an astonishingly ordinary living room. Two armchairs, a small dining room set for four. A heavy old Chinese chest—it was what was keeping the hatch closed. A silk screen with Japanese fabric prints and, behind it, a fireplace and a copper bathtub. Faded chintz wallpaper and a mantel clock made of marble. Everything was a bit worn and dusty but otherwise entirely normal. Nothing gave away the cellar downstairs.

I pushed the chest aside and opened the hatch. Realizing Falchenberg would need something to stand on, I fetched a chair and lowered it through the hatch until he could reach it. It was not quite enough.

"Is there another one?" he asked.

It required a small pyramid of three before we succeeded.

The living room door led to another room that also looked entirely ordinary—a bedroom with a bed, dresser, and wardrobe. Then a small hallway and an equally tiny kitchen.

The front door was locked. But this was a castle gate the battering ram could reach. The doorframe splintered at his first assault.

By modifying the internal nutritional environment [of an embryo], and by holding the organized matter in some way in a nascent state, we may hope to change its direction of development and consequently its final organic expression.

—CLAUDE BERNARD, *"LE PROBLÈME*
DE LA PHYSIOLOGIE GÉNÉRALE," 1867

October 5–11, 1894

Everyone seemed to believe that it was appropriate for me to go to bed. You would think there was a handbook on the treatment of women who have been subjected to mortal danger. (1) If the woman is reasonably unharmed and unravaged, tell her countless times how fortunate it is that unspecified "worse things" didn't happen. (2) Offer her vast quantities of chamomile tea and chicken broth. (3) Send her to bed with a hot-water bottle, regardless of the time of day. (4) If there is an even minimally relevant male figure nearby, thank him profusely for saving her.

I was not quite sure which part of this regimen irritated me the most. At least Falchenberg was honest enough to look uncomfortable and mumble that we might be said to have saved each other. But no one tried to send him to bed with a hot-water bottle and a cup of tea. Instead he was installed in the Commissioner's favorite plush armchair and plied with cognac.

I could tell that my father was a bit confused as to who this young German actually was, and how he fit into the picture—by silent agreement he had been presented simply as "one of Madeleine's fellow students." If Papa had known the full picture, he might have been a little less generous with both his cognac and his gratitude. But at least it seemed that Papa and August had found each other again in their mutual concern for me.

They had arrived home almost simultaneously from their respective wild-goose chases, only to be met by a devastated Madame Vogler, an ether-befuddled Elise, and three representatives of Varbourg's gendarmerie that Madame Vogler had called. Elise could tell them nothing except that she had been in the middle of preparing Mademoiselle's bath when she had heard someone outside the back door. She had opened it—and had been overpowered by a masked man armed with a rag soaked in ether. As to my whereabouts, they had been able to find no clues except for the wet jacket I had discarded.

Papa immediately sent for both the Commissioner and Police Inspector Marot. A search was instigated, but at first no one thought of questioning Althauser. Not that it would have made much difference. He was hardly the type to break down and confess at the first hostile questions. He had not done so, for example, when Marot and I confronted him with the files from the Commission for Public Health and Decency and what they revealed about his connection to Rosalba.

It had been almost noon, explained Papa, before they had received a useful tip from "some journalist—he claimed he knew you?"

"Christophe?" I said in surprise.

"Yes. Him. Peculiar man, something of a flâneur, I shouldn't wonder. It turned out that he had considerably more knowledge of what you have been doing for the last few days than I."

It was hard to explain. I chose not to try.

"Yes," I said. "Go on."

"Are you sure it wouldn't be better for you to lie down? You look pale."

"Come on, Papa. What did Christophe say?"

"Among other things, that you had been extremely interested in the tenement block in Rue Colbert where the coal merchant's yard is. A part of the search was thus focused there."

Perhaps that was why we had not seen any sign of Althauser. Madame Arnaud could come and go more easily without attracting attention; she lived in the building, after all.

Something kept bothering me when I thought of the saddlery shop and the bricked-up windows. Something hovering just under the surface of my consciousness but unwilling to come forward and speak its name. But Christophe's information explained why Falchenberg and I had run directly into the arms of two gendarmes as soon as we had emerged into the street.

After a brief questioning, we had been permitted to go home to Carmelite Street. The search continued, but now it was Althauser they were looking for, so far without success. He was neither at home in Rue Faubourg, at the university, nor at the Institute for Child Care and Nursing.

But that was not where they ought to be searching, peeped that insidious little anxious voice in my head. I rubbed one temple.

"Are you in pain?" asked August.

"No," I snapped. "I'm fine!"

"If you don't want to go to bed, could you at least rest a little?"

"For heaven's sake! I'm not sick!"

It came out with such vehemence that everyone in the salon stared at me—Falchenberg, the Commissioner, Papa, Madame Vogler, and of course August as well. The worst thing was that the moment I had said it, my insides began to wobble and a prickling, stinging feeling right behind my eyes told me that a crying jag was on its way.

I *refused* to sob like a hysteric while they were all looking at me. I got up with as much dignity as I could muster.

"Fine," I said. "If it means so much to you, then I will go upstairs and lie down."

I fled up the stairs before anyone had time to comment on my capitulation. As soon as I had closed the door, the tears came pouring out. I grabbed a pillow and tried to muffle the loudest sobs, but I had an awful feeling that they could still hear me in the salon.

The emotional storm was violent and abrupt, but it did not last very long. My hysterical tears dried up almost as suddenly as they had begun. I lay fully clothed on the bed for a little while, staring at the ceiling. It *had* been a very long night, and a long day both before and after. Perhaps it wasn't entirely unreasonable to provide body and mind with a little rest.

As soon as I closed my eyes, there it was again.

The saddlery shop. The cold cellar. Ether-fogged dreams and a voice that whispered, "Where is the child?"

I placed both hands against my abdomen but felt no response there. Time would show whether I was right, but this endless afternoon I felt sure that my body still belonged to me and that no little stowaway had taken over my uterus.

But if this strange protective urge was not some kind of early pregnancy warning, what was it? And what *was* it I was missing about that coal cellar?

I could almost hear a collective "Oh no!" pass through the assembled men when I came down the stairs. Just when they had finally managed to get me where they thought I belonged . . . I was painfully conscious that I was not properly corseted, that I was still wearing the cellar-stained skirt, that my hair looked like a stork's nest, that my eyes were shiny and red rimmed. All in all, I probably looked like I belonged in an asylum for severe cases of female hysteria.

I strode through the salon as calmly as was possible.

"Where are you going?" exclaimed my father.

I considered saying that I needed a bath—it was true enough and hard to argue against. But Elise was at home with her mother, being justifiably fussed over, and I was not at all sure I would ever feel like going down into that laundry shed again, not even if it was just to leave the house by the back door.

"I am a grown woman," I reminded him. "I can come and go as I please. Wasn't that what you said?"

August had risen.

"Then you won't mind if I accompany you?" he said quietly.

And because he said it in that quiet voice, so completely devoid of disparagement or command, it struck me how comforting it would be to have him with me.

"Very well," I answered, and then, because I felt that sounded a little cold, added, "Thank you."

The streets were darkening when we reached the saddler shop. August looked at the bricked-up windows.

"Are you sure you want to go in?" he asked. "I know you are strong, but . . . most women would run screaming from this place if they had experienced what you have."

I thought of the women in the Decency Commission's custody—both the ones who had been subjected to Pro Patria's experiment and the ones who had "only" undergone the usual forced examinations.

"There are many who *cannot* run screaming," I said, "or run away at all, even though they are put through worse horrors. It is, in fact, only women from higher walks of life who can really afford to be frail. The others just have to pick themselves up and get on with it, if they and their children are to survive."

He acknowledged this with a slight nod. "You may be right. But . . . what is it that you *want* here?"

There it was, the question I could not answer. I did not know what I was doing here; I just knew I had to come.

"Let us just go in," I said. "It looks as if the door is open."

The door was open because it could not be otherwise—Falchenberg had reduced the doorframe to kindling.

The rooms were dim and shadowy, and felt dusty and damp at the same time. In the few hours that had passed, the cellar smell had risen through the open hatch and the hole in the floorboards, and I shuddered in spite of the wool coat I had put on as protection against the evening chill.

"Is there any light?" August asked softly.

"Not electric," I said. "But there is probably a lamp some-where."

Gaslight from the streetlamp outside bled through the part-ing of the heavy plush curtains, and we managed to light a lamp that stood on the table by the armchair in the salon. August raised it like a torch above his head and stared down through the open hatch into the cellar prison I had shared with Falchenberg.

"What is it you want here?" he repeated.

"Shush," I quieted him. I stood completely still and concen-trated my hearing to the utmost. "Can't you hear it?"

"What?"

A faint mewling cry, so weak that it was hard to believe it could emanate from a living creature.

"There!" I said.

"What are you talking about?"

"You must be able to hear it!"

Apparently he could not. But I tore the lamp out of his hands and rushed back to the bedroom. I thought the sound was stron-ger there, even though August still looked baffled. I squatted and tried to push the carpet to the side. I did not succeed—it was stuck somehow. When I examined it more closely, I saw that it had been nailed to a floor hatch similar to the other one, so that it would automatically rise when the hatch rose and fall back into place when it closed.

August put his hand on my shoulder.

"Leave it," he said. "Let us call the gendarmes."

But I could not stop. Not with that cry in my ears. I opened the hatch.

There was a room down there, smaller than the cellar room and with a lower ceiling. I got a shadowy sense of shelves and cupboards, books, boxes, a worktable, a row of glass cabinets full of jars and instruments—all in all an odd mixture of laboratory and storage room.

There was someone down there. Madame Arnaud stood directly under the hatch, looking up at me with a hand shielding her eyes against the light.

"I thought you would come," she said. "You cannot be stopped."

She seemed quite calm, despite the slumped figure at her feet.

It was Adrian Althauser, and he was clearly stone-dead. Few people survive having a scalpel driven so deeply into their left eye that only a few centimeters of the handle are visible.

"He said we needed to clear the room," Madame Arnaud continued in her oddly calm voice. "He said we would have to terminate the experiment, that it was too risky now, and we had to remove the evidence. That is what he called her: 'the experiment.' He wanted to discard her. But I have taken care of her for almost three months now. She is no 'experiment.'"

Between the two glass cabinets stood one of Althauser's specially developed incubators. The crying was louder now, and there was no longer any doubt where it came from. It tore at me, that cry, dragging me down through the hatch, past Madame Arnaud, past Althauser's stiffening corpse.

In the incubator lay a wrinkled little girl with gigantic eyes and the tiniest nose I had ever seen. She looked straight up at me and stopped crying. She wanted me to pick her up.

It was the first time Catherine made me do precisely what she wanted. It would not be the last.

"That young girl in the coal cellar? He forced the photographer to do it. To get rid of her, I mean. Made him do it."

"How?" Police Inspector Marot asked patiently. He could be surprisingly gentle when he questioned witnesses.

"How?" Madame Arnaud looked confused. "M'sieur, he could make anyone do anything. Sooner or later, once he knew how they functioned inside, they could wriggle as much as they liked, it did no good. I wriggled too. But not for very long. It was easier just to do what he said." She looked over at me and Catherine.

"You'll take care of her, won't you?" she said. "Mademoiselle, you know that she is a child, a human being and not an experiment, don't you?"

"Yes," I said. "I will take care of her."

The police inspector looked ill at ease. He was having a hard time looking at Catherine, I noticed.

"How did Monsieur Althauser and Monsieur Gilbert know each other?" he asked.

"He needed someone to take pictures of all those mothers and children," said Madame Arnaud. "For his research. And of other things. Things that . . . he did not want . . . that many photographers would not take pictures of."

The police inspector had at that point already seen some of the photographs Althauser had collected in the room's many filing drawers. Some of them were the raw material for the posters he had used in his lecture. Others were less suitable for public presentation. He had let Gilbert photograph his operations and dissections step-by-step. Later the police found a series of pictures of his attempt to carry out Porro's procedure on Rosalba Lombardi.

Marot cleared his throat. "And the . . . uh, child. How did it happen that . . . ?"

"She was desperate," said Madame Arnaud. "The mother. The Italian girl. She could not take care of it, she said, but she could not kill it either. It was a sin. And they had refused her at the institute because she was . . . you know, not a decent woman. But then he promised her that he would take it out alive. That it would live, and be cared for. And she believed him. Or perhaps . . . perhaps she had to believe it because she had no other options. He did it here. And he had that ready." She pointed at the incubator. "But the mother started bleeding, and then she died. And that was when we put her in the yard . . . There were so many people everywhere, we had to just leave her there even though it was much too close."

They could have left her in the cellar, I thought, with no one any the wiser, at least until the uproar after the president's murder had died down. If a living Fleur could be hidden there, why not a dead Rosalba? But perhaps an unforeseen death could create panic even in a man as calculating as Althauser. It might even be *because* he was normally so calculating—he was not used to having to act without a preexisting plan.

Fleur's murder, on the other hand, had been meticulously planned. Aristide Gilbert had received exact instructions about when he was to collect her from the cellar, what he must do to her, where he should leave her, and how he was to mark her body so as to provide the most plausible substance for the Ripper theory. While Althauser had stood at the rostrum in the lavish halls of the Brotherhood of Freedom giving his speech about the nation's future—while the audience applauded and his fellow patriots drank to his toast—he had known that Aristide Gilbert was murdering Fleur on his orders.

"He told him to cut her throat," Madame Arnaud explained. "So that it would look like that girl from Bruc. But then he read in the paper that she had drowned. That made him quite angry."

That had been the only mercy that Aristide Gilbert had dared to show, I thought. *I thought the water would be kinder than the other thing,* he had written. But since Fleur was in no way similar to his "poor Alice," it had been a dubious mercy. Her death would probably have been quicker if he had done as Althauser commanded.

Fleur's endless hours in the cold cellar, the smashed hands, the suffering her thirst had caused her—it was all so that she could die at precisely the moment that Althauser had ordained.

It was just as well that Madame Arnaud had killed him, or I would have been tempted to do so myself.

Two gendarmes came to lead Madame Arnaud up to the prison transport that waited—colloquially christened a *panier à salade* because the vehicle's cages were reminiscent of the baskets in which one slings lettuce to dry it. On the threshold, she turned and stopped for a moment.

"You will take care of her, won't you?" she asked again. "She is not an experiment . . ."

"I know," I said, and pulled the woolly blanket higher around the hairless little head. I could feel her heartbeat against my un-corseted chest. "I thought we would name her Catherine . . ."

Madame Arnaud nodded. The gendarmes hustled her toward the waiting wagon, and she did not resist.

Dowager Constance Heering-Dreyfuss was angry. That much was evident from the sharpness of her gestures and the way her lilac eyes had narrowed.

"If you think, mademoiselle, that you can fob off the random offspring of some prostitute on me, then you are very wrong. I did not think it was possible to misunderstand our arrangement. I want an heir, not some freak of nature. I'm given to understand she is even bred in an entirely unnatural way on some deceased whore."

"Grandmama," said August, "that is enough."

My future husband's grandmother stopped in the midst of a furious turn.

"Enough? I haven't even started."

"I mean it," he said. "If you wish to be invited to our wedding, then these insults must stop. I do not require you to understand our choice, but if you wish to continue to be a part of my life, you will have to accept that I have a daughter and a wife, and that they deserve some respect."

I rose. "Constance," I said, "don't you want to hold her for a little while?"

"No, I most certainly do not!"

Despite her protests, I extended Catherine's tiny, well-swathed form toward her, with a clear sense that what I was handing her was not so much an infant as a secret weapon.

Five minutes later, Catherine was asleep in her great-grandmother's arms, and there was no more talk of freaks and whores.

How can I explain it? She is not the child of my own body. I have not carried her for nine months—no woman has. I believe that had she not willed herself to live, had she not been such an armful of concentrated survival power, then her miracle would not have occurred. She should have been dead. She just refused to be. And that will to survive is so strong that it drags the rest of us in. We do what it takes. We comply. We care for her needs, we give her what her survival demands. In return, she occasionally rewards us with a look. And most of the time this seems to be an entirely reasonable bargain.

With August, I can make agreements, demand equality, claim my independence. With Catherine, I cannot.

Perhaps it is because she is so tiny. Perhaps it is because I never saw her mother alive. For whatever reason, it is a fact that when I look at Catherine, it is not Rosalba's features I occasionally believe I can recognize. It is Fleur's.

Most of the time she is merely herself. By rights, she should not be alive.

But she is.

Author's Note

"Eugénie Colombe" is in fact Eugénie Delhomme, the first victim of France's own "Jack the Ripper," Joseph Vacher. She was found abused, murdered, and disfigured on May 20, 1894, near the town of Beaurepaire. Joseph Vacher was able to murder at least twenty people, primarily women, girls, and young boys between the ages of thirteen and twenty-one, before he was executed on December 31, 1898, in Bourg-en-Bresse, just twenty-nine years old himself.

A huge thank-you to the people without whose help this book would have had far more mistakes and deficiencies:

Eva Kaaberbøl
Michael Thorberg
Rudi Urban Rasmussen
Lotte Krarup
Bent Lund
Berit Wheler
Esthi Kunz
Lars Ringhof

AUTHOR'S NOTE

Bibs Carlsen
Agnete Friis

And finally, my thanks to the Danish Centre for Writers and Translators at Hald Hovedgaard, and to Peter and Gitte Rannes, for five weeks of unrivaled peace, hospitality, inspiration, and occasional laughter.